The Lesson at Hand

◇

"Come, if we hurry we should have time for one private lesson." Brant's arm slid about her waist as he held her in the traditional waltzing position. "Show me what you have learned."

"That might be a trifle difficult." Sara laughed, her eyes going to the silent pianoforte. "Monsieur Dechamps's sister always provided the musical accompaniment for us. I'm not at all sure I can waltz sans music."

"Look upon it as a challenge," he ordered, his blue eyes bright with laughter. "Now, the most important thing you must remember is to follow your partner's lead. Usually he will signal his intentions by squeezing your hand so"—his fingers gently tightened around hers—"or by varying the pressure of his arm about you. If he wishes you to move a certain way . . . let us say forward, then he will do this." His warm arm pressed against her back, pulling her closer to his strong chest . . . and Sara trembled with an emotion that was half fear and half anticipation.

◇

The Prodigal Spinster

by Joan Overfield

PAGEANT BOOKS

PAGEANT BOOKS
225 Park Avenue South
New York, New York 10003

PAGEANT and colophon are trademarks of the publisher

Cover artwork by Mitchell Hooks

Printed in the U.S.A.

First Pageant Books printing: August, 1988

10 9 8 7 6 5 4 3 2 1

*Many thanks to my friends and family,
who have always provided me with the love and
encouragement I needed to write this book.
A special thanks to my agent, Adele Leone;
my editor, Arlene Friedman;
and a very big thank-you
to all the members of the Inland Empire Chapter
of Romance Writers of America.*

I AM A PART OF ALL THAT I HAVE MET.

—TENNYSON

Chapter One

"We are ruined," Agatha Deverleigh, Lady Mallingham, announced, placing one hand over her ample bosom, "quite, quite ruined. And I should like to know what you intend to do about it."

Brant Deverleigh, the Earl of Mallingham, raised a dark eyebrow inquiringly, casting about in his mind for some new peccadillo of his which may have reached his aunt's ears. The opera singer, he decided glumly, shifting his athletic frame in discomfort. Like the rest of the ornate green-and-gold parlor done in the Empire mode, the chair was designed more for effect than comfort, and he mentally consigned its maker to the devil.

It wasn't just the chair which annoyed him. It infuriated him that he should have to answer to his late uncle's troublesome wife, and he wished he

dared tell her so. His aunt was possessed of the uncanny ability to make him feel like a wet-nosed
lieutenant being dressed down by a superior officer.
It wasn't a feeling he cared for, and it took all of his
control to answer her in a civil manner.

"Really, Aunt Agatha," he drawled, sprawling
back against the lyre-backed chair, "surely you are
doing it a shade too brown! I fail to see why you are
so concerned. She is of little consequence after all,
and Society isn't likely to . . ."

"*She* may be of little consequence," his aunt interrupted, her nose quivering in outrage, "but *you* are
not. You're the earl now, as I am always forced to
remind you, and you may be very sure that your
every action is noted, your every association scrutinized. I shudder to think of the unpleasant speculation it would cause if the ton were to become aware
of the minx's existence. You must do something!"

Brant's blue eyes darkened in anger. He had endured his aunt's vapors and silly passions out of
respect for his uncle's memory and a grudging fondness for her. But he'd be damned if he would allow
her to interfere in his private life.

"Indeed, ma'am," he said, adjusting his starched
cuffs with a flick of his tanned wrists. "And pray,
what would you have me do? Marry the creature?"

"Of course not!" Lady Mallingham was horrified.

"Well then?" He took a deep draught of the Madeira his aunt had provided for him, grimacing at its
cloying sweetness. Perhaps if he got bosky enough
he could survive the next hour without going mad.

"Have her move in with me. It's the only possible
solution, and so I . . . good heavens, boy! What-

ever is the matter with you?" Her sharp blue eyes widened in alarm as Brant choked on his wine.

"Move in!" he wheezed, gasping for air. "With you? My God, what on earth for?"

"Well," the countess acknowledged in a grudging manner, "we *are* related, although 'tis not something of which I'm particularly proud. Nonetheless I am willing to do my duty and sponsor her entry into Society despite her advanced years and dubious choice of occupation."

"You wish to introduce her to Society?" Brant asked, appalled. He wasn't ashamed of his golden Felicia by any means, but that didn't mean he would welcome her into his world. Good Lord, if such were the case he would be forced to marry her. "Aunt, you can't be serious about this," he said at last. "It would never do."

"And why not?" She tossed her head back, causing the large plume adorning her turban to bob dangerously. Like the rest of her ensemble it was a bright orange, a color which did little to enhance her sallow complexion. "I have always held a certain fondness for Katherine, and I should be only too happy to sponsor her daughter. That is what I told Sara, and you know what that impudent . . ."

"Sara?" Brant leapt to his feet, bumping the tea table with his knee and sending the empty wineglass tumbling to the gold carpet. "Who in Hades is Sara? And what has she to do with Felicia?"

"Felicia?" The countess frowned in bewilderment. "Whoever is Felicia? Really, Brant, weren't you attending? We were speaking of your third cousin, Katherine Belding, and her daughter, Sara. And I will thank you, sir, to mind your tongue," she added in starchy tones. "You aren't on the battle-field now."

Brant shook his head as if to clear it. "Aunt Agatha," he said carefully, smoothing out the tails of his blue coat of Bath superfine and resuming his seat. "I have no idea what you are talking about. First you say we are ruined, then you dare to make mention of my personal life, and now you're prattling on about some unknown cousin and her brattish daughter. What is going on? How are we being ruined? And what has this Sara creature to do with anything?" His normally husky voice had risen with his confusion until he was all but shouting. He had to be drunk, he decided wildly. Either that or he had run mad. He had been accused of many things during his two-and-thirty years, but being a slow top wasn't one of them.

Lady Mallingham maintained an injured silence before sighing heavily. "Katherine was the eldest daughter of your uncle's cousin Waldo," she began in the patient tones of one explaining things to a not-overly-bright child. "You wouldn't remember him, of course, as he died when you were a lad. Well, Katherine fell in love with an upstart physician from Surrey. His birth was good enough, but he hadn't a feather to fly with. Naturally Waldo forbade the match, and when Katherine eloped to Gretna Green he cut her out of his will and never spoke her name again."

"Go on." Brant fortified himself with more wine, wishing his aunt would serve him brandy or some other strong spirit. Instinct warned him he would be needing it.

"Elias was a stiff-necked fool who might have

done quite well if he hadn't been so proud," the countess continued once she was certain she had her nephew's full attention. "His family was well connected, and he was offered an excellent post in London. But he turned it down to act as a country sawbones. Poor Katherine, she died some twelve years later of the fever. Waldo was dead by then, and naturally the family offered to take Sara in. But Elias was very bitter and he refused to be parted from his daughter. There was a rather unpleasant scene, as I recall," she added reflectively, refreshing herself with a sip of tea.

"Now it seems Elias, too, has died," she continued. "And Sara, she must be all of two-and-twenty now, and not a quarter of the beauty her mother was, has come to London to make her way in the world. When she wrote me of her arrival I was quick to offer my assistance, and do you know the little minx refused me? Refused! She said she had made 'other arrangements' and didn't wish to bother me. 'Other arrangements' indeed!" she snorted. "Serving as a schoolmistress in some pokey little village in Cornwall!"

There was an expectant pause as Brant waited for her to continue. After several seconds had passed he stirred himself. "Is that all?"

"Is that all?" His aunt repeated incredulously. " 'Tis more than enough, I should think! A Deverleigh reduced to teaching fishermen's brats . . . why, it's not to be borne! Only think of the scandal it will cause when it becomes known that you allowed a relation . . . and an unprotected female at that . . . to earn her bread in so humiliating a manner."

"I'm not 'allowing' her to do anything." Brant rubbed a weary hand across his eyes. "This is the first I have heard of it. Still, I don't see what is so shameful about becoming a teacher. It seems a fitting occupation for an unmarried female."

"Yes." His aunt leaned forward from her Chinese chair, causing her stays to groan in audible protest. "If she were to associate herself with a respectable school. Lady Tillingford's in Hampton, for example. That is where *I* went to school, and I'm sure if we asked them they could find something for her to do. Or she could become a governess; that has always been a suitable occupation for impoverished gentlewomen. At least then she would be associating with her own class; she might even make a decent marriage. But if she continues on her present course, she will be quite beyond the pale."

"What can I do about it?" Brant asked when his aunt paused for breath. "You say she's already rejected your assistance, and I don't see that I could do anything else. She can hardly stay with *me*."

"You could speak to her." Lady Mallingham ignored the last part of his remark. "Go to her, point out the folly of her ways, and urge her to return to the bosom of her family. You're the head of the family now, and she's certain to follow your counsel. And if she shouldn't . . . well, at least we may truthfully say you did your duty. If it comes to that, we can only hope no one connects her to us."

It sounded simple enough, he brooded, studying the shiny toes of his Hessian boots. And for once, Aunt Agatha was right. This was precisely the sort of thing the gossip-mongers thrived on. He could well imagine the stir it would cause.

"Where does Cousin Sara stay?" he asked, coming to a swift decision.

"I have her address here." She withdrew a slip of paper from the folds of her gown and handed it to him. "As you can see, she is living in Chelsea; in a public boarding-house if you will, where any creature with a farthing in her pocket might beg a room. She's such a willful little thing, I shouldn't wonder that she's unmarried. What intelligent man would wish to shackle himself to a shrew? And as I've said, she is on the plain side."

"You've met her then?" Brant glanced up in surprise. From what she'd said, he'd formed the impression his aunt had never seen this Sara.

"Only briefly." The countess was suddenly preoccupied with the contents of her teacup. "I called upon her shortly after her arrival."

"I see." Brant frowned. He had the oddest feeling he had missed something. Oh, well, he supposed it didn't signify. "Very well, Aunt Agatha," he said, pocketing the piece of paper. "I shall pay Cousin Sara a visit. But I make no promises," he added warningly. "If she is as stubborn as you say, then I shall wash my hands of her."

"Of course you shall," his aunt soothed, all sweetness now that she had won her way. "You're such a dutiful young man and so responsible. I've always thought so." She gave him a smile that revealed a row of yellowing teeth. "And now, since we are speaking of responsibility, there is another matter I should like to discuss with you. I've been hearing the most disquieting rumors concerning you and a certain blond opera singer . . ."

* * *

"I'm sorry, Miss Belding, but you must understand my position." Miss Minerva Larkin plucked nervously at the fichu adorning her plain gown. "I have the other tenants to think of, you know. Having a diseased person in residence seems so . . . unhealthy."

Sara Belding bit back an angry retort as she glared at the flustered landlady. "I am not 'diseased,' Miss Larkin," she told the other woman in clipped tones, her light brown eyes blazing in fury. "I have a cold, that is all."

"That might be true for now, but colds can lead to consumption, can't they?" Miss Larkin pointed out anxiously. She was a tall, raw-boned woman who wore her graying brown hair scraped back in a tight bun and had the timid, hesitant air of a startled mouse.

"Perhaps," Sara conceded, rubbing her hand across her throbbing temples. She had been lying down when Miss Larkin tapped on her door, asking if she might come in. Had Sara known what the dratted woman wanted she would never have admitted her.

"Well, then, you can surely understand that it would be better for all concerned if you were to seek accommodations elsewhere. Your rent is all paid up until the end of the week, but after that, perhaps you . . ."

"What?" Sara dropped her hand. "Do you mean to say you are *evicting* me!"

Miss Larkin jumped at Sara's strident tones, her eyes blinking rapidly in alarm. "I . . . well . . . the other ladies . . ."

"I am *not* a consumptive, Miss Larkin, I assure you," Sara said, her voice cold with displeasure. "You forget my father was a physician and I am not unacquainted with the symptoms of the disease." The look she flashed the landlady would have done her high-born kin proud. The poor lady was fairly quaking with fright.

"Oh, yes, I am sure you are," Miss Larkin stammered, her jaundiced cheeks darkening with color. "I certainly didn't mean to imply . . . that is . . . I was concerned for your health . . ." She began inching toward the door.

"Thank you for your concern." Sara rose to her feet, ignoring the waves of dizziness washing over her. Her legs trembled as she walked to the door and pulled it open.

"If that is all, Miss Larkin, I should like to rest now." Sara's small chin came up as she gave the landlady a pointed look. "I'm sure it would be best for us both if we were to forget this conversation ever took place."

"Certainly, Miss Belding." The other woman scurried past, her thin hands waving in apology. "You are quite right. Pray forgive the intrusion. If there is anything I can do to be of assistance . . ."

"You are too kind," Sara replied in a falsely sweet voice as she swung the door closed in the landlady's face. "Good day, Miss Larkin!"

After expending the last of her energy in a childish display of temper, Sara tottered back to her bed and collapsed upon the faded comforter in a boneless heap. *Lord, I'm tired,* she thought, closing her eyes to shut out the sight of the dreary little room. It seemed as if she had been sick forever, even though scarcely a week had passed since she had contracted the heavy cold. But a poor diet and the constant strain of worrying about her finances had taken their toll on her health. She had managed to salvage a few of her papa's medications from his medicine bag, but was too afraid to dose herself. The thought of her father brought weak tears to Sara's eyes and she crawled beneath the covers, too weary to remove her gown.

It had been a little over a year since his death, but she still felt his loss like a stunning blow. They had grown so close after her mother had died, often working together in his surgery. Had she been a man, nothing would have given her greater pleasure than to have followed in his footsteps. But since that was not possible, Sara contented herself with being his assistant. She knew the local gentry wondered that a gently bred girl such as herself should enjoy the grisly practice of medicine, but she hadn't cared.

She remembered how her mother's distant relations had descended upon her and Papa following her mother's death. One woman, Agatha Deverleigh, the Countess of Mallingham, had been particularly insistent that Sara make her home with her. It wasn't until Sara had threatened to run off and join the gypsies that the countess had finally relented. When she had turned eighteen Lady Mallingham had written her a lovely letter inviting her to London for the Season, but Sara had never answered. Now Agatha Deverleigh was once again intruding in her life, arrogantly assuming Sara would welcome her charity.

"You're rather old for a first Season," the countess

had commented, studying Sara through her quizzing glass. "And you ain't the beauty your mother was. Still, I suppose we shall manage." She dropped her glass and gave Sara a satisfied smile. "Have the maid pack your bags. You'll be staying with me, of course."

The conversation had taken place in Miss Larkin's best parlor. The dear lady was so overwhelmed at having a genuine countess under her roof she had built a roaring fire in the grate. Sara had been standing in front of the fireplace, her chilled hands held out to the comforting warmth of the flames. When the countess's words pierced her thoughts, she had turned around in surprise.

"I . . . I beg your pardon, my lady," she stammered, staring at the older woman in confusion. With the exception of the cook and the scullery maid, the only servant was the housemaid, and she was too old to be packing trunks about.

"I said I wish you to live with me," Lady Mallingham repeated impatiently. "You can't stay *here*." She glanced about the tiny parlor with its threadbare carpets and faded drapes with obvious disdain.

Sara had bristled at the countess's words. To be sure, the boarding-house was not overly elegant, but it was clean. It was also respectable, and given the precarious state of her finances that was as much as Sara could hope for.

"That is very good of you, Lady Mallingham." Sara had managed a civil smile. "But as I have already explained, you needn't concern yourself with me. I have made other arrangements."

"If you are referring to that nonsense about becoming a schoolmistress, then I am afraid I must disagree," Lady Mallingham snapped, pulling her orange shawl tighter about her shoulders. "I stood godmother to your dearest mamma, and I refuse to stand idly by while her daughter suffers in poverty! Since your father is dead you are all alone in the world, and your rightful place is with your mother's family. I insist you abandon this folly at once and come with me."

They had quarreled violently after that, and the countess had finally stalked out, announcing to the eavesdropping Miss Larkin that she was washing her hands of the errant child. Sara had retired to her rooms and within hours she was down with the feverish cold.

Now as she lay in her unheated room shivering with the cold and the fever, Sara tried convincing herself she had done the right thing. Anything was better than acting the grateful poor relation, she decided. Besides, she had promised her father she would never go to her mother's high-born relations with her hat in her hand. He had never forgiven the Deverleighs for disinheriting her mother. As his illness progressed he became obsessed with the matter, making Sara give her word she would never take charity from a Deverleigh.

Sara closed her eyes wearily and snuggled against the lumpy mattress. Soon she would be well again, and then she would pack her bags and return to the country, where she belonged. It had been a mistake to come to London, she realized. But she had been running low on funds and a friend had told her it would be easier to find a position in London. It had taken most of what remained of her inheritance to pay for the journey and for her lodgings, but she had been desperate. When she had been offered the position in Cornwall it seemed an answer to her prayers. And then she had written to Lady Mallingham.

Sara smiled ruefully. She'd forgotten what an old harridan the countess was. Life with her would have been unbearable. Sara's last thought as she drifted into a heavy sleep was that she had finally settled the matter of her mother's family. The Deverleighs would never trouble her again.

Two days later Brant set out for Chelsea in his coach-and-four. He seldom used it in town as he considered the heavy black carriage with its ornate silver crest to be pretentious, but he thought his cousin would enjoy riding in it. After he'd left his aunt he'd written Cousin Sara advising her of his arrival. He knew his aunt to be notoriously poor-mouthed, and decided his tiresome cousin feared inflicting herself upon a penniless old woman. Well, he thought as he settled his broad shoulders against the plush squabs of his coach, she was better apprised of the situation now.

Miss Larkin's Boarding-House for Respectable Ladies was located in the less fashionable area of Chelsea. One look at its crumbling and faded facade and Brant found himself in total agreement with his aunt. No Deverleigh could stay in such a place. Cousin Sara would doubtless welcome him with open arms, tearfully proclaiming him her savior. He only hoped she would refrain from embracing him; he detested excessively emotional scenes. Pulling his curled beaver hat over his brows he stepped out of his carriage and set forth to rescue his cousin.

The parlor to which the ingratiating Miss Larkin guided him was a cluttered melange of faded and mismatched furniture. He was reluctant to expose his immaculate pantaloons to their dusty surfaces, and stood with his back to the door. He was studying a copy of a gory hunting scene when the door opened behind him.

"Good afternoon, my lord. You wished to see me?" A soft voice made scarcely discernable by a heavy cold brought Brant face-to-face with his cousin.

His first thought was that he had never seen a more remarkable pair of eyes. They were a bright gypsy gold, fringed with thick lashes and tilted at the corners like a cat's eyes. Her thick dark hair had been pulled back in an untidy bun, throwing the delicate bones of her face into sharp relief. She was dressed in a hideous, ill-fitting gown of black bombazine. His next thought was that she was thin, far too thin by half. Aware he had been staring, he stepped forward to greet her.

"Ah, Cousin Sara." He swept her painfully frail hand to his lips in a familiar salute. "How good it is to meet you at last. Aunt Agatha has told me so much about you."

Sara stared at the well-groomed man in front of her, scarce believing the evidence of her own eyes. With his blue coat of Bath superfine and intricately tied cravat, the earl looked as out of place in Miss Larkin's humble parlor as an Indian chieftain would have looked at a formal ball. She stared at the toes of his glossy Hessians, searching for something to say.

When the letter in its crested envelope had arrived by special courier yesterday afternoon, she had been more curious than anything else. She'd made her position quite clear to the countess, and she couldn't imagine what they would have left to say to one another. Her curiosity was laid to rest when she opened the envelope and read the letter inside.

The message—an order—really, commanded her to pack her things and await the Earl of Mallingham's arrival. The very tone of the letter was an affront to her pride and she could only wonder at the audacity of the man who had written it. Now, looking at the earl, she could easily picture him as the author of the arrogant missive. He was every inch the high and mighty lord, and Sara stiffened in resentment.

"I am Lord Mallingham," Brant continued, moved to pity at the stunned expression upon Sara's face. Poor thing, he thought with a softness quite foreign to his nature. She was so relieved to see him, she had been rendered speechless. He gave her an encouraging smile. "But I pray you will call me Cousin Brant."

Heavens, what a lofty popinjay! Did he really think she was some timid little female who would meekly do his bidding? Well, Sara thought as she straightened her shoulders in determination. She would soon set him straight on *that* score!

"Lord Mallingham." She stressed his title with hard-edged irony. "I fear you have made a mistake. I thought I had made it quite clear to the countess that I desired no part of her offer. I have no wish to live out my days as anyone's poor relation. Now if you will excuse me, I . . ." She broke off as a bout of coughing overcame her.

Brant was at her side in a moment, assisting her to one of the sagging chairs. Once he assured himself she was comfortably seated he stalked over to the door and bellowed for Miss Larkin.

"I want some tea, my good woman," he ordered when the landlady came scurrying from her hiding place. "Then send someone for a doctor. I wish my cousin tended to at once."

"No, no, that's not necessary." Sara had controlled her cough and was struggling for breath.

"Dr. Rivers has been treating Miss Belding," Miss Larkin provided eagerly, thrilled at being ordered about by a handsome lord. "Shall I bring him?"

"Please," Sara protested in a breathy voice, "I would rather you did not. I haven't paid him for his last visit and I . . ."

"Fetch him!" Brant's roar sent the landlady rushing out the door and down the front steps. She was almost to the street when she realized she had forgotten her cloak and had to turn back.

In the parlor Brant was kneeling before Sara, chafing her small hand in his. "This decides it, then," he said, gazing down into her flushed face worriedly. "Aunt is right, you can't continue staying here. You are much too ill."

"I am fine, sir." Sara stared up into the dark depths of Brant's blue eyes. His genuine concern for her well-being surprised her and she revised her opinion of him. Perhaps he wasn't so bad after all.

"Pray forgive me for my sharp tongue," she said,

venturing a shy smile. "But truly, my lord, I am more than capable of caring for myself. I tried to explain this to Lady Mallingham, but she—"

"You're coming with me," Brant interrupted, his lean jaw hardening with resolution. He thrust a hand through his black hair and glared at her. "I'll hear no more of the matter."

Sara's goodwill vanished in a flare of temper. She had survived too much in this last year to allow some dandy to order her about. Her amber eyes narrowed in defiance.

"I am almost three-and-twenty, sir," she announced between clenched teeth. "And I have no use for a misguided guardian! I repeat, I am more than capable of managing my own life, and I will thank you to keep out of it!"

Brant's jaw dropped in amazement at the defiant anger in Sara's voice. He hadn't wanted her to grovel in gratitude, but that didn't mean he was averse to common courtesy. Her rude rejection of his assistance flicked him raw on his pride, and his own temper blazed in response.

"Capable!" He sneered, his azure eyes raking over her emaciated form. "Is this what you call capable? You're no more capable of caring for yourself than a babe is. You *will* accompany me to Aunt Agatha's, or I swear to heaven I shall strap you atop my carriage and carry you there!"

"Oh, you odious bully!" Sara refused to be cowed. She struggled to her feet and met Brant's glittering gaze. "If you think I shall allow myself to be carted off like a sack of grain, then you very much mistake my character! If you so much as touch me, I vow I shall—"

"Miss Belding, what is all this shouting?" A white-haired man hurried into the room, a black bag clasped in his hands. He moved quickly to Sara's side, his wrinkled face grave with anxiety. "I couldn't believe it when Miss Larkin told me you were out of bed."

"I am sorry, Dr. Rivers." Sara allowed the doctor to help her back into her chair. "But my idiotish cousin insisted upon seeing me and Miss Larkin doesn't allow male callers above-stairs . . ."

"You are feverish again." Dr. Rivers laid a skilled hand upon Sara's forehead. He picked up her slender wrist and held it between his fingers. "And your pulse is far too rapid. You have no business being out of bed, no business at all.

"Really, sir." He turned toward Brant in disapproval. "Have you no consideration for your cousin's health? Calling her out of a sick-bed and shouting at her . . . !"

That tore it. Brant had had enough of being treated as if he was a villain out of one of those silly gothics his aunt was forever reading. He was tired of being raged at by a willful little spinster and scolded by an impertinent physician. He crossed his arms across his chest and glared at the doctor.

"I am the Earl of Mallingham," he said in the voice he had used to discipline his troops. "I am Miss Belding's cousin, and I assure you, Doctor"—he spat out the word in contempt—"Sara's health is of the greatest concern to me. I am here on behalf of my aunt, the Countess of Mallingham, to fetch my cousin home so that she might live in more . . . agreeable surroundings." The look he cast about the parlor was eloquent with scorn.

"I shan't go with him," Sara insisted weakly. "Lady Mallingham made it embarrassingly plain that she regards me as nothing more than an object of Christian charity! Well, I told her, and so I shall tell you, sir, that I would as lief be dead than take charity from a Deverleigh! I shall stay here."

"Now listen to me, you little devil—"

"My lord, can't you see you are upsetting your cousin?" Dr. Rivers interrupted, gently assisting Sara to her feet. His wise gray eyes met Brant's hostile gaze. "Whatever your plans, I'm afraid they will have to wait until Miss Belding is better able to deal with them . . . and you."

Brant hesitated, reluctant to yield the field but equally reluctant to continue the battle. The doctor was right. Sara was in no condition for a fight.

"Very well, Doctor," he conceded harshly. "But I shall return later. I mean to remove my cousin to my aunt's house as soon as it can be arranged."

"I won't go with him," Sara vowed, her eyes closing in weariness. "I won't."

"Of course you won't," the doctor said soothingly, shaking his head at Brant. "Come, let's get you into bed. The parlor's no place for you in your condition." He began guiding her skillfully out of the room. "Ah, I believe I see Miss Larkin standing by the door. Perhaps she will be good enough to assist us. Miss Larkin, if I could trouble you but for a moment . . ." And the door closed behind them.

"Blast it all to hell!" Brant cursed furiously, bringing his fist down upon the mantel and toppling over the cheap bric-a-brac. "That stubborn little vixen!"

Whatever his feelings when he'd undertaken this

mission for his aunt, Brant was now committed to the task. He would take Sara to Aunt Agatha's even if he had to drag her there by the hair of her head! He was damned if he would let a willful little spinster make a May game of him. He was the man here, and Sara *would* obey him. With that final thought he turned and went in search of Miss Larkin, determined Sara receive the care befitting a member of his family.

Upstairs Sara allowed Miss Larkin to help her into bed. She closed her eyes and dozed fitfully, only to be awakened by a light tap on the door. Dr. Rivers walked in, followed by a beaming Miss Larkin, who was bearing a heavily laden tray.

"Here you are, my dear," Dr. Rivers said after Miss Larkin had everything arranged to her liking. "With the compliments of your noble cousin. He left strict instructions that you were to eat every bite." His eyes sparkled in amusement at the expression on Sara's face.

She eyed the tray with resentment, determined to ignore the greedy rumblings of her stomach. Her mouth watered at the sight of Miss Larkin's carefully arranged cucumber sandwiches. But to accept charity from that man . . .

"Ah, Miss Belding." Dr. Rivers shook his head sadly. "You can be as stubborn as the very devil sometimes. Surely you wouldn't be so foolish as to reject his lordship's kind generosity?"

Sara lowered her eyes, plucking nervously at the quilt covering her. "It's just that I am not very hungry and I . . ."

"No, my dear," he interposed gently, moving to sit beside her bed. "I'm afraid I can't allow your pride to overrule your intelligence. You are ill and quite weak, and you need the nourishment." He eyed her sternly. "Have I your word you will be sensible about this?"

Sara capitulated with a heavy sigh. He was right, of course. It was silly to refuse the food merely because she was too stiff-necked to accept help. And she did need help, she admitted silently. She needed it very badly indeed.

Chapter Two

After withdrawing from Miss Larkin's, Brant went to White's to lick his wounds and plot a new line of attack. As it was still early in the afternoon the club was all but empty, except for an elderly gentleman dozing comfortably in a corner. Brant nodded a greeting to the majordomo and took his usual chair before the fireplace. Within a few minutes the efficient staff had provided him with a copy of the *Times* and a cigar, which he refused, and a glass of brandy, which he accepted.

He had to get Sara out of that dreadful place, he decided, taking a restorative sip of brandy. The question was how, short of murder, he would accomplish it. His cousin was every bit the shrew Aunt Agatha had warned she would be. He'd been in Sara's company for less than half an hour, and they had all but come to blows. She was a sharp-tongued, headstrong, obstinate little fool, and he had no idea what he was going to do with her. He slouched lower in his chair and stared into the dance of the flames.

"Why the long face, old fellow? Bad run at the tables?" A warm hand clasped his shoulder, and he glanced up to find a familiar pair of brown eyes regarding him quizzically.

"Marcus!" Brant set his snifter of brandy aside as he rose to greet his friend. "What are you doing in London?" he asked, shaking the younger man's hand with obvious delight. "I thought you had retired to your estates."

"The life of a country gentleman palls after the first month," the Viscount Cherrington replied as he took the red leather chair beside Brant's. He was dressed rather casually in a jacket of bottle green velvet and buckskin breeches. His blond hair was brushed in the popular windswept mode and added to his boyish appeal.

"Besides," he continued, swinging a booted leg lazily, "my mother has been kicking up such a dust I thought it best to stage a timely retreat." His sherry-colored eyes flashed in amusement. "She has the fever, you see."

Such a lack of filial devotion struck Brant as decidedly callous. He'd always thought his friend to be devoted to his parent, for he was always writing her when they were on the Peninsula. Perhaps he had misunderstood. "Do you mean she is ill?"

"Aye," Marcus agreed, tongue-in-cheek, "with the worst illness that can befall a female: Marriage Fever. Mama has taken it into her head that it's time I took a wife, and she has been making my life a living hell. I have had every eligible female in the country thrown at my head, and a few not-so-eligible ones as well. When she hired some ripe young beauty as her 'companion' I packed my bags and fled to London."

"I hardly think you'll find things much safer here," Brant replied with a husky laugh. "London is hardly bereft of sweet young females and their matchmaking mamas. You may have fled the beehive only to fall into the hornet's nest."

"True, but at least in London I won't be the only target for the swarm. With so many available dukes and earls about I may escape the Season yet unstung," Marcus joked good-naturedly. A servant had brought him a glass of brandy and after partaking of a healthy swallow he said, "But enough of me. You still haven't explained why you're looking so Friday-faced. Haven't been gaming, have you?" He gave Brant a disapproving frown.

"No, Parson Cherrington, I have not." Brant accepted his friend's censure calmly. Marcus could out-drink and out-wench any man in the King's Army, but when it came to gaming he'd always been something of a prude. Considering his father had all but gambled the family into destitution, Brant couldn't fault Marcus for his caution.

"A woman, then?" Marcus pressed, leaning forward to study Brant's face with interest. "Never say you have fallen into the parson's mousetrap!"

"God forbid," Brant intoned piously. "I didn't

spend all those years slipping out of Boney's ambushes only to be taken captive by some simpering chit." He stretched his long legs toward the fire and surveyed the glass of brandy cradled in his hand.

"Actually," he said, lifting the glass to his lips, "there is a woman involved. But I have no intention of marrying this one, I assure you."

"Ah." Marcus nodded in understanding. "Like that, is it? Well, what's the impediment? Is she already enjoying some man's protection? That's never stopped you before."

"She's not *that* sort of female." Brant chuckled at his friend's misapprehension. Any woman less mistress-like than Sara he had yet to meet. He grinned suddenly, envisioning her reaction if his offer had been what Marcus implied. She would doubtless have beaten him to death with her reticule.

"Well, what sort of female is she, then?" Marcus demanded. "There are only the two kinds that I'm aware of."

"She is my cousin," Brant explained. "That is, she is my distant cousin. Aunt found her starving in some wretched boarding-house and offered her the comfort of the family name. But Sara—that is her name—refuses to have anything to do with either Aunt or myself."

"Does she?" Marcus looked somber. As the eldest surviving son, family obligation was something he comprehended all too well. "I can see why you're looking so thunderous," he said, sipping his brandy thoughtfully. "Tell me everything."

Brant was happy to oblige, describing Sara's circumstances as he saw them and emphasizing her poor health. "So you see," he concluded, "I had no choice but to leave her there. She wasn't shy about refusing what she termed my 'charity.' I could hardly toss her over my shoulder and carry her off."

"No," Marcus agreed pensively. "That would have caused a devil of a stir and you might have found yourself explaining things to the watchman. What's next, then?" He cocked his eyebrow at Brant. "I can't see you allowing the situation to continue as it is. Do you have a plan?"

"Not yet," Brant admitted grimly, signaling the hovering servant for more brandy. "But you're right. I have no intention of letting things remain as they are. Sara is coming with me, and that is all there is to it."

They were arguing over possible plans when an old friend and former comrade-in-arms, Hugh Tressmoore, joined them. Hugh was a great bear of a man whose fierce countenance and somewhat disjointed way of speaking hid the mind of a brilliant tactician. When he learned what was afoot, he demanded to be included in their council of war.

"Enough of this senseless prattle," he thundered after several scenarios had been raised and then dismissed. They had also consumed several glasses of brandy, and were very full of themselves.

"Action is what is called for here. Action." He pounded the table for emphasis. "Not words."

"And what would you have me do?" Brant demanded in bellicose tones. "This isn't a military campaign, you know. We can't storm my cousin's hotel as if it were an enemy's position!"

"Why not?" Hugh responded to Brant's sarcasm with a fierce scowl. "Women have always been the natural enemy of man, have they not?" When the others allowed this was so, he continued. "Perhaps we *should* look at this as a military objective rather than worry ourselves with propriety and all that rot. What is needed here is a straightforward solution to a strategic situation. Come, Mallingham," he said, turning to the earl, who was staring blissfully off into space. "You once commanded a brigade. Forget the chit is your cousin. Pretend she is a . . . a French cannon to be captured! How would you do it?"

Brant tilted his dark head back against the cushions of his chair, trying to focus his fuzzy thoughts. He did not usually indulge in strong spirits so early in the day, and his brain was swimming in brandy fumes. It wasn't easy, but after several minutes of concentrated effort he arrived at what seemed to him the perfect solution to their problem. He wondered why he hadn't thought of it before.

"That's it!" he cried, struggling to his feet. "It's the very thing!"

"Eh?" Marcus raised his eyes from his bleary inspection of his boot. "What's that, Brant?"

"An abduction!" Brant announced, his blue eyes glittering with excitement and wine. "I shall abduct Cousin Sara, and you and Hugh shall help me! Now." He plopped back onto his chair. "Here is what we shall do . . ."

Across town Sara was still abed, slowly stirring to wakefulness following her long nap. After she had devoured the sumptuous tea the earl had ordered for her, she had fallen into a deep sleep. Whether it was the effects of a full stomach or sheer exhaustion, she slept better than she had in months, waking to feel rested and alert. She lay against the pillows enjoying a rare feeling of luxury until there was a light tapping at her door.

"Come in," she called out, pulling the comforter up to her chin. The door creaked open, revealing Dr. Rivers's familiar features.

"Ah, you are awake," he said, advancing into the room. Ever mindful of the proprieties, he left the door slightly ajar, speaking in a soft voice so that his words would not easily be overheard. "Excellent. I was beginning to think you meant to sleep the day away."

Sara blinked her golden eyes in confusion. "What time is it?" she asked shyly, brushing her tangled hair back from her cheek. "It feels as if I have been asleep forever."

"Actually, it's been less than four hours." Dr. Rivers sat down beside her bed. "I thought you might be awake by now and stopped to check on you. You had us all quite worried, you know, collapsing as you did." Gentle gray eyes regarded her admonishingly.

"I'm sorry." Sara ducked her head in embarrassment. She was unused to being cosseted and wasn't sure how to react. "It is just . . . oh, I don't know" —she shrugged her shoulders uncertainly—"my noble cousin made me so angry. Tossing me crumbs from his table and expecting me to bow and scrape in gratitude . . . !"

"That seems a rather harsh condemnation." Dr. Rivers's tone was chiding. "Lord Mallingham's offer seemed an honorable and generous one. From the little you have told me your connection to the

Deverleigh family is distant at best. You have no real claim on their generosity. That they are willing to help you is hardly an insult, my dear."

"Perhaps not to you," Sara protested softly, her soft gold eyes meeting the doctor's gentle gaze. "But if you knew how they treated my father . . . and my mother, I'm sure you would understand why I feel I must refuse. They disinherited my mama for marrying against their wishes, and after she died they tried to take me from my father. Don't you see," she implored, "I feel I would be betraying them if I accepted charity from the Deverleighs! Papa made me swear I would never go to them . . ."

"Your papa was suffering from a debilitating disease that slowly robbed him of his reason," Dr. Rivers said as gently as he could. "From what you have told me of his illness he doubtlessly became more and more confused as his sickness progressed, is that not so?"

Sara nodded, recalling the terrible days when her papa hadn't recognized her.

"That was the disease," the doctor explained, patting Sara's hands in a comforting gesture. "You mustn't feel bound to your word. I am sure your father would not wish you to suffer because of his pride."

Sara blinked at the tears filling her eyes. Was it just the disease? she wondered hesitantly. It had only been in the last few months of his life that he had grown so adamant. When Lady Mallingham had invited her to London for the Season he had urged her to go, saying it was what her mother would have wanted. And yet she had promised. . . .

"Come, Sara," Dr. Rivers urged, "at least promise me you will think about it. I am not suggesting you would need to be dependent upon them for the rest of your days. But surely it wouldn't be so terrible to accept their help for a little while. Only until you are well again," he added when he thought she would protest. "Will you at least consider what I have said?"

Sara closed her eyes in weary defeat. Perhaps Dr. Rivers was right, she mused. Pride, whether it be her pride or her father's, was a luxury she could ill afford. She had pared her expenses to the bone, and there was still less than thirty pounds in her purse. Even assuming she was strong enough to accept the post in Cornwall it would be months yet before she could expect to receive a salary. Months during which she would be expected to feed and clothe herself, pay for lodgings and the few feminine fripperies she allowed herself. A large lump of self-pity lodged in her throat as she faced her bleak prospects.

"Very well, Doctor," she said, swallowing painfully. "I promise to consider what you have told me."

"Thank you." He squeezed her hand gratefully. "Now, I have some medication I want you to take." He took out a brown vial and placed it on her night table. "Take one spoonful after dinner and another before bed if you wish. It's likely to make you drowsy, so don't be alarmed if you should sleep till morning."

Sara thought she had slept enough for three fe-

males, but she said nothing. She had the greatest
respect for Dr. Rivers and didn't wish to insult him
by questioning his orders. She supposed a few more
hours of sleep wouldn't hurt.

"Thank you again, Doctor," she said with a grateful smile. "I appreciate all you have done for me."

"It's no trouble," he assured her softly. "Now,
Miss Larkin has prepared a nice mutton broth and I
want you to drink every drop. Remember," he
added, his gray eyes full of affection, "the sooner
you are well again, the sooner you will be rid of
your cousin."

"That's true," Sara agreed as she bid the doctor
good night. It was only after he had gone that she
realized what she had said. She had just agreed,
more or less, to accept help from the Deverleighs.

"Now remember," Brant instructed as he stepped
down from Hugh's carriage, "you are to protect my
flank. In the event we should be followed, you're to
provide a diversion until we can escape. Is that
clear?"

"Aye, Captain!" Marcus sketched a jaunty salute.
"I say, this is the most fun I've had since resigning
my commission. Eh, Hugh?" He turned to Tressmoore eagerly.

"Indeed," Hugh grumbled in agreement, his dark
eyes scanning the streets expertly. "Peacetime
might be safer for a fellow, but it's a dashed bore."
He stiffened suddenly as he spotted a lone figure
rounding the corner. "There's the watch. Best hold
off fetching your cousin until he's gone. He might
interfere if she should scream."

"There's no time," Brant hissed between clenched teeth. "Get rid of him! Tell him you saw a cutpurse or some such thing, but get him away from here!"

"Very well." Hugh nodded once. "I understand." He gave Brant one of his rare smiles. "Reminds me of that time in Alexandria. A watchman may not be a squad of French dragoons, but these days a man can't be too choosy."

Brant grinned in understanding. He, too, missed the excitement of battle. He'd hated resigning his commission, but when he had inherited the title his aunt had insisted upon it. Besides, Napoleon had been routed and sent to St. Helena's and England no longer had need of her soldiers. It had been a long time since he had gone on a mission, and he enjoyed the familiar surge of anticipation.

He straightened his cuffs as he reviewed the plan they had laid out. It was a brilliant plan, as such plans go, and he had no doubt but that it would succeed. Every contingency had been carefully provided for. Except for one: the enemy had posted a sentry. A timorous woman in brown serge stood between him and the staircase, brandishing a candlestick as if it were a sword of fire.

"I warn you, madam, if you don't stand aside I will be forced to do something ungentlemanly!"

"D . . . .Dr. Rivers said Miss Belding was not to be disturbed," the poor woman stammered, staring at Brant through terror-filled blue eyes. "Now g . . . go away before I set my dog upon you. Shoo!" She waved her hand at him.

At any other time Brant would have found the prospect of being routed by a diminutive female vastly diverting. But at the moment he was too filled with brandy and pride to find much humor in the situation. He took a deep breath, forcing himself to think as a soldier would think.

A good commander never gave in to circumstances, he told himself sternly. A good commander adapted to the situation and made it work for him. Since a frontal attack had failed to dislodge his opponent he would try a diversionary tactic instead.

"Ma'am." He favored her with a honeyed smile which had been known to melt the coldest of feminine hearts. "Allow me to explain. I am Miss Belding's cousin. I only wish to assure myself she is receiving the best of care. Surely you can understand," he added in a wheedling tone.

"No!" The good lady hefted the candlestick warily. "M . . . Miss Larkin told me quite plainly that I was to allow no one to see Miss Belding tonight. No one! If you are truly her cousin, then you may call upon her tomorrow. But you shall not pass by me!" She flung her arms out wide, her eyes squeezing shut in fear. "Do to me what you will, but I shall not budge."

"Oh, for . . ." Brant bit off an impatient oath and was reaching out to physically remove the staunch defender of the staircase from her position when the door opened behind him. Dr. Rivers stepped inside, his eyes widening as he beheld the tableau before him.

"Oh, Dr. Rivers, thank heavens you are come!" The agitated woman lowered her arms in relief. "This . . . this ruffian attempted to force his way past me. But I stood firm in my sacred duty . . ."

"Did you now, Mrs. Goodeve." Dr. Rivers stepped forward and plucked the candlestick from her fingers. "That was very brave of you." He turned to Brant, his eyes bright with merriment despite his solemn expression.

"Ah, Lord Mallingham," he said, smiling, "I rather thought I might find you here. I have taken the liberty of bespeaking the private parlor from Miss Larkin. Perhaps you would care to join me for a little chat? But first, if you will excuse me, I will escort Mrs. Goodeve to her room. I fear all this . . . excitement may have been too much for her."

Brant shot the stalwart sentry a final glare before stalking from the entryway. Once in the cramped parlor he began pacing restlessly, pausing every now and again to look at his pocket watch. What the devil could be keeping the dratted man, he fumed with mounting impatience. He had been gone long enough to calm a dozen hysterical females. Or—Brant halted as a sudden thought occurred to him—warn one particularly stubborn one.

Perhaps that was what was delaying the doctor's return. He was keeping him cooling his heels in the parlor while Sara was smuggled down the back stairs! Well, Brant thought and thrust his jaw forward in anger, he would soon put a stop to *that.* He turned toward the door fully prepared to charge up the stairs and carry Sara away, when Dr. Rivers made his belated entry.

"I apologize for the delay, my lord," he began politely, "but I—"

"Where is my cousin Sara?" Brant interrupted harshly. "I demand you take me to her at once!"

"Peace, Lord Mallingham." Dr. Rivers held his hands up in a placating gesture. "I am on your side, sir, I assure you."

Brant tipped his head back in disbelief. "You're on *my* side," he repeated, his tone laced with sarcasm. "Since when?"

"Why, since the very beginning, of course," the doctor said, ignoring Brant's dark scowl as he took a seat upon the settee. "I quite approve of your desire to remove Miss Belding to more agreeable surroundings and to offer her the protection of your noble family."

Brant studied the doctor through half-lowered lids, alert for any potential traps. "What of your assurances to my cousin that she need not accompany me?" he demanded.

"Mere empty words of comfort, I fear." Dr. Rivers sighed, shaking his head. "Miss Belding was extremely overwrought at the time, and I wished only to calm her. Your cousin, my lord, is very ill. Nothing must be allowed to disturb her."

The doctor's words had a sobering effect upon Brant. He sat down on a faded beige-and-green chair, his eyes steady on the doctor. "Is it consumption?" he asked fearfully.

"No," the doctor assured him quickly. "At least, not yet. Your cousin is suffering from an inflammation of the lungs which, left untreated, might lead to pneumonia. With rest and proper care she should recover. Without it . . ." His shrug was eloquent.

Brant swallowed uneasily. He knew Sara was ill, of course. But he hadn't known matters were quite so serious. Perhaps it was just as well the plan had fallen through. An abduction was likely to send even the healthiest of females into the vapors. If Sara was as ill as Dr. Rivers implied . . .

"How long has she been ill?" he asked the doctor in confusion. "And why was I not informed?"

"She first fell ill less than a sennight ago," Dr. Rivers explained. "At first we thought it was a simple cold, but as she grew steadily worse I realized matters were more serious than that. Miss Larkin summoned me to treat Miss Belding about two days ago, and at that time I asked if there were any relations she might stay with until she was well. She said there were none."

"I see." Brant frowned, feeling strangely at a loss. He couldn't leave Sara here in her condition, and yet the doctor had warned him against upsetting her. He sighed and gave Dr. Rivers a bleak look. "What shall I do?"

"I have already spoken with Sara," Dr. Rivers said with a slight smile. "I do not say that she will welcome your help with open arms. But she has agreed to consider the matter, and for Sara, that is saying a great deal indeed. I am sure she will come around once she is established in your aunt's home. That *is* why you are here, is it not?"

Brant squirmed beneath the doctor's steady regard. The effects of the brandy were wearing off, leaving him with a pounding head and uncertain disposition. The plan he'd thought so clever now seemed absurdly childish. "I had thought to discuss the matter with her," he mumbled, sinking lower in the chair.

"I see." Dr. Rivers's lips twitched in amusement. "That would explain the rather large gentleman outside who did his best to . . . er . . . dissuade me from entering. Was he your guard, perhaps?"

The tips of Brant's ears reddened in embarrassment and he felt like a small boy caught snatching meat pies. "We thought it might be prudent not to have witnesses in case Sara . . . resisted."

"An excellent notion." Dr. Rivers applauded. "Knowing Miss Belding as I do, I can assure you, sir, she would have resisted. In fact, she would have kicked up a devil of a dust. That is why I chose to take certain precautions."

"Precautions?"

"I administered a mild sleeping draught to her earlier this evening," he said calmly. "Miss Belding is extremely strong-willed and although I admire her determination to make her own way, I feel she is being foolish beyond permission by refusing your aid. She is a female after all, and her place is with her family; especially given the state of her health. It is best for her to be with your aunt, and once she is recovered, I know Sara will agree with me."

"Is she sleeping then?" Brant wasn't certain if he approved of the doctor's drugging Sara. Although it would make his task much easier, he thought. Abducting a peacefully sleeping woman was infinitely preferable to carrying off one who screamed and fought every inch of the journey.

"Yes, that is why I was so late in joining you. I peeked in on her and she was sleeping like a babe." He paused. "If you like, I will have Miss Larkin pack her things. I would advise against dressing her, however. It is bound to wake her, and in any case you would just have to reverse the process once you got her to your aunt's. We shall wrap her in some nice warm blankets."

Brant nodded in agreement. As Dr. Rivers said, once Sara was settled with Aunt Agatha she would soon accept the situation. His aunt might be an interfering old crone, but she did like her creature comforts. Sara would lack for nothing. A derisive smile touched his lips. Luxury, or so it had always been his experience, was a most effective persuader; especially where females were concerned. Cousin Sara would sing a different tune once she awoke to find herself surrounded by the wealth of the Deverleighs.

"Well, do you mean to sleep all day?"

The demanding voice pierced the thick mists of sleep filling Sara's brain. She snuggled deeper beneath the soft, scented covers, willing the voice to go away. It was so warm, and for once her chest didn't ache as if a load of bricks had been dumped upon it. She'd just lie here a few more minutes and then . . .

"Sara, child, wake up! It's gone past noon, and I want to talk to you."

Sara's eyes flew open at the strident command, and she found herself face-to-face with a gilded cherub smirking at her from the post of the bed. What on earth . . . ? She stared at the carved creature in bewilderment. Where was she? This wasn't her room at Miss Larkin's! Nor was it her old room in her father's house. She raised her eyes and gazed around the rose-and-gold opulence in mounting alarm. She'd never been in such a room in her life!

The room was decorated in the rococo style, and even her inexperienced eyes could see that no expense had been spared. The walls were hung with heavy rose damask, and paintings or mirrors framed with gold leaf seemed to take every inch of available space. The floor was covered by a carpet of lush maroon, and out of the corner of her eye she could see a pair of heavy cream-colored brocade drapes. Glancing down at the counterpane of rich gold silk, she struggled to understand what was happening. Her eyes lifted to study the gilded cherub. Perhaps she was still dreaming, she told herself. Either that or she had died during the night and gone to heaven. She glanced at the frolicking cupid with its simpering expression and prayed she was dreaming. The notion of spending eternity with that monstrosity was more than she could bear.

"Aren't you going to say hello, my dear? I've been sitting here forever."

Sara's head whipped around to stare at the elderly woman sitting beside her bed. "Lady Mallingham!" she gasped, feeling a fresh wave of dizziness tugging at her consciousness. "What are you doing here?" For a brief moment there loomed the terrifying possibility that her eternal abode might be someplace other than heaven.

"What sort of question is that?" Lady Mallingham asked, shaking her head indulgently. "I live here, of course. And now, so do you." She frowned at Sara's dumbfounded expression. "I fear that drug has addled your mind," she sighed. "I don't approve of such heathenish potions as a rule. They are the devil's own brew and—"

"What heathenish potions?" Sara propped herself up on the pillow. Her eyes narrowed on the countess as a sudden suspicion dawned. "Are you telling me I was *drugged*?" she demanded incredulously.

"Well, it wasn't my doing," the countess said,

looking genuinely hurt by Sara's accusation. "Nor was it Brant's, come to that. It was all your Dr. Rivers's doing. He explained it all to Brant before you were brought here. He said you should be allowed to sleep until you awoke naturally, but it has been so long I became concerned."

"Dr. Rivers brought me here?" Sara sat up, ignoring the spinning blackness that threatened to engulf her. The doctor had left some sort of medicine for her. She remembered that much quite clearly. But after that, things got decidedly fuzzy.

She closed her eyes, a sudden memory surfacing. She was being held in a pair of sturdy arms, while a gentle hand brushed her hair back from her cheek. Someone was bending over her, and she had a distinct impression of the warm smell of spice mingling with the faint odor of brandy and tobacco smoke. It was a distinctly masculine fragrance, and it reminded her of her father. She remembered snuggling closer to a hard chest, feeling safe for the first time in many months.

"No, child." Lady Mallingham's voice shattered the memory like fragile glass and Sara opened her eyes to find the elderly woman smiling at her gently. As on the first occasion Sara had seen her, the countess was dressed all in orange. "That would hardly have been proper, you know," she continued chidingly. "You were in your nightclothes."

"Whereas it is perfectly acceptable for my cousin to have me drugged and then abducted!" Sara replied with some asperity.

"Well, of course." Lady Mallingham gave her a sweet smile. "He is your cousin, after all. As the head of our family he is your guardian."

Sara's lips thinned at such arrogance. "I have no need of a guardian, Lady Mallingham," she told the countess in frigid tones. "And I protest that I should be treated in such a manner. I insist that I be taken back to my rooms at once!"

To her surprise the countess burst into noisy tears, burying her face in an orange lace handkerchief. For one moment Sara was simply too stunned to do anything other than stare at the elderly lady's distress.

"I . . . I mean," Sara said weakly, feeling wretched at having made the countess cry, "I am sure you can understand . . . that is . . . It is very nice of you to be concerned, but I must insist . . ."

"I am sorry." Lady Mallingham was dabbing at her eyes, her wrinkled cheeks alarmingly pale. "I truly hadn't meant to be so selfish. But I did promise your mother I would have a care for you and I . . ."

"You promised my mother you would take care of me?" Sara stared at the countess in disbelief.

In reply Lady Mallingham withdrew a letter from her pocket and handed it to Sara. It came as something of a shock for Sara to see her mother's handwriting after so many years, and she opened the letter with trembling hands.

The letter was more than twenty-two years old, and judging from the date, it had been written shortly before her birth.

The letter was a happy one, filled with descriptions of her mother's life and her joy in the coming child . . . Sara. Toward the end, however, the tone grew melancholy. Her mother feared she would die in childbirth, and she asked the countess to help her unborn child in the event something should happen to her. When Sara finally lowered the letter, her eyes were bright with unshed tears.

She blinked her eyes rapidly, trying to sort through the confusing tangle of emotions. Learning of her mother's request had left her badly shaken, unable to think. Had her father known of her mother's desires? she wondered. Was that why he had borne the Deverleighs such animosity? Or had his hatred been a product of his illness, as Dr. Rivers had suggested? She closed her eyes, tears spilling down her cheeks as she was torn by conflicting loyalties.

"I know you have no great liking for me," Lady Mallingham was saying, her tone soft. "And after the way I behaved at your boarding-house I cannot say that I blame you. It was just such a shock seeing you like that . . . in that terrible place. You must have thought me a disagreeable old harridan," she added with a rueful laugh.

Sara slowly opened her eyes. The countess was smiling at her hesitantly, and for the first time she saw beyond the eccentric clothing and aristocratic manner. Lady Mallingham was perhaps one-and-seventy, and her wrinkled face and faded blue eyes revealed every one of those years. She looked old and alone, and Sara sensed she was desperately trying to do what she thought was best. That was something she could understand only all too well. She had spent the past year trying to do what she thought was right, and look where it had brought her.

"Not a 'harridan,' my lady," she corrected with a slow smile.

"A veritable crone," Lady Mallingham insisted. "I was as haughty as a duchess at tea and I shouldn't wonder that you refused to come with me. Although I do hope you will stay now that you are here . . . if only for a little while."

Sara glanced down at her hands, her mind working carefully. The job in Cornwall was all but lost to her, she acknowledged with a sigh. In her present condition there was no way she could possibly accept it. And it might take months before she could find another position. She stole a surreptitious glance at the countess's wistful face.

Perhaps it wouldn't be so terrible if she were to stay for a few weeks, just until she was on her feet again. That way she could help Lady Mallingham keep her word to her mother without breaking her own promise to her papa. She really wouldn't be accepting charity from the Deverleighs, she assured herself. If by staying she could be of assistance to the countess, well then, it was *she* who was being charitable. Satisfied at the way she had resolved things, she flashed the countess a warm smile.

"Very well, my lady," she said, reaching out to take the countess's hand. "I should like to stay with you, if I may. But only until I am well again," she added cautiously.

"Until you are well again," Lady Mallingham echoed, lowering her blue eyes to hide their smug expression.

Chapter Three

Sara spent her first two weeks at Lady Mallingham's in her rose-and-gold bedroom, recovering her health and fending off the countess's attempts to cure her. The older lady was well versed in every ill imaginable, and she was determined to quack Sara back to good health. When she began pressing purgatives on her, Sara rebelled.

"I'm quite well, ma'am, I promise you," she told the countess, resisting the urge to pull the bedclothes up over her head. "And I really don't care for any more medication."

"Oh, but I had this made up just for you," Lady Mallingham protested. "The doctor assures me it's just the thing to put you on your pins again." She poured some of the thick brown mixture onto a spoon and held it to Sara's lips. "Won't you try a taste," she coaxed.

Sara averted her head, her nose wrinkling in distaste. As a physician's daughter she had often helped him prepare his medications and she was familiar with most of their ingredients. Judging from the potent odor coming from this foul stuff, it contained brandy or some other strong spirit, and very little else. One swallow of the liquid, and she would doubtless be in a stupor for the rest of the day.

"No, thank you, Lady Mallingham." Sara stood firm. She had grown quite fond of the countess during the weeks she had been there, but there were limits as to how far she was willing to go to please her. "I had thought to get up today, and I should like to have all my wits about me."

Lady Mallingham's brow cleared as if by magic and she poured the medicine back into the bottle. "Oh, how wonderful!" she exclaimed with pleasure. "Brant is coming for a visit, and I know he is anxious to see you. You're not still angry with him, are you, my dear?" She gave Sara a worried frown. "I know what he did was very naughty, but it *was* for your own good."

Sara considered the earl's actions a great deal more than "naughty," but she held her tongue. She and the countess had had this conversation before, and it always ended with Lady Mallingham dissolving in tears. "No, my lady," she lied judiciously, "I'm not angry."

"There's a good girl." Lady Mallingham patted her hand. "For I should hate to have my two little ones at daggers drawn. Now," she rushed on excitedly, "we must discuss your wardrobe. I don't wish to be critical, my dear, but it is a trifle limited."

Sara colored in embarrassment. Her belongings had already been unpacked and placed in the wardrobe, and Lady Mallingham had been hinting that she would like to replace several garments.

"Well, I am still in mourning for Papa," she said, not meeting Lady Mallingham's gaze. "It wouldn't be seemly for me to wear colors for several more weeks. Besides, when I begin teaching a simple wardrobe will be better suited for my position."

Lady Mallingham's face crumpled in disappointment. "I'd forgotten you meant to leave me," she sighed, plucking at the ruffle on her morning gown.

"But you are right, of course. I am sorry if I upset you."

"You haven't upset me." Sara squeezed the countess's hand gently. It was obvious Lady Mallingham was lonely. Her husband was long dead, and from what she could glean from the servants there had been no children. Apart from herself the only family the countess had was Lord Mallingham, and he only came to visit once a week . . . selfish mushroom.

"What dress do you think I should wear?" she asked in a bright voice, hoping to distract the countess from her sad thoughts.

Lady Mallingham pursed her lips, and for a brief moment Sara had a glimpse of the coldly autocratic woman who had called upon her at Miss Larkin's. But before she could say anything the expression was gone, and the countess was smiling with her customary sweetness.

"The gray wool with the lace collar, I think," she said, shaking out the folds of her gown. "Now if you will excuse me, I must go speak with Cook. Good day, Sara. I will see you at tea."

After she had left Sara settled back against her pillows and rang for the maid. Servants were an all-but-forgotten luxury, and their eager ministrations often left Sara feeling uneasy. Any attempts to do for herself usually ended in exclamations of dismay from the staff, and Sara was learning to accept their presence. Besides, she admitted as the smiling maid came hurrying in to do her bidding, it was rather pleasant being pampered. She would enjoy it while she could.

The maid who had been assigned to her was a

talkative woman in her mid-thirties by the name of
Matty, and she chatted gaily as she helped Sara
with her toilet.

" 'Course I've only been with her ladyship these
last two years. Afore that I worked for a merchant
and his wife," she confided as she brushed Sara's
waist-length brown hair to shiny order. "She had
long hair too, though it weren't nearly so pretty as
yours. I used to dress it for her, and she said I was
every bit as good as the man they hired from town.
Lady Mallingham said I was to arrange your hair
today. If you don't mind, miss." Her anxious brown
eyes met Sara's in the cheval glass.

"That would be fine, Matty, thank you," Sara
murmured, not wishing to hurt the maid's feelings.
She had heard two other servants whispering how
Matty had been promoted from downstairs maid to
act as her personal maid, and she was afraid the
woman would be demoted again if she showed any
displeasure in her services.

"If you don't mind my saying so, miss, it's grand
having a young lady in the house," Matty continued cheerfully. "I've never seen the countess happier, all full of plans and such. Cook is that pleased
because her ladyship is talking of a dinner party.
She ain't never had one, not since the old earl, God
bless him, passed on. That's what Jemma says, and
she's been here a good ten years or more."

"Lady Mallingham is planning a dinner party?"
Sara asked in surprise. Only the other day the
countess had been sighing how all her dear friends
were dead and buried. Whomever did she mean to
invite?

"Oh, my, yes." Matty pulled the gray dress over

Sara's head and began lacing up the fastenings with nimble fingers. "It's only proper is what Mr. Jenks says. He's the butler, you know, and he's been with the countess since he were a lad. He says since my lady is sponsoring you we'll be having balls and soirees and all them lovely things as well. It will be ever so much fun, don't you think?"

Sara thought nothing of the kind, but she could hardly say as much to the maid. She listened in growing alarm as Matty described the countess's plans for the coming Season. To hear her tell it, Lady Mallingham was planning a full-fledged assault on Society.

"Now me, I likes the idea of one of them fancy-dress balls," Matty said as she began arranging Sara's hair in a loose chignon. "All them pretty gowns and the men in their silks and satins. But Jemma thinks a midnight supper would be better. After all, it ain't like you was fresh out of the schoolroom . . . begging your pardon, miss."

Sara mumbled a reply, her mind on what Matty had let slip. This was the first she had heard of anything. To be sure, she had agreed to stay part of the Season with Lady Mallingham, but she hadn't thought she would be expected to participate in the festivities.

"There you are, miss." Matty stepped back to admire her handiwork with obvious satisfaction. "Will there be anything else? Some rouge, perhaps?"

"What?" Sara gazed blankly at the fashionably attired young woman reflected in her mirror. "Oh . . . No, thank you, Matty. That will be all."

"Very good, miss." Matty bobbed a curtsey and departed, leaving Sara alone with her troubled thoughts.

Brant arrived at his aunt's almost half an hour later. He was rigged out in a new coat of mulberry velvet, his hair brushed to ruthless perfection by his valet. Lady Mallingham had written that Sara would be joining them, and he was anxious to see her again. He hadn't seen her since the evening he had carried her into his aunt's home. He'd called upon her several times, only to be told she was too ill for visitors. He was concerned for her health, and Lady Mallingham's first words upon entering the drawing room did little to ease that worry.

"Ah, Brant, I'm so glad you've come." The countess collapsed upon the green brocade chair set before the cheerful fire. "I'm worried to death about Sara. Things are even worse than I feared."

Brant resumed his seat on the gold-and-white-striped settee. "Do you mean she won't be joining us?" he asked, his brow wrinkling in concern. "I thought you'd written she was much improved."

"Oh, her health is good enough, I suppose." Lady Mallingham settled the skirts of her orange silk dress about her ankles. "Or as well as can be expected, considering she refuses to consider any sensible course of treatment. I don't know what ails these modern gals," she grumbled, turning her attention to the lavish tea that had been set out on the wooden cart. "We were never so missish about disorders of the body in *my* day. But as it happens, I'm referring to Sara's financial circumstances. You would not credit it, but the poor child has been left penniless."

Brant silently accepted the cup his aunt offered him. Sara's strained finances came as no surprise to him. He'd had his man of business investigating Sara's affairs this past week, and he confirmed what Brant had suspected. The death of her parents had left her virtually destitute. It did surprise him that she would confess as much to his aunt, however. He would have thought Sara would have died sooner than admit as much to anyone.

"How do you know that?" he asked, folding his arms across his chest. "Did Sara tell you?"

Lady Mallingham gave him a sagacious look. "Credit me with a little sense," she told him dryly. "I saw where she was living, and in any case, one look at her wardrobe would be enough to tell me her pockets are to let. Well, I shall have to see to it, I suppose. Sara is a good child for all her hoydenish ways, and I hate to think of her cast off in the world."

"As should I," Brant replied. He had an idea—well, it was Marcus's idea actually—but he had improved upon it, and he had been wondering how to broach the subject.

"I have been thinking, Aunt," he said, after clearing his throat. "If you and Sara are getting along together, perhaps you might hire her as your companion. She would then have a comfortable home, and you would have someone to take care of you. It would be an ideal solution to all our problems, don't you agree?" He gave his aunt a hopeful smile.

"No, I do not." Lady Mallingham rejected his plan with a curt shake of her head. "For your information, I have no need of someone to take care of me! Companions are only suitable for either very young ladies fresh out of the schoolroom, or doddering old women. As I am neither, I would hardly have use for such a creature, now would I? Besides, Sara and I would be at each other's throats within a sennight. I can't maintain my pose as a saintly old lady indefinitely."

The notion of his meddlesome aunt as a "saintly old lady" was almost Brant's undoing. "Indeed, ma'am," he said, once he had regained control of his composure, "I had no idea you felt it necessary to . . . er . . . employ such a pose."

"Well, I have," the countess retorted with a sour look. "And believe me, it was highly necessary. Sara was in such high dudgeon when she awoke, she would have bolted straight for the border if I hadn't thought to show her a letter Katherine had written to me before she was born." She shook her head in disgust.

"Why you men must insist upon doing things in such a havey-cavey manner, I know not. 'Tis a wonderment to me how you ever manage to win your silly wars. But be that as it may," she continued before Brant could let fly with a blistering reply, "I don't think hiring Sara as my companion would solve anything. Servants have been known to resign. No, there is only one solution to our problem, and I think you know it as well as I. We must marry her off, as quickly as it can be arranged."

* * *

Had it not been for the footman Sara would have never found her way to the drawing room. It was only the second time she had been out of her room without someone to escort her, and she quickly became lost in the twisting maze of corridors. Despite its small size the countess's town house was a confusing jumble of rooms, each filled to overflowing with exotic artifacts and doo-dads.

The Deverleighs evidently had a passion for collecting every manner of useless things, and they had spent the better part of two centuries indulging themselves with little regard for either economy or good taste. Sara had just backed out of a tiny room containing several examples of Hindu erotica when she collided with the footman. After she had recovered from the severe shock to her sensibilities she allowed the grinning servant to escort her downstairs.

The sight that greeted her when she walked into the room was straight out of a domestic novel. Lady Mallingham, clad in what was for her a demure gown, sat before a cheerful fire, her head bent over her needlework. Lord Mallingham sat facing her, a teacup balanced in his large hand. Lady Mallingham lifted her head at the sound of the door opening, her eyes softening in a pleased smile when she saw Sara.

"There you are, my dear," she said, setting her knitting aside as she rose slowly to her feet. "I was wondering what was keeping you. Come and say hello to your cousin."

Sara turned to face the earl, determined to be pleasant if only for the countess's sake. "Good afternoon, my lord," she said, proffering her hand with a polite smile. "How nice to see you again."

"Cousin Sara." Brant took her hand in his and raised it to his lips. The rest and good food his aunt had provided had removed the pinched look from Sara's face, and her fine eyes glowed with health. He noted the plain gray dress, and decided he would have to discuss her wardrobe with his aunt. "I'm glad to see you are recovered from your illness. I trust you are feeling more the thing?"

"Yes, my lord." Sara freed her hand as soon as politeness allowed. She was watching him through wary eyes, not quite sure she trusted his dimpled smiles and easy charm. Handsome is as handsome does, her papa used to say, and the earl was a great deal too handsome for Sara's comfort.

"I am relieved to hear it," he said, assisting her to her chair with the reverent care usually shown to fragile old ladies. Once she had been seated he continued standing, a warm smile lighting his blue eyes as he stared down at her.

"I want to apologize, Cousin, for my somewhat unorthodox behavior in bringing you here," he began, making Sara start in disbelief. "I realize you have every right to be upset with me, but in my own defense I would like to say that I was very concerned for your health. That is why I felt it necessary to . . . er . . . remove you as I did." He tilted his dark head to one side, a dimple flashing in his cheek as he asked coaxingly, "Dare I hope you might forgive me?"

It would have taken a harder heart than Sara possessed to withstand so charming an apology. Besides, she disliked discord of any kind. If the earl was willing to offer so pretty an apology, then the very least she could do was accept it.

"Of course, sir," she replied, responding to Brant's dazzling smile with a shy offer of her own. "And may I apologize as well? I was most uncivil, as I recall." She added the last part for good measure, deciding that if the earl could be magnanimous then so could she.

"Not at all," Brant denied with a soft murmur. Secretly, he was delighted at how well things were progressing. His aunt was right; a direct confrontation wasn't always the best way to defeat an opponent. The last thing in the world he had expected was that Sara would actually return his apology. Emboldened by his apparent success, he leaned down to pat her hand. "You weren't quite yourself," he said in soothing tones. "I do understand. Although I am not at all sure that you *have* forgiven me."

"Oh, but I have, my lord," she assured him, firmly squelching the resentment his words caused. Now that they had arrived at a truce of sorts she was determined not to fly up into the boughs. She swallowed her anger enough to say, "I am sure you did what you thought was best, and I appreciate your concern."

"Then why are you calling me 'my lord'?" he asked, lowering his voice to an intimate whisper. "I thought it was agreed you would call me by my Christian name."

Actually, he had commanded her to call him "cousin," but in the interest of family harmony Sara decided not to mention that now. If it was tranquillity he wanted, tranquillity he would have.

"Very well . . . Brant," she said in dulcet tones, "consider yourself forgiven."

"Thank you, Sara." Brant's eyes narrowed in sudden suspicion. There was something in her sugary voice that made his senses tingle. That little frisson of warning that all was not as it seemed had saved his life on more than one occasion, and he wasn't about to ignore it now.

"Thank heavens that is settled," Lady Mallingham sighed, busying herself with the tea. "Now we can discuss the coming Season. There is much to be done, starting with a voucher from Almack's."

"Almack's!" Sara exclaimed in horror, trying to juggle the cup of tea and plate of cakes Brant had given her. Almack's was the holiest of holies and she had never thought to visit there. Evidently the countess's plans were even more elaborate than she had feared. "Are you quite sure that is proper, my lady?" she asked weakly. "I've never been formally introduced, and . . ."

"Nonsense!" Lady Mallingham snorted derisively. "And please, my dear, you would honor me if you would call me 'Aunt' as Brant does. As to the other, there is no doubt but that you will be accepted. After all, you're my cousin and a Deverleigh. I have already written Lady Jersey and the other patronesses, and they have agreed to overlook the fact you have never been properly launched. Don't worry, child, we shall see to it."

"Aunt Agatha is right." Brant leaned forward in his chair to better study Sara's reactions. He could see that the thought of entering Society dismayed her, and he felt a sudden wave of fierce protectiveness. There was no need for her to be afraid, he thought, fighting the urge to reach out and take her hand. With Aunt Agatha's help and his influence they would have no trouble establishing her. He gave her a smile and succumbed to the need to touch her hand.

"Don't be afraid," he said gently, seeking to reassure her. "Now that you are under our protection no one would dare snub you. I will take care of you."

The temptation to dump her scalding tea over her cousin's head was proving almost too great to resist, so Sara set the cup hastily aside. Of all the arrogant, overbearing— She gave him a fulminating glare. How dare he patronize her as if she were some timid little mouse! Did he really think she cared a whit what a group of snobbish strangers thought of her?

"That is very kind of you both," she said in a controlled voice. "But I fear it would not serve. I'm still in mourning for my father, and it wouldn't be proper for me to enter Society just now."

There was a tense silence as Lord and Lady Mallingham exchanged knowing glances. "Forgive me, my dear," the countess said mildly, "but it has been over a year since your father died. I know you grieve him still in your heart, but it is time you came out of mourning. I'm not suggesting that you dispense with it entirely, but it would be permissible if you were to attend a few select functions."

Mourning her father's death had been Sara's last hope of dissuading her aunt. Despite her own reluctance to enter a gay social whirl, she could see it was something the countess wanted very much. After all her aunt had done for her, she couldn't bring herself to refuse. It would only be for a little while, she told herself, just until she found a new position. Also it wouldn't hurt her to experience a bit of the world.

"Very well, Aunt," she capitulated with a small sigh. "If you are sure it is acceptable."

"Thank you, my dear." The countess was dabbing her eyes with her handkerchief. "You have made an old woman very happy. Well, thank heavens that is settled," she said, blowing her nose for emphasis before turning her blue eyes on an unsuspecting Brant.

"Brant dearest," she spoke in honeyed tones. "Why don't you tell Sara about your plans for next Wednesday evening."

Brant stirred uneasily. His plans for next Wednesday involved a delightful tête-à-tête with the beautiful Felicia. But that was hardly the sort of thing he could confess to Sara.

"Plans?" He raised his teacup to his lips, assuming his most innocent expression.

"You know." Lady Mallingham was having none of his shilly-shallying. "For the theater." She turned back to face Sara. "We were discussing the newest production of *Macbeth*. It is said to be quite good. I thought perhaps you would enjoy attending. Do you like Shakespeare?"

Sara brightened at once. Like most girls of her class she had been raised with a healthy respect for the Bard's works, and *Macbeth* had always been a particular favorite of hers. "Oh, yes, Lady . . . Aunt Agatha," she replied, her light brown eyes sparkling with interest. "Papa and I often read his plays aloud. We talked of coming to London to attend a play, but there was never enough time."

Brant silently cursed his aunt for her clever maneuvering. Faced with Sara's genuine enthusiasm for the proposed outing there was no way he could cry off without appearing the veriest villain. He cast Sara a considering look, noting her flushed cheeks and bright eyes speculatively. It was the most animated he had seen her and it gave him an odd feeling of pleasure to see her so happy. He hoped Felicia would understand. This would make the second assignation he had canceled in as many weeks.

"Then we shall consider the matter settled," he said, repressing his own feelings. There was much more to this guardian business that he had first thought, but he supposed he could make a few concessions in the line of duty. "What time shall I call for you next week?"

"Seven," the countess supplied. "We shall dine here first. Oh, and do bring the Viscount Cherrington with you. I have heard from his mama that he is in town. I daresay he is as fond of the theater as anyone."

Actually, Marcus detested the theater and would rather be drawn and quartered than endure an evening of Shakespeare, but Brant held his tongue. It was obvious Aunt Agatha was hoping to arrange some sort of match between Sara and his friend, and Brant thought it might prove interesting to oblige her.

They spent the rest of the hour discussing their plans, and Brant was preparing to take his leave when his aunt rose to her feet.

"I am sure you two young people must have a great deal to say to one another," she said, straightening her turban deftly. "Sara dear, don't let this naughty boy tire you out. You are still recovering, and I don't wish you to overtax yourself. Brant, I shall see you and Lord Cherrington next Wednesday evening." She gave them a maternal nod and departed in a swish of orange silk.

After the door closed behind Lady Mallingham, Sara and Brant sat staring at each other in an uncomfortable silence. For two people with so much to say, they were both surprisingly silent. Finally Brant stirred himself to ask, "How are you settling in with Aunt Agatha? Is everything satisfactory?"

"Everything is fine, my lord," she responded hesitantly, perhaps too hesitantly, for his wide eyes had narrowed as they rested on her upturned face.

"Are you certain?" he pressed, wondering what was going on behind her honey-gold eyes. It was obvious something was troubling her, and in a flash he knew what it was. "Are you still worried about the coming Season?"

Sara blushed at his perceptivity. He really was the most exasperating man, she thought, glancing away from his probing look. One moment he was so impossibly arrogant she longed to box his ears, and the next moment he could be so gentle and understanding.

" 'Tis not the prospect of the Season that alarms me," she confessed, raising her eyes to his. "But rather, it's the matter of my wardrobe. I know Aunt has ordered me several gowns, and although I appreciate her generosity I cannot possibly accept them."

Brant breathed a silent sigh of relief. Here he had been envisioning Sara quaking in terror at the thought of facing the ton, and all the while she was fretting about her gowns. Not that he wished to make light of her worries. He more than anyone knew just how much her pockets were to let. Nor did he fool himself into believing she would allow him to pay for them . . . unless . . .

"Sara," he began in a casual tone, "do you mind if I make a suggestion?"

"Not at all, sir." She gave him a hesitant smile.

"Brant," he corrected automatically. "I want you to accept the gowns from Aunt Agatha. I know you don't wish to," he added when she opened her mouth to protest, "but if you will only listen to me, I am sure we can arrive at a satisfactory arrangement. Now, when we first met you spoke of going to Cornwall to be a schoolmistress. Is that not so?"

"Well . . . yes," she confessed in confusion. "But circumstances have forced me to write and refuse the position. What has this to do with Lady Mallingham's extravagances?"

Brant forced himself to remain calm. He had only just got Sara settled with his aunt, and didn't wish to jeopardize that by any imprudent action. He would have to proceed very carefully or he could ruin everything.

"My point, Sara, is that you were once willing to work for your keep. Since that is the case, I should like to make you a counter-offer. I will pay for your wardrobe out of my own pocket if you will agree to act as Aunt's companion for the time you are in London."

"But . . ." Sara was stunned by the unexpectedness of the earl's proposition. Her fondness for the countess aside, she thought there was something decidedly mercenary about accepting payment for staying with a relation. "I cannot do that," she managed at last. "Lady Mallingham is my cousin. I cannot allow you to pay me when I am already living in her home. If anything, sir, I should be paying *you*."

Brant had been expecting this argument. Even though his aunt had already refused even to consider accepting Sara as her companion, he saw no reason to abandon the plan entirely.

"You *can* repay me," he said urgently, "by acting as Aunt's companion. I know how lonely she has been and how hard it is for her rattling around this place, alone except for the servants. I've offered to pay for someone to stay with her, but up until now she has refused. I have been at my wits' end wondering what to do about her.

"Don't you see," he continued, taking her hand in his and squeezing it firmly, "the cost of your gowns would be as nothing to me! But my aunt's happiness means everything. I would willingly pay for a dozen wardrobes if it would keep Aunt happy."

This much at least was true. Sara's arrival in his aunt's home had produced the side benefit of decreasing the countess's demands upon his time. In fact, if he hadn't written to remind her of his weekly visit, he wondered if she would even have missed him.

"Won't you consider my offer?" he added on a pleading note.

The eloquence of his appeal left Sara with nothing to say. She knew he was an exceedingly wealthy man, and as he had said, the cost of her gowns would be as nothing to him. He probably lost as much or more at the gaming tables and never gave it a second thought. But his aunt's well-being did matter to him, and it was the one thing his money could not buy. She bit her lip, turning the matter over in her mind.

She would be staying with the countess anyway, and common sense told her she would be needing several new gowns if she were to attend even half of the entertainments her aunt was planning. Perhaps, if she regarded the gift of clothing as a sort of uniform like her friend Mary Digby wore at her private school, she could better swallow her pride and accept the earl's offer. She frowned as a sudden thought occurred.

"Won't the countess think it odd when you pay my bills instead of her?"

Brant cursed beneath his breath. He hadn't thought of that. He scowled furiously until the solution came to him. "She won't even realize what is going on," he assured her with a smooth lie. "My man of business handles her accounts as well, and I'll instruct him to pay your modiste's bill out of my funds. She need never know."

Sara lapsed into another thoughtful silence. It hurt her pride to be forced into the position of having to accept charity . . . even charity that was lovingly offered, as it was in the countess's case. On the other hand, if she were to agree to her cousin's plan, then the wardrobe would be in lieu of a salary. It would mean, indirectly at least, that she would be paying her own bills.

"Very well, Cousin," she said, accepting his offer before she lost her nerve. "I agree to your plan, and I promise I will do everything in my power to make the countess happy."

"Thank you," he murmured, raising her hand to his lips for a brief salute. He rose to his feet, gently tugging her out of her chair. "I am more grateful than I can tell you. Now, I have just one more thing to ask of you."

"Of course, sir. What is it?"

"Don't tell Aunt of our arrangement," he said. "It would only hurt her, you see. This will be our little secret. Do you agree?"

Even though she found the thought of such deceit distasteful, Sara nodded her head in agreement. "Very well, sir, but . . ."

"Shhh." He laid his finger on her lips. "Not another word. The matter is settled. Now if you will excuse me, I must be off. I have to find Marcus and warn . . . er . . . inform him of the outing to the theater. Oh, and Sara?" He flashed her one of his wide, dimpled grins.

"Yes?" She didn't trust that charming smile of his.

"My name is Brant . . . remember? Or Cousin Brant, if you insist upon the formalities. You might practice saying it so that by next week it will come more naturally to you. Until then, Cousin, adieu."

Chapter Four

Marcus's lodgings were in Mayfair, not far from Brant's own modest town house, and after stopping to explain matters to his petulant mistress, the earl hurried to his friend's rooms. He surprised Marcus in his shirtsleeves, and while the viscount finished donning a new jacket of fawn-colored velvet, Brant waited in his sitting room, helping himself to brandy with the familiarity of long friendship. Marcus joined him a short time later, and as he expected, the viscount was less than thrilled with the proposed agenda.

"The theater," he groaned, flinging himself on his blue-and-cream-striped Sheraton couch. "And Shakespeare, no less. Really, Mallingham, you do ask a great deal of your friends. Wouldn't your cousin be happier at a nice ball or soiree?"

"Perhaps." Brant rose lazily to pour his friend a generous portion of brandy. "But she's going to *Macbeth*." He handed Marcus the snifter with a mocking bow. "And you needn't glare at me," he continued, resuming his seat in the dark blue wing chair. "It wasn't my idea, I assure you. I'd already made my plans for that evening, and they had nothing to do with theatrical productions."

"The fair Felicia." Marcus gave an envious sigh as he gazed into the flames flickering in the fireplace. "Well, I can understand how you may have found your aunt's meddling ill-timed, but is that any reason to involve me? You know how much I dislike watching grown men capering about onstage."

"Look upon it as an onerous but necessary duty," Brant advised, amused by Marcus's good-natured grumbling. "As for 'involving' you, you may lay the blame for Aunt's invitation on your mother's doorstep. She apparently wrote to my aunt telling her of your presence here in London."

"Did she?" Marcus grimaced, leaning his back against the casement. "Oh, Lord, I am a doomed man, then. I may have circumvented Mama, but if she joins forces with that formidable aunt of yours then my days of carefree bachelorhood are numbered." He took another sip of brandy before cocking a dark blond eyebrow at Brant. "And what of you?" he challenged. "You are years older than I. Isn't it time Lady Mallingham had you safely leg-shackled?"

"Bite your tongue, puppy. So far I've been singularly fortunate in that Aunt has spared me any matchmaking proclivities she may be harboring. And now that she has Cousin Sara to marry off, she'll be far too busy to bother with such an old crusty bachelor as I."

"Speaking of your fair cousin, how is she?" Marcus inquired politely. "She must be feeling more the thing if your aunt is planning on trotting her off to the theater."

"She is much recovered," Brant agreed, a thoughtful frown darkening his face. "Although she is still somewhat thin. Do you suppose it is too soon for her to be out? I hadn't thought of it, but perhaps you are right. I wonder if I should speak with her physician and . . ."

Marcus's crack of laughter stopped Brant in mid-sentence, and he looked up to find his friend gazing at him with obvious amusement.

" 'Lo, how the mighty are fallen,' " he mourned, shaking his head sadly. "I never thought to see the day when I should hear you clucking over a sick relation like a mother hen. Now I would expect such behavior from *me,* but from you . . ." He gave another delighted chuckle.

Brant stiffened, cut by Marcus's teasing words. He set his glass on the table and glared at him through narrowed eyes. "I fail to see what you find so amusing," he said, the ice in his voice matching the glacial sheen in his blue eyes. "I should hope that I am as capable of fulfilling my family obligations as any man, and I wonder that you should imply otherwise."

The laughter faded from Marcus's face at the harsh words. "I say, Mallingham, I meant no offense," he mumbled uncomfortably. "It is just . . . well . . . you have never seemed overly fond of your relations, few as they may be, and you are forever complaining about your aunt's interference in your life. I merely meant that you aren't as close to your family as I am to mine."

"Just because I don't choose to live in my aunt's pocket doesn't mean I am totally without affection for her." Brant was aware he was overreacting to Marcus's innocent teasing and softened his tone accordingly. "As for Sara, I am determined to do my duty by her, and I cannot like your implying I have been derelict in carrying out my responsibilities."

At first Marcus was puzzled by Brant's response to what had been, after all, a playful jest. Then he remembered how Brant had been during the war.

He was the consummate officer, putting his duty to his men above all else. Even when he had been wounded he'd refused to relinquish command, urging his men on until the battle had been won. Such a man, Marcus knew, would not take kindly to any suggestion that he had failed in his duties. He was searching for an appropriate apology when Brant gave a weary sigh.

"I'm sorry, Marcus," he said, rubbing a hand across his forehead. "I shouldn't have torn into you like that. And you're quite right, my actions toward my family do me little credit. My aunt, for all her troublesome ways, has been very good to me. She wrote me every week while I was in Spain, and when I was wounded and brought home, it was she who nursed me. I owe her much, Marcus, and I mean to repay her."

"Does this mean you shall assist her in her endeavors to marry off your cousin?" Marcus tactfully refrained from commenting on Brant's quiet apology. "Somehow I can't envision you as a matchmaker. Not after all the years you've spent dodging every marriage trap in the kingdom."

"Ah, but it is precisely that experience which will aid me now." Brant appreciated Marcus's discretion in not mentioning his sullen behavior. "Having successfully avoided such traps I am an expert on how best to bait them. By the time I have finished preparing her, Sara shall have her pick of any man."

"Indeed?" Marcus was thoughtful. "But I understood you to say she is a shrew, and a plain one at that. Unless you intend bestowing a sizable dowry on her, you may have your work cut out for you."

"Of course I will see that Sara is well dowered,"

Brant replied, his brow puckering at Marcus's words. "And as for her being a shrew, well, I fear I may have misjudged her. She is a trifle strong-willed perhaps, but a bit of spirit is to be desired in a woman. And since moving in with my aunt, her conduct has been most becoming."

"But she *is* plain?"

Brant considered the question. "Not really," he said at last. "She is no beauty by any means, but I wouldn't go so far as to call her plain." He conveniently forgot this was his own description of Sara, and continued in a reflective tone. "She is very thin, as I have said, with no figure to speak of. But dressed in the proper clothes she should do quite well. Her eyes are a beautiful shade of gold, and her hair is quite lovely. If we take care to play up these assets I daresay we'll give a good accounting of ourselves." He lifted his glass to his lips for another sip.

"It's rather like a battle, you see. If your infantry is weak, then you reinforce your artillery. That's all the marriage mart is, really; a war fought upon the battlefield of Society."

Marcus was much struck by this. "Do you know," he said in a bemused tone, "I have never thought of it quite like that, but you're right. Setting aside all the taradiddle about love and family obligations, the marriage mart is a war, and like any war it can be won. The most important thing is deciding upon a course of action, and then seeing it through to the end."

Brant nodded, pleased at his friend's acuity. "My sentiments exactly. In our time, Marcus, you and I have carried out some brilliant operations against the enemy. Between the two of us, I daresay we should have no trouble marrying off one little spinster. What do you say? Are you game?"

"Begad, I will do it!" Marcus set his glass down with a thump. "It will be our greatest challenge!"

"Then I may count upon you for support?"

"Short of marrying her myself, I'll do anything within my power to help Sara snag a husband. Here's my hand on it."

"Thank you." They shook hands solemnly before Brant said, "Now down to business. The first thing we must do is to scout out the lay of the land and learn what we can of the enemy."

"Enemy?"

"The other marriageable females. I have few acquaintances amongst the debs, so I fear I am not all that familiar with this year's crop of beauties. We must rectify that if we wish to succeed. At the theater we must pay close attention to the other ladies, especially those hanging about for a husband."

"I say." Marcus snapped his fingers. "Tressmoore has a sister, Prunella or some such thing. She is to make her bows this year, and as they are using Hugh's town house I'm sure he must have a great deal of information he would be willing to share with us."

"An excellent suggestion," Brant approved, going to Marcus's desk and extracting a piece of stationery. "We'll invite him and his sister to join us in my box. I've worked with Hugh before, and even though he's a bit of a slow top, he's a brilliant tactician. He'll have that sister of his married off before the Season's end, I'll wager."

"Sooner." Marcus took the sheet of paper from Brant and began penning an invitation. "She's rather a pretty little thing, as I recall. I met her briefly when I was down there last year on a hunt. Now," he said, glancing up at Brant expectantly, "what shall I say?"

"Tell him to meet us here tomorrow night for a council of war. That should bring him here *tout de suite*. While we're waiting for him we can make up a list of provisions: ball gowns, hats, that sort of thing. Although"—he paused as a sudden thought occurred to him—"perhaps it might be best if Aunt Agatha were to arrange all that. I'm an old hand at dressing mistresses, but one can't rig one's cousin out like a ladybird, I suppose."

"Not if the offer one has in mind is an honorable one," Marcus agreed, tongue-in-cheek. "But you are right. Such things are best left to females. After all, what could go wrong?"

By a late afternoon of the following week, Sara was beginning to regret ever having expressed an interest in Shakespeare. During the course of the week she had been poked, prodded, and pinned by a veritable army of servants, all telling her to stand this way, or hold out her arms just so, as various swatches of material were pinned to her person. Even cheerful Matty had turned into a martinet, scolding her to sit perfectly still while she submitted to the discomfort of having her long hair curled with the tongs.

By the night of the theater party, Sara was drooping with weariness. She wanted nothing more than to crawl into bed and sleep until morning, but Matty set up such a howl at the very suggestion that she quickly discarded the idea. She was sitting before the mirror while Matty added finishing touches to her coiffure, when Lady Mallingham walked into the room, a maid carrying a large box trailing at her heels.

"Why, dearest, how charming you look!" the countess exclaimed, surveying Sara's reflection with a pleased smile. "With your hair all curled like that you look the veriest angel. Matty, you are to be congratulated."

"Thank you, m'lady." Matty was aglow with pride. " 'Twas my pleasure, I'm sure."

Sara remained silent, although she thought she looked a perfect cake. Her thick brown hair had been coaxed into a tortuous arrangement of cork-screw curls fashioned to cascade over one shoulder. An acceptable style for a young debutante, she decided, studying her reflection in the cheval glass, but hardly one suitable for a spinster of her advanced years. Her wide gold eyes looked somewhat apprehensive in her wan face, and she gave careful consideration to dipping into the rouge pot before shrugging her shoulders. The lily was already sufficiently gilded, as far as she was concerned.

"I have brought you a surprise, my dear," Lady Mallingham said, gesturing for the maid to set the box on Sara's bed. "Just a little something to wear this evening. Please say you will accept it."

Sara turned from the mirror and moved toward the bed. The maid had already unpacked the gown, and when she held it up Sara was unable to repress the tiny gasp that escaped from her parted lips.

The gown was fashioned in a sheer gauze that floated like an apricot-colored mist. Small brilliants had been sewn across the bodice and full skirts, so that the dress sparkled in the light. Sara reached out a tentative finger to touch one of the small stones.

"Oh, Aunt," she whispered, her eyes glowing with wonder, "it is the most beautiful dress I have ever seen."

"Do you think so?" The countess was obviously pleased with her reaction. "Does this mean you will accept it, then?"

"Of course I shall." Sara emerged from her trance long enough to remember her promise to her cousin. Besides, she admitted with rueful honesty, even if she hadn't struck her bargain with the earl, there was no way she would have refused the stunning gown. It was so breathtakingly exquisite that she simply had to have it. She lowered her finger at last as she turned to embrace her aunt.

"Thank you, ma'am," she said, drawing back to bestow a soft kiss on the withered cheek. "You have been so very good to me."

"Stuff." Lady Mallingham's blue eyes were suspiciously bright. "I am good to myself. It makes me feel young again to buy such pretty things. Now," she spoke in brisk tones, "it is time you were dressed. We mustn't keep your cousin and his guest waiting. I'll send my maid in with my small set of diamonds. They are just what you need to show the gown to its best advantage. Mind you wear them. We can't have you going about half clothed, now can we?" She gave Sara's face an affectionate pat and left the room.

"Oh, miss, have you ever seen such a gown?" Matty fairly snatched the gown from the other maid and was holding it up to study with a knowing eye. "You'll look like a fairy princess to be sure."

"It is lovely," Sara agreed, scarce believing the dress was hers. A vague memory stirred in her mind, and she had a sudden image of her mother unpacking an old-fashioned ball gown in bronze-colored brocade. She remembered her mother's lilting voice describing the ball to which she had worn the gown.

"For it was there that I met your dear father. His cousin had invited him at the last minute to make up our numbers. He was standing by the doorway looking quite ill at ease in his borrowed finery, but I took one look at him and knew no other would ever do. A year later, we were wed."

At the time Sara had thought the story terribly romantic, but it wasn't until years later that she realized the true depths of her mother's love for her father. By marrying the man she loved rather than the one chosen for her, her mother had turned her back on a world of wealth and privilege. A world Sara had vowed always to disdain . . . until now.

"I'll see to Miss." Matty dismissed the other maid with a jealous glare and began helping Sara out of her dressing-gown. Since she had already bathed, Sara had only to don her new and deliciously feminine undergarments (an earlier present from Aunt Agatha) before stepping into the dress.

"Such a lovely gown," Matty sighed as she laced the delicate fastenings. "And so modest too, not like when my sister Liza was in service. She said the ladies used to dampen their muslins to better show their bodies to the men . . . can you imagine such a thing? She was employed by an actress, and the stories she can tell ain't fit for proper ears . . ."

A brisk rap at the door heralded the arrival of Miss Pimms, Lady Mallingham's formidable maid. The dour creature had been with the countess longer than either woman cared to remember, and the entire household went in fear of her acid tongue.

"Here be the countess's jewels," she grumbled, thrusting the square velvet-covered box into Matty's hands. "Mind she don't lose 'em, and bring 'em to me directly she comes home." Her stone-colored eyes slid over Sara consideringly before she snapped, "Fix the neckline of her gown proper so's her shoulders show. The Deverleigh women all have fine shoulders, and they ain't a bunch of Quakers to be coverin' 'em up."

After Miss Pimms departed in a swish of starched cotton, Matty closed the door and hastened to Sara's side. She opened the case and extracted a set of diamond ear-bobs which she fastened carefully in Sara's ears. The necklace she draped about her neck was a delicate chain of golden roses, each containing a small diamond at its heart.

"There be a selection of rings for you too, miss." Matty dug through the glittering collection of jewels until she found one to her liking, which she slid onto Sara's finger. When she was satisfied with her charge's appearance, she picked up a crystal bottle of perfume and misted her with the light floral scent.

"Will you be needing anything else, miss?" she asked, folding her hands in front of her, smiling at Sara with smug pride. "A plume for your hair, perhaps?"

Sara gave her reflection a final glance, feeling a

pleasant thrill of surprise at her appearance. She looked every inch the proper young lady, and she could not help but be pleased. "No, Matty," she said, rising from the padded bench. "That will be all, thank you." Taking a deep breath, she smoothed the skirts of her gown and turned to go join her aunt and their guests in the parlor.

Blast it all, where was the chit? Brant stood with his back to the fireplace, his dark brows knitted in a scowl as he watched the door leading into his aunt's parlor. Lady Mallingham had joined him and Marcus some fifteen minutes earlier, assuring them Sara would be along momentarily. He hoped she wasn't one of those dratted females who delighted in keeping a man dangling until she could make a grand entrance. If so, he would have a sharp word with her on the matter. As her guardian it was his duty to ensure she always presented herself in the most favorable light.

He had just pulled his watch from his pocket to check the time when the footman opened the door, and Sara hurried in. After making her bows to Lady Mallingham, she came to his side, her thin face lit with an apologetic smile.

"I am sorry to be so shockingly late, Cousin," she said, holding out a bejeweled hand to him. "I trust I haven't kept you waiting?"

The lecture Brant had been rehearsing withered at the look of honest embarrassment he saw shining in the golden eyes which sought his. "Not at all," he murmured, lifting her hand to his lips for a brief kiss. "And in any case, your charming appearance makes any wait I may have suffered more than worthwhile. You look most fetching in that gown."

Sara's cheeks warmed at the compliment and the intimate smile lighting the earl's eyes. Rigged out in proper evening dress of a somberly cut black velvet jacket and cream-colored silk pantaloons, he seemed to her even more handsome than usual. A ruby the size of a pigeon's egg glowed from the folds of his elegantly tied cravat, but he was saved from the charge of dandyism by the shock of black hair which fell across his broad forehead, adding a certain rakish air to his sartorial splendor. Aware she had been staring at him, Sara turned a hesitant smile on the stranger who had walked over to join them.

Brant caught her shy smile and was quick to make the proper introductions. "Sara, this is my very good friend, Marcus, Viscount Cherrington. Marcus, allow me to make you known to my cousin, Miss Sara Belding."

"Miss Belding." Marcus bowed over her hand, light brown eyes studying her with obvious approval. "May I say what a pleasure it is to meet you? Brant has told me much of you, and I have been longing to make your acquaintance."

"Sir." Sara curtsied, responding instantly to the viscount's easy charm. Like Brant, he was dressed in evening clothes, a single watch-fob and gold signet ring providing his only adornment. Unlike Brant's, his wheat-blond hair was worn in a fashionable mode, making him look very much like a man of the town. He was perhaps eight-and-twenty, with a boyish nature she found utterly relaxing.

"My cousin has also told me much of you," she

told him, her soft voice gently teasing. "I hear you are a great aficionado of Shakespeare." Her gold eyes slid to Brant's, who was doing his best not to laugh. "Is that not so, my lord?"

Clever minx, he thought, realizing she had caught his slip of the tongue when he'd mentioned warning Marcus of the trip to the theater. "Marcus's devotion to the theater is indeed well known," he drawled, blue eyes twinkling in acknowledgment of her saucy wit. Privately, he was pleased to see her doing so well in company. Perhaps marrying her off wouldn't be as difficult a chore as he and Marcus had feared. Even the plainest of women could benefit from a lively charm, and Sara was far from plain. "He has been known to sleep through some of Kean's most brilliant performances."

The sound of the dinner bell interrupted Marcus before he could defend himself, and Lady Mallingham rose majestically to her feet. "Well, he had best not nod off tonight," she said, shaking a gnarled finger at him in playful warning. "Or it will be a sharp elbow in the ribs for him. I'll not tolerate such behavior in my presence."

"Fear not, dear lady." Marcus bowed to her. "With two such lovely ladies to bear me company I assure you I shall have no trouble remaining awake. Now, if you will do me the honor of escorting you into dinner, we shall begin our evening."

The streets surrounding Hazlitt's Theatre were clogged with carriages, and it took them almost twenty minutes to reach the entryway. The crowds inside were even worse, and Sara feared they would be crushed long before they reached the earl's box.

"Lord, I'd forgotten what a squeeze these things can be," Lady Mallingham grumbled, straightening her turban with a shaking hand. "Every cutpurse and ne'er-do-well in London must have been in that crowd tonight." She shot her nephew an angry glare. "Really, Brant, I should have a word with the manager if I were you. Surely there is something that can be done."

"Yes, Aunt." Brant replied to his aunt's complaining automatically, although he wondered what she expected him to do. The theaters were public entertainment, after all. He turned to check on Sara's welfare only to find Marcus already bent over her, patting her hand and inquiring after her health.

"I am fine, sir." Sara smiled up at Marcus shyly. "Although I must allow this all seems so strange to me. Being from the country I am unused to such crowds."

"Well, you'd best get accustomed to them, and soon," Lady Mallingham advised tartly. "This is nothing compared to the crushes at Almack's or one of the more important balls. 'Tis the rage amongst the London hostesses to invite two times the number of people their homes will safely hold."

"Good heavens, ma'am." Sara's eyes widened in dismay. "Isn't that rather dangerous?"

"Only if a lady neglects to leave on her stays," the older woman cracked, "in which case she finds herself thoroughly pinched and pawed before she ever reaches the dance floor."

Sara paled at her aunt's words. Although she herself had not been molested, she'd seen several other ladies subjected to the most indelicate of touches as they fought their way through the crowds. Still, it did make her wonder if this was the sort of treatment she could expect each time she ventured out. If so, she would soon teach the culprit a lesson in manners he would not easily forget. Her papa had taught her what to do should a man ever attempt to make free with her person, and she wasn't averse to using such knowledge.

"I've arranged for some champagne to be delivered," Brant said as they took their seats. "Shall we open it now, or wait for the others?"

"I can't speak for the ladies, but I, for one, would welcome a glass," Marcus replied, brown eyes twinkling. "I've found that I require no fewer than three glasses of the stuff if I am to endure Shakespeare with any degree of enjoyment."

"But if you so dislike the theater, then why have you come?" Sara asked, turning to him with a puzzled frown.

"Why, because I wanted to meet you, of course." Marcus laughed, sweeping her hand to his lips. "After hearing Mallingham speak so highly of you, I knew I would do anything to meet you, including sitting through one of these dreary tragedies. There, are you not moved by my noble sacrifice?"

At first Sara was uncertain how to respond to such flowery talk, but then she realized he was only twigging her, and gave a soft chuckle. "Indeed, dear sir, I am quite moved by your heroic efforts," she said, fluttering her lashes at him coyly. "You would soon turn my poor head if I didn't already know you for a flirt and a rake."

"You wound me, ma'am." Marcus contrived a

pained expression. "I admit freely to being a flirt, but I deny categorically that I am a rake."

"Is there a difference?"

"Oh, yes, though at the moment I can't recall the exact specifications," Marcus admitted with a careless shrug. "Only take my word for it, dear lady, there *is* a difference."

The arrival of the Tressmoore party provided a diversion, and the next few minutes were taken up with the necessary business of introductions. Sara found Lord Tressmoore to be more than a little intimidating, with his coal-black hair and the piercing, jet-colored eyes of his Cornish ancestors. He was as tall as the earl, but much heavier, with broad shoulders and a large barrel chest. The seams of his elegant evening clothes were strained to the limits of their endurance, and he kept plucking at his cravat, destroying whatever sense of style the garment may have once possessed.

In contrast, his sister, Miss Priscilla Tressmoore, was as tiny as a fairy child, with masses of golden hair and wide-set green eyes that peeped out of a face that was breathtakingly beautiful. She was as soft-spoken as her brother was loud, and Sara and the countess had to strain to catch her gentle tones.

"It was very good of you to invite us, my lady," she said to the countess once she had been seated and presented with a glass of lemonade (she had demurely refused the champagne). "I am very fond of Shakespeare, and I was hoping to attend at least one play during my stay in London."

"Not at all, my dear." Lady Mallingham took the news that she had invited the Tressmoores with her customary calm. "You have something in common

with my niece then, for she is a great admirer of his,
are you not, my love?"

"Yes, Aunt." Sara gave the younger girl an encouraging smile. She was so prettily mannered that
it was impossible not to like her, and Sara had
hopes of furthering her acquaintance. Despite a
span of almost five years in their ages, she thought
it would be nice having a friend in Society. "And
may I say how much I welcome the presence of a
fellow devotee? I fear there are others present who
do not share our appreciation." She cast the viscount a meaningful look.

"I believe I hear my name being slandered," Marcus protested, leaning over to smile at both ladies.
"Come, Mallingham, you must defend me. Your fair
cousin is maligning my sense of taste."

"You ain't got a sense of taste," Lord Tressmoore
interrupted with a gruff laugh. He gave Sara an ap-
praising look before adding, "Glad to see you on
your pins again, Miss Belding. You was sick as a cat
last I heard."

"That's right, Hugh had mentioned you were ill."
Priscilla settled her filmy white and gold skirts
about her. "I do hope it was nothing serious?"

"A slight cold," Sara assured her quietly. "But tell
me, how long will you be in London? I believe Lord
Mallingham said this is your first Season?"

That was enough to set Priscilla chattering, her
soft voice breathless as she described her impres-
sions of the city and the preparations for her coming
presentation. "But what I enjoy most is shopping
for clothes," she confessed with an artless sigh. "At
home we have only Mrs. Pettigrass to sew our
clothes for us, and although she is a very accom-

plished seamstress, she isn't nearly so clever as the modistes here in London. I have been meaning to compliment you on your toilet, Miss Belding. I think it charming that you and your aunt are dressed in matching colors. Don't you agree, Hugh?" She turned to her brother for confirmation.

His lordship, who was deep in conversation with Brant and Marcus, glanced up at the sound of his name. He blinked like a startled owl. "Eh, 'Cilla?"

"Miss Belding's attire," his sister pressed gently. "Don't you think it lovely?"

"Oh." Lord Tressmoore gave the matter ponderous thought. "Dashed fine," he agreed at last, turning back to his companions. "Always liked orange."

Brant almost choked on his champagne. Orange! He turned and gazed at Sara in alarm. Good God, why hadn't he realized it until now? Sara *was* rigged out in orange. An attractive shade of orange to be sure, but orange nonetheless. He shook his head in disbelief. It had never occurred to him that his aunt would impose her rather bizarre sense of style on his hapless cousin. And Sara, bless her, would never think to protest. His aunt's next words confirmed his worst suspicions.

"As do I, Lord Tressmoore. Such a vibrant color, don't you think? Not that I have anything against pastels, mind you. They are quite suitable for younger gals. But a woman of my years can be more adventurous when it comes to selecting her wardrobe. And since Sara is a trifle older than most debutantes, I see no reason why she must be rigged out in white and sprig muslins." She gave Sara's hand an affectionate squeeze. "I have some delightful surprises in store for you, my dear."

Brant shuddered in horror, a sudden vision of Sara moving through the ton dressed from head to foot in a bilious shade of orange filling his mind. How Society would laugh, he thought worriedly. Such behavior was acceptable in an older woman; in fact, he rather suspected that his aunt enjoyed her reputation as an eccentric.

But for a woman of Sara's years to attempt likewise would mean social ruin. If that happened, Brant reasoned, then they would never be able to find her a suitable parti. He turned the matter over in his mind, reaching what seemed to him the only possible conclusion.

He would have to see to Sara's wardrobe himself. He was a man of fashion, and who better to know what sort of gowns would best attract a man? Yes, he decided, setting his glass aside as the house lights dimmed to indicate that the performance was about to start. He would see to the matter himself. He was, after all, in charge of the operation.

Chapter Five

At first Sara enjoyed the play, enthralled with the skill of the performers. But as the evening wore on she found it increasingly difficult to concentrate on the stage, as people drifted in and out of their box. During intermission there were so many people jammed in the tiny space, Sara feared it would surely collapse. When the crowd began dispersing at the start of the third act, she settled back with a sigh of relief. Perhaps now she could enjoy the play in peace.

Her hopes were quickly dashed, however, when a young captain, who had taken the seat beside hers, began rambling on about his newest racehorse. His sonorous tones all but drowned out the voices from the stage, and when Sara had borne all she could she turned to him with a polite smile.

"I beg your pardon, sir, but would you be so good as to lower your voice? I fear I cannot hear the actors."

The young man drew himself up, the row of medals adorning his thin chest fairly quivering with outrage. "Well, 'pon my soul," he sniffed, rising to his feet. "Chit's a dashed bluestocking!"

Sara's jaw dropped at the captain's words. Well, really, she thought, turning her head back to the stage, London manners certainly left a great deal to be desired. There was the rustle of clothing and the jangle of a dress sword as the captain took his leave, but she scarce paid him any heed. The sleep-walking scene was next, and she leaned forward as a tormented Lady Macbeth drifted onto center stage.

"What, will these hands ne'er be clean?"

"What the devil was that all about?" A warm hand descended upon Sara's shoulder, and she gave a sharp squeal of fright. She clapped a hand over her mouth, and whirled around to find her cousin glaring down at her.

"Sara, have you run mad?" he hissed, glancing around the darkened theater self-consciously. "What do you mean by squalling like a scalded cat? People are staring."

"You startled me," she gasped, placing a gloved hand over her heart to quiet its thunderous beating. "Whyever did you sneak up on me like that? I am trying to watch the play."

"Never mind the blasted play." Brant took the seat recently vacated by the pompous captain. "I want to know what you said to Evingvine."

So that was the man's name, Sara thought. Not that it mattered, she supposed, for she doubted she would ever see the dratted man again. "I didn't mean to upset the captain," she said, not wishing to engage her cousin in an argument. "But I couldn't hear the performers, and I asked him to lower his voice. That is all."

"That is . . ." Brant was stunned by his cousin's confession. "Sara, the man stands to inherit a dukedom when his uncle dies!"

"That doesn't excuse him from common courtesy," she replied staunchly. "I think it very rude of people to prattle on while others are attempting to watch a play. I wonder why London people ever bother attending the theater for all the attention they pay the performers."

"Goose." Lady Mallingham had overheard Sara's remark, and leaned over to scold her errant niece. "No one comes to the theater to do anything so vulgar as watch a play. One comes to be seen. I should have thought you knew that."

"But that doesn't make any . . ."

"We shall discuss this later," Lady Mallingham interrupted, her voice dripping with icy disapproval. "We are already attracting far too much attention as it is. Hush now and watch the play."

"But that is what I have been trying to do!" Sara's voice rang out in indignation.

"Shhh!" Her angry outburst was drowned out by a chorus of hisses from the adjoining box. Sara threw herself back in her chair, her arms crossed and her shoulders hunched, as the play rushed toward its bloody conclusion.

Once the villainous Macbeth had been routed and his severed head gruesomely displayed on a pike, the theater lights were turned up. Sara was still feeling ill used by the night's events, but she was unfailingly polite as she made her good-byes to the Tressmoores.

"Please say I may call upon you on the morrow," Priscilla pleaded as the young ladies shook hands. "I've only been in London a few weeks, and except for my sister Fanny I know so few people."

"That would be very nice, Miss Tressmoore," Sara replied, flicking Lady Mallingham a questioning glance. "I am staying with my aunt, but . ."

"We shall expect you for tea," the countess interjected smoothly. "And by all means, do bring your sister with you. She is sponsoring you, I believe?"

"Yes, my lady. She and her mother-in-law Lady Burnstead are sharing the duties."

"Indeed?" Lady Mallingham looked pleased. "How interesting. Lady Burnstead is one of my dearest friends. I will send a note around tomorrow inviting her and your sister for tea."

Priscilla murmured her thanks, and after she and her brother bid the earl and Lord Cherrington good night, they took their leave. Marcus sensed a family squabble brewing and also departed, ignoring Brant's frantic signals that he remain. The press of the crowd precluded any attempts at conversation, and it wasn't until they reached the privacy of the carriage that Sara could give vent to her feelings.

"Aunt Agatha," she began in a firm voice, determined to have her say. "About what happened this evening, I . . ."

"Tomorrow, Sara, if you please," the countess interrupted, leaning her head against the plush squabs and closing her eyes. "I have the headache, and I simply can't endure another scene. You may come to me in the morning to make your apologies."

Sara bit her lip to keep from shouting that she had no intention of apologizing. She had done nothing wrong, after all, she reminded herself sulkily. If anyone was to blame for tonight's fiasco, it was her graceless cousin. If he hadn't invited that toy soldier into their box, then none of this would have happened. She slid a resentful glance in his direction only to find him glaring at her. Even in the poor light his anger was evident, and her own anger stirred in response.

Odious toad, she thought, turning her head to stare out the darkened window. How dare he sit there glowering at her like a disapproving papa! Just because she had agreed to let him provide her with a wardrobe, that didn't give him the right to sit in judgment on her actions. She'd told him at their first meeting that she had no need of a guardian, and if he thought that had changed, then he was very much mistaken.

By the time they reached the countess's town house Sara's temper had cooled somewhat, although her pride was still stinging. Lord Mallingham escorted them inside, his hand closing over Sara's elbow when she would have followed her aunt up the stairs.

"One moment, Sara," he said, his strong fingers closing on the sensitive flesh of her upper arm. "I'd like a word with you, if you will."

She raised an eyebrow at the imperious command. Aunt Agatha had told her of Brant's years in the army, and his experience of command had never been so obvious. It was evident he meant to get her alone so he could dress her down in private. Well, she decided, her chin coming up in defiance, she'd be hanged if she'd oblige him.

"My apologies, *Cousin.*" She freed her arm with an angry jerk. "But I'm afraid I'm rather tired. I should like to retire now, if you don't mind."

Brant's lips thinned in ominous warning. Why, the little devil, he thought with incredulous anger. Did she really think she could escape him by using that time-worn feminine ploy? "This will only take a moment," he promised silkily, reaching out to recapture her arm. "It is very important, and I fear I must insist."

She evaded him with a deft twist of her slender body. One moment she was standing there beside him, and the next she was halfway up the stairs, tossing him a triumphant smile over her shoulder. "Thank you, Cousin," she cooed in dulcet tones. "I knew you would understand. Good night."

Brant let fly with a blistering oath as he watched her scamper up the stairs. For a moment he was tempted to go after her and haul her back downstairs, but he reluctantly dismissed the notion. Aunt Agatha was sure to interfere, and he was in no mood to deal with two obstreperous females. He turned toward the door, ignoring the impassive footman who had witnessed the small drama.

Let the little minx think she had bested him, he decided with a grim smile. Tomorrow was another day. Sara was his ward, and he would see she conducted herself with proper decorum, even if it killed them both. Giving the footman a curt nod, he stalked out the door, his mind already active with thoughts of how to tame his cousin.

He rose early on the following morning, eager to begin his day. The Season would be starting in less than two weeks, and there was a great deal left to be done. He sent a message to Marcus's rooms requesting the viscount join him for a strategy session. After consideration he also sent a similar invitation to Hugh, reasoning three heads were better than two. Besides, Hugh had the experience of outfitting two sisters to call upon.

Once his correspondence was out of the way, he donned a cutaway of dark broadcloth and a pair of light gray morning trousers. His tailor assured him they were the coming thing, and Brant had to admit they were a dashed sight more comfortable than breeches. Since it was such a lovely morning he decided to take his breakfast in the morning room, as he disliked eating alone in the vast dining room. He had just sat down to his food when the butler announced Lord Cherrington.

"I came as soon as I received your message," Marcus said as the door closed behind the butler. "What is the plan, then? Your note said it was important."

"The matter isn't so important it can't wait until after we have eaten," Brant assured him, waving Marcus to one of the vacant chairs. He picked up the silver bell beside his plate and rang it. "I'll tell you about it over breakfast."

The butler had already alerted the kitchen staff of Marcus's arrival, and when the footman entered he was carrying a second place setting and a fresh pot of coffee. Brant waited until his guest had been seen to and they were alone before saying, "I hadn't thought of it until Hugh mentioned it, but did you happen to notice what Sara was wearing last night?"

"Of course." Marcus helped himself to the fluffy eggs and grilled kippers. "Some sort of gauze thing, wasn't it? And dashed attractive as I recall."

"But did you notice the color?" Brant pressed, leaning forward to study Marcus.

"Well . . . yes . . ." Marcus paused, his fork suspended in midair. "It was a peach color, wasn't it?"

"It was orange." Brant's mouth tightened in disapproval. "And so was her cape."

"So?" Marcus was obviously perplexed. "What is wrong with that? As your aunt pointed out, Sara is hardly a deb fresh out of the schoolroom. She can wear whatever color pleases her."

"Yes, and out of the rainbow of colors available to her, what must she choose but orange. Or rather, Aunt Agatha has chosen orange. Don't you see," he exclaimed as Marcus continued staring at him in confusion, "Aunt Agatha means to make Sara over in her own image! *Orange,* for heaven's sake!"

Comprehension dawned in Marcus's brown eyes. "Good Lord," he said, whistling softly. "I can see your concern. She would be the laughingstock of London."

"I realize that," Brant replied grimly, "and I refuse to let that happen. It would destroy all our plans. I'd hoped I could trust Aunt to supervise the selection of Sara's wardrobe, but since I can't, it's up to us. That is why I have asked you here."

Marcus looked uneasy. That "us" had an ominous sound, to his way of thinking. "Us?" he repeated, hoping he had mistaken Brant's meaning.

"Us." Brant nodded. "You did say you would help me."

"And so I shall," Marcus responded with alacrity. "I will dance with her, flirt with her, fight duels in defense of her honor; but dash it all, Mallingham, I draw the line at acting as a lady's maid! I don't know the first thing about outfitting a female!"

Brant leaned back in his chair, his mouth lifting in amusement at Marcus's discomfiture. "I seem to recall a little singer in Spain who enjoyed the fruits of your . . . er . . . expertise," he teased, his blue eyes shining at his friend's obvious chagrin.

"That was different," Marcus muttered, the tips of his ears turning bright red. "You said yourself that we can't rig your cousin out as if she were a ladybird."

Before Brant could torment his friend any further, Hugh was announced and came ambling into the dining room. Since he had already breakfasted he declined to join them, but did help himself to the hot coffee.

"Head's like a damned anvil," he complained gruffly. "The whole house is at sixes and sevens with m'sister's coming-out. Carpenters and painters everywhere you step. 'Tis enough to drive a man to drink." He took a sip of coffee, then cocked a bushy eyebrow at Brant. "What's the emergency? Note said to come to Mayfair at once."

Brant explained the situation, and unlike Marcus, Hugh was quick to understand the gravity of the problem. "I've married off one of m'sisters already, and hope to fire off the other one before the Season's done," he said smugly. "Reckon I know as much about feminine doo-dads as the next fellow. Glad to help you out, Mallingham."

"Thank you, Hugh." Brant turned to Marcus expectantly. "Well?"

"I'm in," Marcus sighed in defeat. "If Hugh is game, then so am I. What's the plan?"

"First we'll call upon a modiste and have her design a new wardrobe for Sara. I've heard of a Mme Truffant on Bond Street who is said to be quite good; we'll go there. I'm sure that for the right price we can convince her to handle the matter for us."

Brant took another sip of coffee. "Then I thought we might call upon Lady Jersey."

"Lady Jersey . . . not that old prattle box!" Marcus groaned in protest. "Must we? The woman's tongue runs like a wheel, and you know what a scheming matchmaker she is. Last year she tried matching me with Crenshaw's oldest girl. She was so obvious about it I had to leave the city."

"You're lucky." Hugh studied the toes of his boots morosely. "Paired me with some blasted bluestocking. Her name was Jane, as I recall. She was a widow, you know, who doubtless plagued her husband to death. Spouted radicalism like a fountain. Good figure though," he added reflectively.

"Nonetheless we shall still call upon Lady Jersey." Brant was resolute. "She is in a position to do Sara a great deal of good. If tongues are already wagging after last night, then old Sal will know about it. I intend to nip any rumors firmly in the bud, and to do that I'll need to be in Sally's good graces."

"Oh, very well." Marcus made a face. "I suppose for Miss Sara's sake I shall risk it. But I warn you, if she pushes even one chit in my direction I'm bolting for the door."

Mme Truffant was a tiny woman of indeterminate age whose skill with a needle was surpassed only by her business acumen. She had started out as a seamstress in a small shop in Bloomsbury and had quickly worked her way into her own shop. She had outlived two husbands and a score of lovers, and thought herself proof against any shocks life cared to toss her way. Lord Mallingham's request, however, stunned her to the roots of her artfully dyed hair.

"You want me to design an entire wardrobe for a young lady and 'ave it ready in less than two weeks?" she asked, her acquired French accent giving way to the coarser inflections of her Cockney youth. "Cor!"

"You will be well compensated for your time," Brant assured her, surveying the dazed seamstress with knowing eyes. "Shall we say . . . double your usual prices?"

Madame almost swooned, her agile mind quickly calculating her possible profit. The sum she arrived at warmed her mercenary heart to such a degree that she cast Brant a simpering smile of delight. "I should be only too 'appy to accommodate you, m'lord," she said, her gray eyes shining with avarice. "The young lady in question is your fiancée, perhaps?"

"My cousin." Brant lifted an eyebrow at the question. "Does that present a problem?"

"Oh, not at all, monsieur," she assured him anxiously. "It is just that if this were to be a trousseau, then I would need to design a wedding gown as well. When may I expect your cousin for a fitting?"

"I will arrange to have some of her clothing brought to you so that you may size it." Brant had grown bored with the conversation, and began leafing through a book of patterns lying on the table. He stopped when he came to a particular drawing.

"This dress," he said, tapping the page with his finger. "I'd like you to sew it up for my cousin."

"Of course, monsieur." The modiste peeked at the sketch, pleased to see it was one of her more costly designs. The cut of the gown was deceptively simple with its rounded bodice and full skirts. "Have you any preference as to color?"

"Anything but orange." Brant continued flipping through the book, finding several other patterns to his liking. Hugh and Marcus soon grew bored just sitting, and began exploring among the bolts of materials Madame had spread out through the room. Hugh found one fabric, a soft silk in a delicate shade of rose, particularly attractive, and held it up for Brant's approval.

"What do you think, Mallingham?" he asked, stroking the gossamer silk with a blunt fingertip. "Rather pretty, eh? Ought to make a fine riding habit."

Madame blanched at the sight of her precious French silk being pawed by so large a gentleman, and was making to rescue it when Marcus took the bolt from Hugh and spread it on a table.

"Idiot," he told Hugh in good-natured derision, "you don't use silk for a riding habit. But it is a lovely shade of pink." He flicked a thoughtful look at Brant. "Mallingham? What do you think?"

Brant bent to examine the silk, running its softness through his fingers. "Lovely," he agreed quietly, envisioning Sara in a pink ball gown, her brown hair curling about her face. "Yes," he murmured in agreement, "I like it. An excellent choice, Hugh. Madame"—he turned to the dressmaker—"I want the ball gown I picked out made up in this material."

"Mais oui." Madame snatched up the silk and clutched it to her bosom protectively. At this point she would have agreed to anything if it would have

emptied her workroom of the disruptive gentlemen. She ventured a hopeful smile. "I am sure your lordships must find all this *très* boring, *non?* If you will leave your card I would be happy to . . ."

"This is what you use to make a habit." Marcus had located a length of velvet and was showing it to Hugh. "The color is good, too. This topaz is just the thing to bring out Sara's eyes."

They spent the next hour poring over the pattern book and pawing through rolls of materials until Madame was all but prostrate. Finally the men had had enough, and made to take their leave.

Brant was pleased at the speed with which he had discharged his obligations. He had ordered several gowns to be made up as well as a riding habit in the topaz velvet Marcus had discovered. On a whim he also commissioned Madame to design a bridal gown. Since the ultimate objective of the campaign was to get Sara married off, he thought it prudent to have all in readiness.

"Have those dresses made up and sent to my aunt's house. I would like the pink ball gown made up in time for Lord Tressmoore's ball," Brant instructed as he pulled on his gloves. "I'm also commissioning you to arrange for some appropriate jewelry to be sent to my aunt's home as well. That should be all."

"Thank you, m'lord." The modiste had collapsed upon a chair and was fanning herself in exhaustion. "I will attend to the matter personally."

"Excellent." Satisfied with the arrangements, Brant collected his friends and departed, promising to be back within the week to check on the progress of his order.

"You were quite right, Marcus," he remarked to the viscount once they were on their way again. "This matchmaking business is quite simple, really. All you need is a plan."

Sara and the countess spent a quiet morning preparing for their guests. Rather than use the drawing room, Lady Mallingham decided to use the morning parlor. She had recently redecorated it in the rococo style she favored, and she was anxious to show it off. Sara thought the gold walls, thick cream-colored rugs, and ornate furniture rather too much, but out of fondness for her aunt she kept such opinions to herself.

At her aunt's suggestion she was wearing one of her new gowns. This was a sprigged muslin with violets scattered across the white cloth, and a violet ribbon tied beneath her breasts. A matching ribbon was threaded through her light brown hair, and Sara had to admit the effect was pleasing. Lady Mallingham was in her usual orange, but in a style more sedate than usual. In honor of Lady Burnstead (who, she privately admitted to Sara, was a dreadful stickler for such detail) she was also wearing a starched cap, and looked every inch the grande dame.

The marchioness was a wizened gnome of a creature with a shock of white hair and snapping black eyes. She was draped from head to foot in unrelenting black, and reminded Sara of a crow, in the way she kept hopping about, inspecting the parlor with malicious curiosity. Priscilla's sister, Fanny, was as dark as her brother, and she wore a modest gown of deep blue as befitted a married lady. Although she was only some five years older than Sara there was a comfortable, matronly air about her, and her conversation was filled with constant references to her husband and children. She seemed a pleasant sort, but it was evident to Sara that the poor woman was very much under her mother-in-law's thumb.

When Sara was presented to her, the tiny marchioness surveyed her through her quizzing glass until Sara felt like an exotic creature on loan from the Royal Menagerie. "You'll do," the elderly lady announced in a raspy voice. "You ain't near the beauty your mother was, but you'll do."

"Thank you, my lady." Sara was unsure how best to respond to so blatant an insult. Lady Burnstead put her strongly in mind of her aunt when they had first met, and she found it difficult to maintain a polite demeanor.

Once the social amenities had been dispensed with, Lady Burnstead turned her back on the younger girls and began conversing with Lady Mallingham. While they were busy comparing notes as to who was alive and who had died, Sara and the others withdrew to the far end of the morning parlor.

"You must forgive my mother-in-law," Fanny apologized, settling her skirts while reaching for a gooseberry tart. "I fear her ague is plaguing her, and she is not herself."

"That is quite all right, my lady." Sara accepted Fanny's apology with a graceful smile. "I am sure the marchioness meant no harm. But tell me, I heard you mentioning to my aunt that you are only recently returned from Scotland. I have always longed to go there. Is it as lovely as they say?"

Fanny took the hint, and they spent the next quarter hour sipping tea and discussing the rigors of travel. Sara and Priscilla were listening to Fanny's somewhat disjointed account of her stay in Edinburgh when the marchioness called out, imperiously demanding that Fanny bear her company. After her sister had bustled off, Priscilla reached out shyly to touch Sara's hand.

"I do hope you weren't upset by what Lady Burnstead said," she whispered, her green eyes soft with distress. "I am sure she meant well. It is just that she is so very old, and sometimes she doesn't comprehend what she is saying."

"I wasn't upset." Sara was touched by the younger girl's genuine concern. It was obvious Priscilla had a warm nature.

"I am go glad," Priscilla sighed in relief. "Marcus . . . Lord Cherrington, that is"—her creamy cheeks pinked in embarrassment—"told me you have just come out of mourning for your father. I lost both my parents when I was but a babe. I don't know what would have become of me had it not been for Hugh. He is the dearest brother in the world." She took a sip of tea and smiled at Sara. "It is wonderful having a family, is it not?"

Sara lifted her own cup to her lips as she considered her reply. For so many years it had been just she and Papa, and when he had died she had felt so terribly alone. She hadn't wanted to become involved with Lady Mallingham and her cousin, but now that she had, she wasn't so eager to return to her solitary existence. She was growing to love her aunt more with each passing day, and when he wasn't being so impossibly overbearing, she even had a certain fondness for her cousin. When she left the countess's house, as leave she must, she would be all alone. . . .

"Yes," she answered at last, her voice subdued, "a family is a wonderful thing."

"The countess says you have received your voucher for Almack's," Priscilla continued eagerly. "Mine arrived this morning, and I must admit I have been in a perfect quake. It all sounds so . . . overwhelming somehow. I have dreaded going."

"But why?" Sara was puzzled by the other girl's timidity. Priscilla was lovely, the very embodiment of young English womanhood, and as a true member of the aristocracy there was no doubt but that she would be accepted.

"I won't know anyone. And London people can be so haughty. So cold. What if no one were to talk to me? Or dance with me?" Priscilla shuddered in delicate horror. "I should die of mortification."

Sara smiled in understanding, for Priscilla's fears so closely mirrored her own. "You will know my cousin," she told her in encouraging tones. "He will surely dance with you. And, of course, there is Lord Cherrington."

To her surprise the color in Priscilla's cheeks rivaled the soft pink of her muslin gown. "Lord Mallingham is very kind," she said in a strained voice. "But I really don't *know* him, do I? As for Lord Cherrington, I fear he regards me as little more than a bothersome child. He told Hugh last night that he considered my gown to be too daring for a girl my age, and now Hugh won't let me wear it."

This came as something of a shock to Sara, who had thought Priscilla's dress to be charming in the extreme. Granted she was unversed in the ways of the ton, but Priscilla's dress had seemed quite modest in comparison to the gowns some of the other ladies had been wearing. She also found it difficult to imagine the viscount saying something so unkind. Now if it had been her cousin who had expressed such an opinion, she would have believed it at once.

"You are quite sure it was Lord Cherrington who said this?" she asked curiously. "It doesn't sound like him."

"I'm sure." Priscilla's sigh was heartfelt. "His lordship has little liking for me, I fear. Well, no matter." She turned to Sara with a bright laugh. "At least I will have you to talk to me. We shall sit all by ourselves in a corner and say terrible things about the other guests!"

Finally the customary hour for a social visit was at an end, and the ladies made to leave. Priscilla gave Sara's hand an impulsive squeeze, promising to see her soon. After the others had gone Lady Mallingham relaxed against her chair with a weary sigh. "Thank heavens that is over," she said, closing her eyes in gratitude. "I'd forgotten how exhausting the social round can be, and it's only just starting. Once the Season begins in earnest, we may expect upwards of thirty callers a day."

"Thirty!" Sara paused in the act of pouring her aunt a cup of tea, and glanced around the gold morning parlor in alarm. "Wherever shall we put them all?"

"Don't be a goose, Sara." Lady Mallingham reached out and took the cup from Sara's hand. "We shan't be here."

"But if we aren't going to be here, why should anyone come to call?" Sara asked, her brow wrinkling in bewilderment. The rules of Society were all so very strange, she mused, sipping her tea thoughtfully.

"Our callers won't expect us to be at home," the countess explained, taking an invigorating sip of the amber brew. "They will just leave their cards and be on their way."

Sara digested this in silence before asking, "Where will we be when they come to call?"

"Out making *our* calls, of course." There was a definite edge in Lady Mallingham's voice as she glared at her niece impatiently. "Really, Sara, how can you be so mutton-headed? It's all so simple even a child can comprehend it."

Simple perhaps, but to Sara the entire notion was utter nonsense. She couldn't envision anything sillier than driving from house to house leaving cards for people who were out doing the same thing. It seemed to her it would be a great deal easier on everyone involved if they just traded cards as they passed each other on the street.

"If you say so, Aunt," she agreed at last. "But it makes little sense to me."

"We are talking of Society, Sara," Lady Mallingham reminded her with an arch look. "It isn't supposed to make sense. Now," she said as set her cup to one side, "there is another matter I need to discuss with you. Do you know how to waltz?"

"No, ma'am." Sara's golden eyes dropped to her hands. "There was never an opportunity to learn. The squire of our village hired a dancing-master to instruct his daughters and invited me to join them, but I couldn't leave Papa."

"I understand." Lady Mallingham reached out to pat Sara's clenched hand consolingly. "Well, no matter. I have wormed the name of Miss Tressmoore's dancing instructor out of that hen-witted sister of hers. I mean to hire him to give you waltzing lessons. I won't have it bandied about that you are a country mouse with no town bronze."

"Thank you, Aunt." Sara smiled in gratitude. "I was thinking of mentioning it to Lord Mallingham, but—"

"Heavens, don't do that!" Lady Mallingham exclaimed in horror. "He would insist upon instructing you himself, and that would only end in disaster."

"But why?" Sara was puzzled by her aunt's vehemence.

"Sara." Lady Mallingham gave her a sagacious look. "Take it from an old lady; there are two things a woman should never allow her nearest male relation to teach her. The first is handling a team of horses, and the second is dancing. We will hire the dancing-master."

Sara was coming to know that determined note in the countess's voice, and bowed to her wishes. "Very well, my lady," she said. "If you think it best."

"I do." Lady Mallingham nodded firmly. "My

Henry once tried teaching me how to drive a gig, and it almost ended our marriage. If I had known how to point a gun, I vow I would have shot him. Trust me, Sara. Nothing makes a man more insufferably arrogant than to think he is the only one to teach you anything."

Chapter Six

The next two weeks passed in a whirlwind of activity for Sara. Brant, after a discreet word with Lady Mallingham, took Sara aside and told her of his arrangements with Mme Truffant. At first she balked at such largesse, but when he reminded her of their earlier agreement, she reluctantly accepted the extravagant wardrobe.

The fittings took up the better part of the afternoon, and in between them and accompanying her aunt on her dizzying round of social calls, Sara worked diligently on her waltzing. The instructor her aunt had engaged was a dark-eyed Frenchman who called himself M. Dechamps. Despite his melodramatic airs and petulant manner he was a fairly competent instructor, and Sara was pleased with her progress.

On the day before Lord Tressmoore's ball she was enjoying a rare afternoon of solitude when the maid came to tell her Lord Mallingham had called and was asking to see her. Setting aside the book she had only just picked up, Sara gave the young girl a quick smile.

"Thank you, Betsy," she said, reaching up a hand to check her hair. As she hadn't been expecting callers she had left it down, and it fell in gleaming curls to her shoulders. "Please tell his lordship I'll join him in a few minutes."

After the maid left she dashed over to her cheval glass, surveying her appearance with a critical eye. The mulberry-colored gown was fashionable but somewhat plain, with a modest neckline and a single row of ruffles adorning the hem and cuffs. She was about to ring for Matty to help her change when something stayed her hand. What on earth was wrong with her? She had never fretted over her appearance before, and she wasn't about to begin doing so now. If her cousin didn't care for her choice of gowns, then he could leave! She wasn't about to primp for him like an anxious schoolgirl preparing for her beau. With that thought in mind she tossed her silver hairbrush onto the dresser and went in search of her cousin.

In the parlor, Brant helped himself to the tea provided for him by his aunt's ever-efficient staff. He supposed protocol dictated he wait until his hostess was there to pour for him, but having forgone lunch he was simply too hungry to wait. Besides, he reasoned, lifting the heavy silver teapot to pour himself a generous cup, he was family, and he saw no reason to stand on ceremony. He was enjoying his second cup when Sara made her appearance.

"Hello, Cousin," she greeted him with a shy

smile. "No, pray be seated," she said when he would have stood. "You look so comfortable, I hate to disturb you." She settled behind the tea cart, filling Brant's plate with more of the macaroon cookies he liked before attending to her own needs.

While her hands were occupied with the familiar domestic chore, she studied Brant through half-lowered lashes. She wondered if he had come to the house directly from Parliament, as he was dressed in a conservatively cut jacket of deep gray, his muscular legs encased in a pair of lighter gray morning trousers. She had been in Society long enough to recognize his cravat as being tied in a mathematical, and she privately thought the style suited his dark good looks.

"Aunt tells me she has hired a dancing-master for you," he said, not seeming to notice her silence. "How are the lessons progressing?"

The question caught Sara by surprise. "Quite well, I think," she said, wondering if he were trying to find fault with her. "M. Dechamps is an excellent teacher, and he seems pleased with my progress." Her chin came up proudly. "You needn't fear I will disgrace you at Lord Tressmoore's ball."

Brant raised a dark eyebrow. "The thought never entered my mind," he assured her in mild tones. "I was merely expressing an interest in your lessons." He lifted the Sevres cup to his lips. "What are your thoughts on your teacher? Are *you* pleased with him?"

Sara ducked her head, embarrassed by her petulant retort. "Yes, my lord," she said, wishing she wasn't so sensitive where her cousin was concerned. "He seems an adequate instructor, although I have very little with which to compare him. He is my first dancing-master, you see." She ventured a conciliatory smile.

Brant noted the shy smile with a thoughtful frown. When she first walked into the parlor Sara had seemed hesitant, almost as if he were a stranger she was meeting for the first time. Then when she thought he had been maligning her dancing skills, she had been the familiar, defiant Sara, her golden eyes sparkling with pride. Now she was softer, more feminine somehow, her lips lifted in a sweet smile and her cheeks delicately tinted.

Looking at her in her pretty gown with her brown hair tumbling down her back, he wondered that he had ever thought her plain. Aware that Sara was expecting some sort of reply, he set his cup on the side table.

"Perhaps we should remedy that situation," he said, rising to his feet and extending a hand to her. "Come, Cousin, let's go test this newfound expertise of yours."

Sara gaped at him in confusion. "I beg your pardon?"

"I wish to apprise myself of your dancing skill," Brant explained, his tanned fingers curling around her hand as he pulled her to her feet. "After listening to your boasting I am anxious to see if you are as accomplished as you claim."

"I didn't mean to boast, my lord," Sara protested, her aunt's admonishments fresh in her mind. "And I'm sure you must be very busy. I wouldn't want to impose upon your time . . ."

"It's no imposition," he replied with an easy smile. "In fact, I am rather looking forward to it."

"But . . ."

"Come now, Sara," he said, his lips pursed in a boyish pout. "Surely you don't mean to imply an English lord is not the equal of a French dancing-master. You must not so insult me."

Sara laughed at his wounded look. "I should never think of saying anything so unpatriotic, my lord," she told him, her eyes bright with amusement. "But I should think even an English lord would find it somewhat difficult to dance without benefit of musical accompaniment. Unless you can play and dance at the same time, of course."

Brant looked nonplussed for a moment before his brow cleared. "That is no problem," he said with a pleased smile. "I asked Marcus to join me, and he should arrive shortly."

"Lord Cherrington is coming?" This bit of news pleased Sara, for although she was not well acquainted with the viscount, she did like him. He was so open and friendly, not at all like her cousin, who was forever throwing her into an emotional turmoil. Even now, when she was no longer angry with him, her heart was still beating furiously, and her senses were tingling with awareness. Her responses to Brant puzzled her, for she had always considered herself the most tranquil of persons. Yet around him she was at the mercy of her uncertain emotions, and the sensation only seemed to intensify each time she saw him.

"Yes, he plans to join us when he has completed his business." Brant pulled his watch from his pocket and consulted it with a frown. "In fact, he should be here soon." The watch was tucked back into his pocket and he slipped his arm through hers.

"Come, if we hurry we should have time for one private lesson. I'm sure M. Dechamps has trained you well, and I look forward to partnering your fair charms."

"Your lordship is too kind," Sara simpered, fluttering her lashes at him. "If the viscount is as free with his praise as you are with yours, I fear my poor head will become swollen beyond all recognition."

The music room had been closed up for several years, but Lady Mallingham had recently had it opened and cleaned in anticipation of her increased social life. A pianoforte and harp stood in opposite corners awaiting use, while a Queen Anne settee and several side chairs, all upholstered in soft blue, lined one wall. The cream-colored drapes were partially open, admitting a small stream of sunlight, which pooled in the center of the parquet floor. Brant led her to the middle of the room and bowed with a courtly flourish.

"Very well, ma'am." His gray-clad arm slid about her waist as he held her in the traditional waltzing position. "Show me what you have learned."

"That might be a trifle difficult," Sara said with a laugh, her eyes going to the silent pianoforte. "M. Dechamps's sister always provides the musical accompaniment for us. I'm not at all sure I can waltz sans music."

"Look upon it as a challenge," he ordered, his blue eyes bright with laughter. "Now, the most important thing you must remember is to follow your partner's lead. Usually he will signal his intentions by squeezing your hand so"—his fingers gently tightened around hers—"or by varying the pressure of his arm about you. If he wishes you to move a certain way . . . let us say forward, then he will do this"—his warm arm pressed against her back, pulling her closer to his strong chest—"and you must, perforce, move—"

"Forward," Sara finished for him, the color in her cheeks deepening as the tempo of her heart increased. She could feel the heat of his body pressed to her own, and she tensed with a mysterious uneasiness. She hadn't felt this way when dancing with her dancing-master, she mused, struggling to concentrate on Brant's careful instructions. Aunt Agatha was undoubtedly right when she warned against accepting instruction from one's male relations, for she had never felt so flustered.

Brant sensed her discomfort and glanced down at her in concern. "Relax, Sara," he said, giving her an encouraging smile. "The waltz is meant to be enjoyed, not endured. Now come, let us try. Close your eyes and pretend we are in a moonlit ballroom with an orchestra playing softly behind us. Don't think about the steps at all, just concentrate on the music and follow my lead."

He whirled her deftly about the room, guiding her with subtle nuances of his muscular body. When they had completed a second turn he halted, and Sara opened her eyes to find him frowning down at her in obvious displeasure.

"You're not relaxing," he chided reprovingly. "I know you are not without grace, and yet you are dancing with all the animation of a toy doll. Don't hold yourself so stiffly; I don't bite, you know."

"I *am* relaxed." Sara defended herself through gritted teeth.

Brant said nothing, but privately he wondered if

Sara's sensibilities were offended by "the wanton waltz," as Byron had called it. There were many in Society who would agree with her, but it was nevertheless expected that a young lady should waltz. He tightened his arm about her with renewed determination.

"We will try again," he commanded sternly, "and this time I want you to relax. I think it will help if you pay more attention to the music. Flow with it, and learn to anticipate the hidden inflections in the rhythm. I—" His voice broke off as a small tremor shook her.

"Sara, is something wrong?" He tried to look into her face, but she kept her head averted, her shoulder shaking slightly. He was about to ask if she was ill when he heard a stifled giggle escape her lips. "Are you *laughing* at me?" he demanded indignantly.

His outrage proved too much for Sara's control, and she dissolved into helpless laughter. "I am sorry, Cousin," she said, wiping tears of mirth from her eyes. "It is just that I find it rather difficult to listen for hidden inflections in make-believe music being played by an imaginary band."

Brant's worried scowl vanished, and he gave a low rumble of laughter. "Minx," he accused, using the pressure of his arm to draw her closer against him. Their hands were still tightly clasped, and he brought them down to rest against his chest. He covered her hand with his, trapping it on his heart. "Don't you know the pupil must never mock the teacher? I'll not tolerate such insubordination in my classroom."

"Will you not?" Sara teased, studying him, her eyes filled with laughter. "And pray, sir, how do you mean to punish me? Will you beat me with your cane and make me stand in the corner for the rest of the day?"

"There's a tempting thought." He tilted his head to one side as if considering the matter. "I shall keep it in mind for the next time you defy me. You, madam, are a shrew masquerading as a lady. But I am wise to you now. You'll not find it so easy to get around me again."

"And you, my lord, are an arrogant tyrant, and I refuse to be cowed by you," Sara retorted with a playful toss of her head. "Aunt Agatha has told me how you fought against Napoleon, but don't think to pull such tricks with *me.* I'm not some poor infantryman under your command, and I will thank you, sir, to remember that."

" 'Tis a good thing for you, my lady, that I don't have you on the battlefield now." Brant slipped his hand beneath the silky fall of her hair, unable to resist its shiny allure. "Or you'd soon find yourself court-martialed!"

He used the pressure of his hand to tilt her face up to his, and when their laughing eyes met, he felt a warm excitement rush through him. He forgot Sara was his cousin, his ward, and that he was holding her in what could only be termed an intimate embrace. All sense of honor and duty fled from his mind as he concentrated on how good her soft, feminine body felt pressed against his, and the way her perfume teased his already inflamed senses. Unable to resist the sweet lips lifted to his, he bent his head.

Sara watched him through wide gold eyes. She could feel the urgent pounding of his heart beneath her palm, and it echoed the wild beating of her own.

She met his burning gaze, trembling with an emotion that was half fear and half anticipation. His warm breath feathered over her lips as her eyes drifted shut.

"I say, what are you doing in *here?*" Marcus's voice exploded into the heavy silence, driving Sara and Brant apart with the force of an explosion.

Brant whirled away from her, his back stiffening as he fought to control the raging hunger that was consuming him. He balled his hands into tight fists and sucked air into oxygen-starved lungs. His own actions appalled him, and he could only wonder what Sara must be thinking. When he had composed himself, he swung around to face his friend.

"It's about time you decided to grace us with your presence," he drawled, his languid tones belying the furious pounding of his blood. "Sara and I have been attempting to make do without you, but we could not get our imaginary musicians to play in tune. Is that not so, Sara?"

"Indeed not, Lord Cherrington." Sara took her cue from Brant, doing her best to appear coolly nonchalant. "I was hearing a light, frivolous waltz while my cousin appeared to be listening to a quadrille. Now that you are here, perhaps you will provide us with some proper musical accompaniment?"

Marcus was no one's fool, but he accepted her glib invitation without comment. "Your confidence in my abilities is highly gratifying, Miss Belding," he said with a courtly bow. "And I shall do my best to fulfill your expectations. However, I must warn you, it has been a number of years since I last played a musical instrument."

"In that case, perhaps it would be best if I were to

provide the music." Brant was quick to volunteer. He had mastered his emotions, but wasn't ready to test that control by taking Sara in his arms again. "Besides," he told Marcus, "it would be best for Sara to learn to handle herself with different partners."

"You'll get no argument from me." Marcus laughed as he faced Sara. "In fact, I should be honored. Shall we, Miss Belding?"

Marcus proved to be an excellent instructor, kind and unfailingly patient as he guided her through the intricate steps. Much to Sara's relief, she didn't experience the same turbulent emotions in Marcus's arms as she had felt in Brant's. By concentrating on the lilting music Brant provided, she was able to relax and enjoy the lesson. When they had completed two dances without a single misstep, Marcus brought her to a halt beside the pianoforte.

"Very good, Miss Belding," he congratulated her with a merry smile. "You are without doubt the most graceful student it has ever been my honor to teach. Of course," he added with a conspiratorial wink, "you are the *only* student it has been my honor to instruct. I found the experience most . . . enlightening." A light kiss was deposited on the back of her hand.

"Thank you, good sir." Sara laughed at his teasing and dropped a graceful curtsey. She was aware of Brant's silent presence on the piano bench and was careful to include him in her warm smile. "And thank *you,* Cousin, for your skillful playing. Your tunes were far more melodious than those of our previous orchestra."

Brant did not return her smile, and his "You are

most welcome" was spoken in a tense, clipped voice. He refused to meet her gaze, and after a few uncomfortable moments she murmured her good-byes and slipped from the room. There was an awkward silence before Marcus turned to confront Brant.

"What the deuce is wrong with you?" he demanded with a heavy frown. "You were rude as the very devil to your cousin! And while you are about it, you might also explain what was going on when I first walked in. Good gad, man, had I been your aunt the pair of you would be betrothed by now!"

Brant's fingers crashed down on the ivory keys. "Don't you think I know that?" he answered fiercely. "I'm aware my actions were beneath contempt, but I . . . oh, hell!" He rose to his feet and began pacing the spacious room. "I can't explain what happened, and bedamned if I know what I'm going to do about it."

Marcus tipped his blond head to one side as he watched his friend. "Are you in love with her?"

"What?" Marcus's question brought Brant whirling around to face him.

"Are you in love with her," Marcus repeated, folding his arms across his chest.

"Of course not!" Brant thundered. "My God, she is my cousin."

"That didn't stop you from trying to kiss her," Marcus pointed out, the sparkle in his eyes belying his somber tones.

A dark mantle of color spread over Brant's cheekbones. "I know that," he said tightly. "And I know there is nothing I can say to defend my actions." He ran a hand through his dark hair and met Marcus's gaze. "Do you think I should offer for her?"

Marcus's amusement with the situation faded at his friend's obvious distress. "Of course not," he protested, clearly appalled by the very mention of matrimony. "Good Lord, man, I was only twigging you! You haven't done anything as bad as all that."

"No." Brant shook his head. "You are wrong. Despite the fact that nothing actually happened between Sara and myself, I *did* attempt to kiss her. I took unfair advantage of my position, and in so doing compromised the lady I had sworn to defend." He drew himself up proudly, his expression resolute. "I am prepared to do the honorable thing."

"Don't be such a cloth-head," Marcus advised, not unkindly. "No need to sacrifice yourself on the altar of duty just yet. Wait and see what Sara has to say. If she sets up a dust, well, then there's little to be done. But Sara seems a sensible enough female to me . . . unless that is a contradiction in terms. She might be green as grass in the ways of the ton, but she ain't a gudgeon. I daresay you'd shock her senseless if you were to offer for her."

Brant hesitated, torn between what he felt was his duty to Sara, and his natural aversion to marriage. All the while he had been playing the pianoforte he had given the idea of marriage to Sara a great deal of thought, and much to his surprise the notion wasn't nearly as distasteful as he thought it would be. The very idea of surrendering his freedom was abhorrent, of course, but if one had to surrender to the inevitable, then the least one could hope for was a comfortable sort of bride.

Sara could be a shrew at times, but she was also unfailingly honest. And, much as he denied it, he admired her fiery, independent spirit. He had seen too many of his friends driven to distraction by their clinging, whining wives, and he was determined never to suffer their fate. He had to marry eventually, if only to ensure the succession, and he supposed Sara would do as well as anyone.

"Brant? Are you all right?" Marcus was peering at his friend anxiously.

"What?" Brant glanced up and, seeing the younger man's concerned expression, managed a weak smile. "You're right, I suppose," he grumbled, his dark frown disappearing. "No need to dash for the border just yet. The thing to do is to wait and see what Sara expects me to do. She is no green girl, as you say, and I am sure she understands . . . er . . . matters."

"I am sure she does," Marcus agreed. "But if she sets up a hue and a cry, I should be honored to stand up with you."

"Thank you, Marcus." Brant was genuinely touched by his friend's offer. "Should it come to that, I can think of no other man I would rather have beside me."

"It would be my honor," Marcus replied with a flourishing bow. "Just remember I shall expect similar assistance when my sisters make their bows."

"But you have four sisters," Brant protested with a teasing grin.

"Precisely." Marcus laughed in delight. "I will see you at White's then, Mallingham. Good day to you."

* * *

Sara spent the remainder of the afternoon in her room. It was easy convincing Matty she had the headache; one look at her white face and shadow-filled eyes, and the attentive maid was tucking her into bed.

"You just lie still now, miss," Matty scolded, drawing the crimson drapes against the watery sunlight. "I'll send word to the countess that you are unwell." She gave Sara a worried frown. "Will you be wanting a supper tray in your room?"

"That sounds fine, Matty, thank you," Sara replied with a weak sigh. At the moment the thought of seeing anyone, especially her sharp-eyed aunt, was too painful to be borne. Although she had always despised women who took to their couches at the slightest emotional upset, she knew she was in no shape to face the world as yet. If hiding in her room could be considered an act of cowardice, then coward she would be. She was simply too heartsick to be anything else.

"Very good, miss." Matty hovered by the doorway uncertainly. "If there is anything else you need, mind you ring."

"I will, Matty." Sara closed her eyes with a low moan.

The maid took the hint and slipped from the room, shutting the door quietly behind her. When she was alone Sara rolled onto her back, staring at the top of her canopied bed with burning eyes.

How could she have behaved so . . . so brazenly, she asked herself in quiet despair. She had clung to Brant like the veriest strumpet, encouraging his kisses and caresses with a boldness which must have shocked him as deeply as it had shocked her.

Despite her inexperience she wasn't ignorant of lovemaking or the special closeness that existed between a man and a woman. As a small child she had often watched her parents exchanging small kisses and private looks. She had known instinctively that they shared something unique, and she had longed to experience it. At eighteen she had fallen in love with Alex Creighton; or at least, she had thought it was love. But when he had kissed her she had felt nothing.

Since then she had been too preoccupied to bother with such things, and had resigned herself to life alone. But when Brant had taken her in his arms, his warm body pressed intimately to hers, she had experienced sensations that burned her with forbidden fire.

She should have swooned, she acknowledged bitterly. She should have drawn back in horror, slapped his face, something . . . anything other than stand there docile as a lamb as his lips hovered over hers. No . . . more than that. More than merely accepting his touch . . . she had encouraged it, and that was her shame. Brant was her cousin, her guardian, and she wanted to know the feel of his lips on her own. If Marcus hadn't come in when he had, she would have known that touch. She wasn't sure if what she felt was relief or disappointment.

A solitary tear freed itself from one of the golden pools in her eyes and wended its way down the curve of her cheek. As degrading as she considered her own actions to be, she could not help but wonder what Brant must be thinking. Their squabbles and differences aside, she liked Brant, admiring him for the man he was. She had teased him about his years in the military, but privately she honored him for the service he had given his country. He had fought in some of the most dangerous battles in the war when his wealth and title might have kept him safely home.

Even now, with the war ended, he conducted himself according to a code of honor that she respected above all else. She knew there were times she exasperated him, but he had never treated her with anything other than the utmost courtesy. The thought of losing his respect hurt her more than she would have thought possible, and she bit her lip to hold back a painful cry.

A second tear ran down her face, then another, and another, until she was sobbing helplessly. She dashed a shaking hand across her cheeks, her eyes closing as she fell into an exhausted sleep, dreaming of a moonlit ballroom and a man with sapphire eyes who whispered to her of love.

Chapter Seven

Society wasn't nearly as terrifying as Sara had feared, and she soon found her footing in the ton. People were quick to accept her as part and parcel of the Deverleigh household, and she never lacked for invitations. She even made a few friends amongst the other young ladies, and as the Season passed she grew complacent with her new life.

Only one thing marred her happiness: the memory of that afternoon in the music room. She and Brant had seen each other almost daily since then, and although he never spoke of what had transpired, she sensed a restraint in his attitude toward her. Oh, he was as polite as ever; she couldn't fault him there. But there were times when he was so distant, so cool, that it made her heart weep. Even his arrogance was preferable to the formality with which he now treated her, but she was at a loss as to what she could do about it.

Lady Mallingham noted Sara's distraction, and put it down to a simple case of nerves. But as the weeks passed and Sara showed no signs of improving, she decided enough was enough. Bedamned if she'd let the chit sulk away the best part of the Season!

"Sara, child, what ails you?" She had judiciously waited until they were in her carriage before confronting her niece. The carriage, drawn by an excellent pair of matched bays, had been her husband's last purchase before his untimely death; and as she so seldom used it, the yellow and black paint gleamed like new. "You have been in a perfect mope for the better part of three weeks, and I demand to know what is wrong with you. Are you ill?"

Sara brushed an imaginary speck of lint from her white velvet evening cloak. "No, my lady," she said, puzzled by her aunt's sharp tone. It was the same tone she had heard when the countess had first visited her at Miss Larkin's, and she wondered if Lady Mallingham was feeling quite the thing. She noticed the older woman often spoke thusly when she was upset or fatigued. Distressed at having caused her aunt undue worry, she hastened to reassure her.

"It's just that I'm unused to the social whirl, and there are times when I find all this"—she indicated the opulent interior of the carriage with a bejeweled hand—"a little overwhelming. That is all."

"I see." Lady Mallingham was unconvinced. There was something going on, all right, and she'd bet a monkey that nephew of hers was involved. He'd been every bit as grim-faced as Sara, and as sober as a country parson as well. A speculative gleam lit her eyes as she contemplated the delightful implications.

"Very well, my dear, if you're certain nothing is wrong." She patted Sara's hand. "Although I still say you are sickening after something. Perhaps you need a tonic." The idea seemed to appeal to her.

"It's just the excitement," Sara replied hurriedly, recalling her aunt's attempts to dose her when she had been so ill. "I fear I still find the thought of Almack's somewhat unnerving. So many people crowded into such a small place!"

"Nonsense, child." Lady Mallingham straight-

ened her turban deftly. "You are a Deverleigh.
There's no reason for you to fear anything. Lady
Jersey has assured me she and the other patronesses
find you delightful. She was quite taken with you
when she came to visit us, you know."

Sara recalled the plump, fading blonde whose
malicious tongue had wagged nonstop during the
course of her hour's stay. The marchioness was well
aware of the power she possessed, and she wielded
it with charming ruthlessness. Still, Sara had to
admit that Lady Jersey had been kind to her, if
somewhat condescending, and at the end of her
visit everyone breathed a collective sigh of relief
when the patroness announced Sara would "do very
nicely."

"Of course, we owe the honor of Sally's visit to
your cousin," Lady Mallingham continued in a
bored voice. "He went to call upon her himself to
personally explain the circumstances of your coming-out. He said she was most understanding of the
matter, which is something of a surprise considering
what a stickler Sal can be. Still, she has never been
able to resist a handsome man, and your cousin,
when he puts his mind to it, has all the charm of the
devil. Don't you agree?"

Sara colored. "Well, I . . ."

"Speaking of that little scamp, don't think I have
forgiven him for refusing to accompany us tonight,"
Lady Mallingham went on as if Sara had not spoken. "It would have been so much better if we had
arrived *en famille.*"

"He didn't refuse, Aunt. The House of Lords was
in special session, and he was required to be there."
Sara felt compelled to defend her cousin, although

privately she couldn't help but wonder if the excuse he had given his aunt was just that: an excuse.

"Stuff!" the countess replied with an inelegant sniff. "There are some things, Sara, which are far more important than mere politics; not that you'd ever get a man to admit as much, of course. It's a great pity they don't allow women to run the government. You may be very sure *they* would never schedule a jawing session in the very middle of the Season. Still"—she sighed thoughtfully—"I suppose I shouldn't be so hard on the poor dears. They're only men, after all."

Almack's was ablaze with thousands of candles as the countess's coach pulled up beneath the covered portico. Liveried servants bowed them into the mammoth entryway, which was overflowing with elegantly dressed people and banks of exotic flowers. Looking at the virtual sea of humanity crowded into the rooms below, Sara thought it was a good thing her aunt had warned her of the London crowds. Otherwise the sight of all those strangers would have sent her fleeing to her home in panic.

It took them the better part of the next hour to fight their way through the mob to reach the reception line. Once they had greeted their hostesses they pushed and shoved their way into the Public Rooms where a small orchestra was playing. Priscilla and Lord Tressmoore were already there, and they hurried over to join the Deverleigh ladies.

"Ah, Lord Tressmoore," Lady Mallingham greeted him languidly. "How refreshing to see a man who comprehends his duty to his family. Has that nephew of mine arrived as yet, or is he still over at Parliament wagging his tongue?"

"M'lady." Lord Tressmoore bowed stiffly, looking uncomfortable in a formal evening coat of black velvet, his cravat bunched untidily beneath his massive jaw. "Mallingham should be along directly. The session was breaking up as I left, otherwise *I* shouldn't be here." He turned next to Sara.

"Miss Belding, you are looking in fine fettle this evening."

"Thank you, my lord," Sara replied, smiling. "It is kind of you to say so."

"Not at all." He waved a beefy hand. "Liked the color the moment I picked it out. As Mallingham said, one mustn't skimp on vital supplies, eh, Miss Belding?"

The arrival of a group of dandies, dripping with rings and fobs, their cravats tied in intricate arrangements and their collars impossibly high, saved Sara from answering Lord Tressmoore's puzzling remark. After securing Lady Mallingham's permission, one of the dandies, resplendent in a bright yellow jacket trimmed with large brass buttons, led Sara out onto the dance floor where couples were already forming for a quadrille. Sara took her place with the other ladies, but even as she began the steps of the intricate dance she was turning the remark over in her mind. She knew Lord Tressmoore seldom engaged in idle chatter, and could only conclude that it must mean something. But what? As the tempo of the music increased she pushed the mystery to the back of her mind, concentrating on the steps and her simpering partner.

* * *

Almack's was filled to bursting as Brant made his belated bows to the patronesses. He had rushed home from the House, barely pausing to bolt down his dinner while his valet helped him into a jacket of sapphire velvet and cream-colored breeches. It was almost midnight when he walked down the marble staircase leading to the Assembly Room, scanning the crowd for some sign of his aunt and cousin. He had just spied his aunt (the orange head-dress she was wearing made his task easier) and was making his way to join her when Hugh appeared at his side.

"About time you arrived," he greeted the earl with a low growl. "That dragonish aunt of yours all but took m'nose off because you weren't here."

"My apologies," Brant murmured, secretly amused by his friend's distress. "But the Home Secretary stopped me on my way out and asked for a word with me. I could hardly refuse."

"I suppose not," Hugh grumbled with a heavy frown. "I know you've been hoping for his support for your bill, but dash it all, Mallingham, you should have been here!" He glanced around furtively before whispering, "We've got trouble!"

"Trouble?"

"Trouble." Hugh nodded. "While you weren't here to stand guard on your cousin, she's been rushed by every rake and scoundrel in London! You should see the fortune hunters that have been making up to her, and your aunt hasn't so much as lifted a finger to help her."

"Where's Marcus?" Brant frowned, searching for

his friend. "He promised to keep an eye on Sara until I could get here."

"Lady Jersey dragged him off to waltz with some dratted female." Hugh dismissed the viscount with a shrug. "And that's another thing, you really shouldn't let Miss Belding take up with the radical element. She's had that Mrs. Broughton to tea twice this week. M'sister, too."

"Your sister is a radical?" Brant was only half attending to Hugh. He'd located Sara, and for a brief moment he allowed himself the luxury of studying her. She was wearing another new gown, this one in a cherry-red silk with a deep décolletage that revealed the pure line of her throat. Diamonds winked from her ears, and a small tiara set with rubies and diamonds held her brown hair in a sleek chignon. He felt a warm stirring of excitement at the sight of her, and he cursed his own lack of control.

"Not 'Cilla, cloth-head!" If Hugh was aware of Brant's distracted air he was too much of a gentleman to mention it. "I meant Mrs. Jane Broughton. 'Cilla's had her to tea several times since the Season began, and the three of them are thick as thieves when they meet out in Society. You really shouldn't allow it, you know. Otherwise people will think she's as blue as that she-devil."

Brant nodded, a forbidding expression crossing his face as he recognized the blond man in the ruby coat bending over Sara's hand. What the devil, he thought savagely. Surely his aunt hadn't given Sara permission to stand up with *that* scoundrel! Well, too bad if she had, he decided, his lips tightening in fury. Because he was damned if he would allow such a thing.

"Excuse me, Hugh." He cut into whatever his friend was saying. "But I believe it is time I claimed a waltz with Sara."

"Eh?" Hugh blinked at Brant's uncustomary rudeness. He turned to see what Brant was glaring at, and his own eyes widened in disbelief. "Braxton!" he exclaimed in accents of loathing. "How the deuce did that black-hearted devil find his way in here?"

"I have no idea," Brant replied softly, moving forward with a purposeful stride. "But I do know how he will be finding his way out." He started across the room.

"Come, Miss Belding, surely one little waltz isn't so much to ask," Anthony Braxton coaxed, his green eyes confident, as he smiled down at Sara. "I have been admiring you all evening, and I simply must have a dance with you!"

"I am afraid that is quite impossible, Mr. Braxton," Sara replied, wondering what it was about the handsome man that made her so leery. "As I have explained, my aunt isn't present at the moment, and I cannot dance with you until she has given her permission. You must know it will not do, sir."

"Nonsense, Miss Belding." Braxton availed himself of her free hand and carried it to his lips for a brief kiss, an intimate act which brought a gasp of outrage from her. "At your age surely you are exempt from the tiresome rules of conduct which govern girls fresh out of the nursery. Granted we haven't been formally introduced as yet, but I . . ."

"Ah, Sara, there you are." Brant materialized at her side as if in answer to her most secret prayers. "I have been looking for you so that I might claim that waltz you have promised me." He held out his hand in a commanding gesture.

"Of course, Cousin." Sara accepted his hand with alacrity, torn between relief at his timely arrival and a lingering embarrassment over the memory of that last waltz. Covering her conflicting emotions she turned to face Mr. Braxton, who was still standing beside her.

"Mr. Braxton, I should like to make you known to my cousin, Brant Deverleigh, the Earl of Mallingham. Cousin, this is Mr. Anthony Braxton of Surrey."

"Mr. Braxton and I have already met." Brant's hand tightened on Sara's, drawing her imperceptibly closer to his side. "He knows me quite well, as I know him. Is that not so, Braxton?" The smile he gave the other man was as deadly as a sword thrust.

"If you say so, m'lord." Braxton didn't pretend not to understand Mallingham's meaning. The earl's skill as a marksman was well known, almost as well known as his devotion to his newfound cousin. In fact, it was his devotion to the heretofore unknown Miss Belding which had drawn Braxton's interest. The word in the clubs had it that Mallingham was prepared to come down quite handsomely on his cousin's behalf, and the figure being bandied about had drawn more than one gentleman whose pockets were to let. Still, no fortune was worth a bullet through the heart, and Braxton decided to heed the earl's warning . . . for the moment at least.

"I do," Brant replied coldly, pleased to see the

rascal was using the modicum of intelligence he possessed. "Now if you will excuse us, I should like to dance with my ward."

"Of course." Braxton bowed sardonically before flashing Sara an ingratiating smile. "Miss Belding, I shall bid you adieu. Now that you know your esteemed cousin and I are such old friends, perhaps next time you won't hesitate to grant me a dance, hmm?"

Brant drew her away before she could reply, and as soon as they were on the dance floor he began quizzing her about Braxton.

"What do you mean by talking to that blackguard?" he demanded in a low hiss as he guided her about the floor. "Aunt couldn't have been so henwitted as to have introduced you to him!"

Brant's tone put Sara's back up at once, killing the warm gratitude she had been feeling. It also destroyed the paralyzing shyness she had been feeling around him these past few weeks, something she failed to notice in the heat of the moment.

"She did not," she replied, her chin lifting a notch as she met his burning gaze. "He introduced himself."

"The devil he did!" Brant thundered, his jaw tightening ominously. "And you were going to *dance* with him? Good Lord, Sara, have you no care for your reputation?"

"I have every care, sir, which is why I had already refused him," Sara reported, her eyes flashing with fury. "I might be a little country spinster, but even I know how rigidly Society judges an unmarried female. I had only just declined his offer when you arrived."

"Thank God for that," Brant muttered, feeling far from mollified. "That man's reputation is scandalous, Sara, and you would soon find yourself cut dead if you allowed your name to be associated with his. I suggest you use a little more discretion in choosing your dancing partners."

"Really, Cousin?" Sara replied with false sweetness, recalling rumors she had heard of Brant and the blond opera singer he was said to keep in considerable style. She supposed she should not know of such things, but she did, and she deplored what she regarded as his hypocrisy. "But if all ladies were to follow your advice and cut any man whose reputation is less than it should be, I fear we poor ladies would soon be reduced to waltzing with one another. An unsavory reputation is considered something of a cachet in a man, don't you agree?"

"I do not, and I want your word you will have nothing further to do with Braxton," Brant continued, warming to his theme with a vengeance. "Now that you are known to be a member of my family, you may find yourself marked as easy prey by those who would take advantage of your innocence. Any suitors you may have must be personally appraised by me. If I approve of their suit you may continue seeing them, but if not, you are to have nothing further to do with them. Is that understood?"

Only the knowledge they were under the watchful eye of the crème de la crème of Society kept Sara from stomping on her cousin's foot and howling with rage, as she longed to do. How dare he treat her with such high-handed contempt! Did he think her so lacking in intelligence and modesty that she would take up with one of the rackety fortune hunters who had been clustering about her for these last few weeks? She had been dealing with their sort quite successfully, and all on her own, too. If he thought he could step in now after ignoring her existence for the last month, then he was as big a gudgeon as he thought her to be.

"Sara?" Brant had felt her stiffening against him and sought to meet her eyes. "Did you hear what I said?"

"I heard." She was barely able to get the words past her clenched teeth.

"And?"

"And if you think I will meekly do as you bid, then you, my lord, have made a grave error." Their eyes met in a fiery clash of wills. "I am my father's daughter, sir, and I have no need of Deverleigh gold! You can't force me to obey you merely by decreeing it so! I will repeat what I have been saying since our first meeting: I have no need of a guardian. I shall take care of myself in whatever manner I see fit, and if I choose to see Mr. Braxton, or any other man for that matter, then there is nothing you can say. Your money might have purchased my agreement to stay with your aunt, but it hasn't bought my heart! Now, my lord, do you understand *me?*"

Brant stopped in midstep, not caring that he was providing the gossip-mongers with a delectable tidbit. "Why, you little shrew," he began incredulously. "How dare you take that tone with me! I'll have you . . ."

"Mallingham, there you are." Marcus's hand closed on Brant's shoulder in silent warning. "And Miss Belding, how delightful. Miss Tressmoore and

I were just remarking what a handsome couple the two of you make. Isn't that so, ma'am?"

"Oh, yes," she agreed, smiling gently at Brant and Sara. She was wearing a ruffled gown of sky blue tulle trimmed with silver ribbons, diamond stars winking from the mass of blond curls pinned to the top of her head. "You are both excellent dancers."

"Something for which I, in all modesty, must claim credit," Marcus said hurriedly. The crowd of dancers swirled around them, and he was aware of their interested stares. "At least, as far as Miss Belding is concerned. It was I who taught her to waltz, and now I am anxious to see how she progresses. Mallingham, with your permission." He whisked Sara away before either she or Brant could protest.

"Neatly done, my lord," she applauded as they completed a rapid turn about the room. "But you needn't have bothered. I'm sure my cousin is far too aware of his own consequence to have made a scene."

"I shouldn't count on that if I were you," Marcus retorted, remembering the fury blazing out of Brant's eyes. "And for your information, ma'am, it wasn't Brant I was concerned about. You looked angry enough to slit his throat. Whatever did he say to throw you into such a temper?"

"Nothing you would regard as so terrible, I am sure. Only that I was a brazen little hussy who hadn't the sense to recognize a fortune hunter when she saw one."

"What?" Marcus's look of incredulity would have been amusing had Sara been in any shape to notice it. "Surely he couldn't have said *that!*"

"Well . . ." Honesty compelled Sara to answer truthfully. "Perhaps he didn't say it, but he implied as much. He ordered me to stop seeing Mr. Braxton . . . whom I had only just met . . . and then he insisted that my suitors must first meet with his approval!"

"What else?" Marcus waited expectantly.

"That is all," Sara said, drawing herself up proudly. "I told him I would do as I pleased, and there was naught he could do about it. He's not my guardian after all, and—"

"Not your guardian!" Marcus interrupted indignantly. "Of course he is! Not legally, I suppose, but morally, and in every other way that matters, he is. He's your only living male relation, and that means he is responsible for you until you are wed. It is the way of our world, Miss Belding, and you would be well advised to accept that. Mallingham wants only what is best for you, and you must allow yourself to be guided by his wiser judgment."

Marcus mistook Sara's frozen silence as acquiescence and continued in a soothing voice. "Brant is a very good fellow, you know, and a dashed fine commander. It was his plan that we approach the matter of finding you a husband rather as we would a military campaign. We have spent weeks drawing up battle plans and strategies, going over lists of supplies . . . all those things. Nothing was left to chance, not even your clothing, and you can see for yourself how successful we have been. Why, with any luck at all, by the end of the Season you will find yourself some fine fellow to wed, and with Brant's approval, you shall marry. That is the end for which we have all labored unceasingly, and you mustn't destroy it all by taking up with some blasted fortune hunter! Don't you see?" he implored hopefully, her unnatural stillness finally penetrating his senses. "It is all for the best."

It took Sara several seconds to master her temper and her tongue. Fury such as she had never known burned in her, and it was all she could do not to scream out her rage. Rage and a burning pain, as she realized how easily her cousin had manipulated her. From the very beginning he had intended to marry her off as if she were no more than an inanimate piece of chattel, and she had let him. She had let him! Drawing a deep breath, she gave the viscount a tight-lipped smile.

"Oh, yes, Lord Cherrington," she said in a voice that shook with feeling. "I understand only all too well."

Marcus peered at her worriedly, wondering if perhaps he had said too much. Brant hadn't sworn them to secrecy, but he was experienced enough to know that one didn't reveal the battle plans to the enemy. He cast Sara a thoughtful glance, but when she didn't sink into a fit of the vapors as he had half feared, he sighed with relief. Perhaps she was going to be sensible about this after all, he thought as he escorted her back to a waiting Lady Mallingham.

The next hour passed with excruciating slowness for Sara, and she found it almost impossible to maintain a polite facade. Her argument with Brant had been carefully noted, and she soon found herself the target of a sharp inquisition by several avid gossips. It took all of her willpower to answer with anything approaching civility the questions being shot at her by a purse-lipped crone. Just as she was certain she must lose her temper, she felt a warm hand on her shoulder. Turning around in surprise, she was relieved to see a tall woman in her early thirties, her soft brown hair worn in an elegant chignon and her slender form encased in a simple gown of gray silk, smiling at her.

"Good evening, Miss Belding, Mrs. Fitzroy." Mrs. Jane Broughton's gray eyes were bright with amused sympathy as she smiled at Sara. "I do hate to interrupt you, but I was wondering if I might have a word with you, Miss Belding."

"Of course, Mrs. Broughton." Sara barely paused to bid the elderly Mrs. Fitzroy a strained farewell before scurrying away with Jane.

"I'm eternally in your debt," she told Jane with a grateful sigh as they strolled about the room. "Another few minutes and I wouldn't have been accountable for my actions!"

"You're most welcome," Jane said, leading Sara to a small alcove set off from the rest of the room by a large potted palm. "But tell me, what really happened between you and your cousin? I have been hearing the most delicious rumors!"

The possibility of a sympathetic ear was all it took to loosen Sara's tongue, and once they were comfortably seated she burst into an angry description of what Marcus had said. "So you see," she concluded with growing indignation, "I am nothing more to Brant than an . . . an objective! Another battle to be won for king and country. He doesn't care a fig for *my* feelings in the matter! Can you imagine anything so . . . debasing?"

"Actually, I find it rather amusing," Jane confessed with a candid laugh. "The notion of three soldiers plotting out and then executing a husband-hunting campaign is almost irresistible! What would they have done if no one had come up to scratch, I wonder. Ordered Almack's bombarded?" And she gave another delighted peal of laughter.

"Jane!" Sara was crushed by her friend's lack of compassion.

"I am sorry, Sara." Jane assumed a somber expression. "You're right, of course. The very notion is debasing, an affront to noble young womanhood everywhere. But in all good conscience you can't hold your cousin totally to blame for what happened."

"Why not?" Sara demanded in bellicose tones. "It was all his doing, every bit of it! He meant to marry me off as if I were a brainless chit without a thought in my head or a will of my own."

"Well, of course he means to marry you off," Jane responded reasonably. "He's a man, isn't he? And that's all a man thinks women are good for. That is why the Season exists, after all. Every year a fresh crop of nubile young virgins is trotted out so that the men may haggle and bargain over them. Men think us creatures without souls whose only excuse for existence is to see to their comfort and give them heirs—male heirs, that is."

"Well, I for one don't mean to oblige them!" Sara tossed her head decisively. "Once the Season is ended I shall find a fine position as a governess or companion. The only reason I am here at all is that I gave my cousin my promise to remain with Aunt Agatha through the Season."

"You promised your cousin you would stay with Lady Mallingham?"

"Yes." Sara nodded, burning with resentment as she realized how easily she had been tricked. "He made me give my word I would act as Aunt's companion, and in return he would pay for my wardrobe. And to think I actually *thanked* him, the deceitful creature!"

"The life of a governess or companion isn't always a pleasant one," Jane said, studying Sara with interest. "Are you quite sure you would find the life suitable?"

"Oh, yes. In fact up until two months ago, I thought it would be my life. My papa had died, you know, and the money he had left me was almost gone. I had already secured a post as a schoolteacher when I fell ill. That is when I came to live with my aunt." She prudently left out the precise details as to how she had come to the countess's house.

Jane raised an eyebrow in surprise. "You were going to be a schoolteacher?" she echoed. "Now that is amazing. I should have thought the earl's pride would never stand for such a thing."

"What has it to do with him?" Sara was indignant. "It's *my* life after all . . . and I'll have you know I'm highly qualified as a schoolmistress. I speak French and German, as well as a smattering of Greek and Latin. I paint tolerably well, and I'm quite good at mathematics. The squire who hired me to teach in his village was most impressed with my skills."

"I didn't mean to cast aspersions on your abilities," Jane assured her quickly. "It is just I am surprised. Most young women of noble families usually prefer posts in private households if circumstances force them to seek employment. Did Lord Mallingham approve of your plans?"

"No," Sara admitted reluctantly. "But it didn't really matter because I was so ill I was forced to withdraw my acceptance. Perhaps I should write to the squire again . . ." Her eyes grew thoughtful as she considered the matter.

"Miss Belding, Mrs. Broughton, what a delightful surprise!" A plump gentleman in a plum satin coat materialized before them, the stays of his corsets creaking as he executed a stiff bow. "But what are two such fair flowers doing languishing in this isolation? Come, you must allow me to escort you back to civilization."

Jane and Sara exchanged an eloquent glance, but managed not to laugh as they rose to their feet to accept their elderly swain's arm. Mr. Parish was known to them both as a determined, if harmless, fortune hunter and they allowed him to lead them back to the others. Sara's dance partner was waiting to claim her, and after bidding Jane and Mr. Parish farewell, she moved forward to meet the waiting young officer.

The rest of the evening passed slowly. Fortunately for Sara the topic of her and Brant's conduct on the dance floor was replaced by the scandal which erupted when the young "sister" of a noble lord was revealed to be an infamous Cyprian. People were so delighted by the latest *on-dit,* that everything else paled in comparison. After dancing several other dances and turning down an invitation to join a rather intoxicated young captain on his morning ride, Sara was more than ready to leave when the countess suggested they do so.

"Well, that was an interesting evening," Lady Mallingham said as she settled against the squabs. "Thank God Ruxford showed up with his latest doxy, or we should soon have found ourselves in a bumble-broth. Whatever your squabble with your cousin, Sara, I must insist that you keep it private. I really cannot like to have our family's differences made the object of so much unpleasant talk. Do you understand me?"

The sharp lecture caught Sara unawares, and she jerked upright in her seat. She had almost convinced herself that her aunt had forgotten what happened, or had decided against mentioning it.

"Yes, my lady," she replied, deciding that for now, at least, discretion was the better part of valor. Besides, avoiding Brant had taken the last bit of energy she possessed, and she simply wasn't up to a scene with Lady Mallingham. "I am sorry."

"That is all right, child." The countess closed her eyes, hiding her expression. "I know Brant can be a provoking devil. But I do wish you would learn some decorum. Will you promise me that you will try?"

"Yes, my lady," Sara repeated, grateful at having escaped so easily. She had been steeling herself for a stern lecture on duty and responsibility. "I promise I shall try to do better."

"There's a good girl," the countess sighed, suddenly looking rather tired. "I knew I could count on you. Now if you will excuse me, I believe I will just rest my eyes until we are home. Those demmed bright candles have given me the headache."

* * *

Sara was enjoying a quiet cup of tea the next morning when the butler announced a visitor. She had barely risen to her feet when Jane rushed into the room, her cheeks flushed with excitement.

"I have found it, Sara!" she announced, waving a newspaper with dramatic emphasis. "The very solution to your problem!"

"What are you talking about?" Sara asked, taking the paper from Jane and studying it with a puzzled frown. "What has Prinny's latest scandal to do with me?"

"Not that, silly," Jane exclaimed, snatching the paper back and rustling through it until she reached the page she wanted. "That." She indicated a tiny advertisement with a gloved finger.

The advertisement was in the *Situations Available* column of the *Times,* and Sara's brows puckered as she read the words. "A young woman of gentle birth is required to act as companion to an elderly lady currently residing in Cornwall. Some knowledge of the German language helpful. Inquire between two and four o'clock at One-ten Grosvenor Square." She glanced up into Jane's eager face. "So?"

"So, it is perfect for you!" Jane enthused, throwing herself onto one of the dining room chairs. She had been in such a hurry she hadn't even removed her pelisse, and only now began unfastening its many buttons. "You said you wished to be a companion, didn't you?"

"Yes," Sara replied, beginning to understand, "but after the Season ends. I told you I had given Brant . . . my cousin, that is, my word that I would remain through the Season. I can hardly leave now."

"Why not? From what you have told me the scoundrel deceived you. Why should you honor your word to such a man?"

"Well . . ." Sara hesitated. She hadn't thought of it in quite *that* light before. "I don't suppose I should. But—"

"Don't you see," Jane said as she leaned forward earnestly, "this position would solve everything! Once you have a post like this you can tell your high-and-mighty cousin to go whistle in the wind! You're an adult after all, and he has no legal hold over you. You may do as you please, and there is nothing he can do to stop you."

"That is so," Sara agreed, Jane's words almost echoing her angry words to her cousin. Then she shook her head. "No, it wouldn't be right. Even if my cousin has tricked me, it wouldn't be fair to make my poor aunt suffer for it. I have grown very fond of her, and it would be cruel for me to leave her without any warning at all. I couldn't do that."

"Perhaps not." Jane rested her small chin on her hand, her dark eyebrows meeting over her tip-tilted nose. "What a pity. The position seemed so perfect for you. You speak German, and you are of gentle birth. Opportunities like this don't grow on trees, you know. In another few months you may not be able to find anything nearly so desirable. Then what will you do? Live with your aunt *ad infinitum?*"

Sara bit her lip, remembering the struggle she had had finding that first post. Jane was right, she realized with a sinking heart. She, better than anyone, knew just how difficult finding adequate employment could be. It could be weeks, even months, before anything half so good came her way. If she didn't at least try for the post then she could find herself forced into remaining with her aunt.

"I suppose it wouldn't hurt to apply for the position," she said, picking up the paper to reread the article. "It doesn't say when the post starts. Perhaps if I explained the situation to them they would allow me to stay with my aunt through the remainder of the Season. I could always join them in Cornwall at a later date."

"That's true." Jane brightened at once. "I remember when my late husband Harry hired a valet from the Duke of Weston, we had to wait almost a year before he was free to come to us."

Sara glanced up at the mention of Jane's husband. She seldom spoke of him, but Sara knew she had been very fond of the man despite the almost twenty-year disparity in their ages. He had left Jane a comfortable inheritance so that she did not need to remarry.

"Where is Grosvenor Square?" she asked, returning her attention to the matter at hand. "Can I get there from here?"

"It's just across the park," Jane replied, smoothing a strand of jet-black hair back into its neat coronet. "I have my coach with me if you'd like a ride."

"That's very kind of you, but I believe it would be better if I walked. How many companions do you know who arrive for their interview in a fine carriage?"

"That's so," Jane agreed. "A carriage would be bound to cause comment, especially when it went to the servants' entrance. What will you wear?" Her agile mind moved on to other matters. "Your new clothes are very nice, but they are hardly the sort of thing a companion would wear, even in the most noble of houses."

Sara remembered the trunk of her old clothing packed away in the countess's attic. Her aunt had suggested throwing it out, but Sara's frugal nature had decried such a waste. Finding it would take some doing, but Sara supposed it could be done. She glanced at the small gold watch pinned to her bodice. It was almost noon now, which meant she had less than two hours to prepare herself.

"I have a little something," she replied with a sudden smile. "But I'm afraid I will have to excuse myself for now. I'll need time to transform myself."

"I'll help." Jane leapt to her feet and began pulling off her gloves. "It was my idea after all, and I demand that I be allowed to witness the transformation. Besides, you may need assistance sneaking from the house."

"I hadn't thought of that." Sara laughed, feeling younger than she had in weeks. "If worse comes to worst, I can always hide in my trunk and have it carried out to your coach. They should never miss me for hours!"

"What an excellent suggestion!" Jane clapped her hands in pleasure. "What fun we shall have, dearest Sara! There, you see? Men are not the only ones who know how to plan. We shall soon see just which is the more clever of the sexes."

Chapter Eight

Much to Jane's disappointment, smuggling Sara out in a trunk proved unnecessary. Lady Mallingham had gone out for the day to visit an old friend who had just arrived in the city, and the servants were busy readying the house for the dinner party the countess had planned. Sara had the footman fetch her trunk from the attic, and with Jane's help selected a dress they deemed suitable for the interview. It was the same dress of black bombazine she had worn the first time she had met her cousin, and while it had hung loosely on her then, now it was a struggle just to get it fastened.

"I can't believe I have gained so much weight," Sara protested as Jane fought to tie the laces together. "Perhaps I should borrow one of Aunt's corsets."

"There's no need for that," Jane assured her, grunting as she completed her task. "We're—oof!—almost done. There." She sighed in relief, stepping back to survey Sara's gown. "Just be very sure you don't eat so much as a crumb should they offer it to you, or you may burst your stays. Now what about your hair? Up or down?"

"Up." Sara sat in front of her mirror while Jane helped her brush her long hair and secure it in the familiar bun. Once this was done Sara leaned forward to study her reflection with a puzzled frown. Something was wrong. In the plain black gown, with her hair pinned back, she looked much like her old self. And yet she didn't.

Oh, she wasn't nearly as thin, of course, and her face had lost its invalid's pallor. But something was changed . . . *she* was changed. She was no longer the grieving daughter of Dr. Elias Belding of Somerset. She had experienced more of the world, learning at last to put the pain of his death behind her and to get on with her life. She would always love and miss him, but the love she had felt for him had been replaced by the deep affection which she had for the countess. Before, she had been alone in a world that wouldn't have even noticed her death. Now she had friends, family; she was loved. . . .

"Sara?" Jane laid a gentle hand on her friend's shoulder. "Is everything all right? You're so quiet."

"Oh, no, I'm fine." Sara shook off her melancholy thoughts and gave Jane a bright smile in the mirror. "I was just noting how much I've changed." She rose to her feet, her hands going to a waist that was still enviably small. "Aunt's French cook is to be commended."

"Well, we had best be leaving, or you'll be late." Jane picked up Sara's gray woolen cloak from the bed and draped it about her. "I think it would be better if I were to drive you at least part of the way there. Will you be able to get back on your own, or shall I wait for you?"

"No, I can manage," Sara replied, remembering the day she had walked all over London, her stomach growling from hunger. "Should I bring the advertisement with me?"

"It might be a good idea," Jane agreed after some thought. "Otherwise the housekeeper might not let you in." She handed the paper to Sara. "Are you ready?"

"As ready as I shall ever be," Sara replied nervously, her heart pounding with sudden fear. "Oh, Jane, are you quite sure I am doing the right thing?"

"Are *you* sure?" Jane wisely reversed the question.

Sara closed her eyes, knowing there was but one answer she could give. "Yes," she replied, opening her light brown eyes with quiet resolve. "I'm sure."

The two ladies crept down the back stairs with a great deal of giggling and hushed laughter. The ubiquitous Mr. Jenks was nowhere in sight, and they were able to slip from the house without being noticed. Sara rode with Jane as far as the park, but elected to walk from there. The gentle drizzle which had been falling all afternoon turned into an icy downpour, and by the time she reached her destination she was shaking from the wet and cold.

Grosvenor Square was all but deserted, the gray cobblestones glistening in the rain. Number 110 was a brick mansion some three stories high, with tall windows flanked by green shutters. Sara barely took time to notice the trio of white Doric columns standing like sentinels before hurrying around to the servants' entrance.

The footman who answered her knock showed a marked reluctance to admit her until Sara showed him the advertisement. " 'Nother one, eh?" he asked, giving her a cheeky grin. "You be the last one, then. Mr. Stampford said to turn 'em away when the parlor be full."

He relieved her of her sodden cloak and escorted her to a small room located off a magnificent staircase. "Mind you don't sit on a chair till you be proper dry," he advised with a wink. "For them chairs be Mrs. Daniels's pets, and she'd skin you sure if you was to spot 'em."

The parlor to which the jocular footman had led her was filled to overflowing with females of every description, some of whom stretched the term "gentle birth" to its breaking point. Sara avoided these obvious creatures and settled herself next to a respectable-looking woman in her fifties. Mrs. Daniels's pet chairs be hanged.

"It's a nursing post, I'll wager," her newfound friend said, nodding wisely. "Can't trust those. The old dearies pop off before you have your bags unpacked, and then where are you? The wilds of Cornwall, that's where, and them people barely civilized."

"Well, it's all very havey-cavey if you ask me." A young woman who looked to be Sara's age cast a suspicious glance about the parlor. "Why, they say the Duke of Langden himself is conducting the interviews! What business has a duke interviewing a companion, I ask you?"

"Perhaps," Sara ventured, eager to converse with her fellow job-seekers, "the post is as companion to his dear wife and—"

"Hiring the companion has always been the responsibility of the lady of the house," the young woman interrupted, her sharp nose fairly quivering in outrage. "Even if that lady is but a poor relation. Of what use are men for such things? They'd only hire the first pretty face they see." Her colorless eyes slid to a rosy-cheeked blonde in a gay blue dress.

"Perhaps there is no lady." Sara's friend rolled

her plump shoulders with disinterest. "Happens sometimes."

"A bachelor's establishment?" A timorous-looking young woman in wire-rimmed spectacles gave a squeak of alarm. "Oh, dear . . . how very awkward . . . our reputations . . ."

"I served in a bachelor's establishment once," the blonde volunteered with a sultry laugh. "It's really not so bad if you've a mind—"

A general chorus of "Well, I never!" rippled through the parlor, effectively ending all attempts at conversation. The blonde was called in shortly after that, but soon returned, the smug look quite wiped from her face. She was followed by Sara's friend, the bespectacled girl, and then by the priggish young woman, until one by one the number of applicants had been whittled down to one: Sara. She was beginning to think she had been forgotten when the duke's secretary appeared at the door.

"Ah, Miss Belding." The young man, who looked to be no older than twenty, gave her a harried look. "You are still here, then. Have you a list of references?" He held out his hand expectantly.

Sara stared back at him mournfully. It had never occurred to her that she would need such a thing. "I . . . that is . . ." She wet her lips nervously. "This is the first post I have ever applied for, and . . ."

"Of course." The secretary bobbed his bright red head in sympathy. "I quite understand. Well, as long as you can speak German there should be no problem. You *do* speak German, don't you?" he added anxiously.

"Oh, yes." Sara was happy she could reassure

him on this point at least. "I had a paternal aunt who taught me and . . ."

"Thank heavens for that." The young man ran a distracted hand through his hair, adding to its wild disorder. "None of the other applicants could speak a word, and the duke has been most displeased." His bright blue eyes swept over her in quick appraisal. "Yes, I do think he will be pleased with you. This way if you please."

He led her to another room, pausing just outside the massive door. "As this is your first interview perhaps there are a few things you should know," he told her, his voice kind. "You may not take a seat unless the duke gives you permission to do so. Also, please don't speak unless asked a direct question, then confine your answers to the matter put before you. The duke dislikes senseless prattle," he added in a conspiratorial whisper. "And pray don't be nervous. Beneath his bluster, His Grace is rather a good fellow." He gave her an encouraging smile before opening the door.

"Miss Belding, Your Grace," he announced, then stepped aside to admit Sara.

She hesitated, the trickle of panic inside of her become a raging torrent. She had no idea what awaited her beyond the door, and the unknown prospect terrified her. She considered turning tail and dashing back to Aunt Agatha's, but then she remembered her cousin and his nefarious plot. How he would gloat to see her fleeing like the veriest coward, she thought, straightening her shoulders with renewed determination. Taking a deep breath, she lifted her chin proudly and marched through the open door.

The room where she found herself was a library, the walls lined with books. With the exception of a few ancient leather chairs and candle tables, the only piece of furniture in the dimly lit room was a massive desk. A small man sat behind the desk, his bald head shining in the faint light. A pair of dark eyes peered from beneath thick, graying eyebrows, and no expression registered in the impassive face as Sara paused before the desk.

"Sprechen Sie Deutsch?" The sharp question made Sara leap with fright, and she blinked at him in confusion. *"Sprechen Sie Deutsch?"* the duke repeated, the sour look on his homely face increasing with each passing second.

The impatience in the man's voice loosened Sara's tongue, and she glared at him angrily. "Indeed I do, my good sir," she retorted in the same language. "My dear aunt was from Bavaria and we often spoke together. How are you, sir?" She added the last in her aunt's rather obscure dialect, perversely hoping he couldn't understand. Really, she fumed to herself, the man was almost unforgivably rude.

To her surprise the duke gave a hearty chuckle. "So you have some backbone, have you?" He reverted back to English, and was regarding her with obvious approval. "Excellent. I can't abide these milk-and-water misses who wouldn't say boo to a goose. My mater would make mincemeat of them. What was your name again?"

"Miss Sara Belding, Your Grace," Sara replied, feeling confused by the duke's abrupt turnabout. She studied his bulldog-like face and decided she liked him better when he was scowling. His physiognomy did not lend itself well to the act of smiling.

"Miss Belding, pray, will you be seated?" The duke rose to his full five feet to bow her into one of the red leather chairs matching his. "Don't want you to think I don't know how to do the pretty with the ladies. I am the Duke of Langden, by the by, and most pleased to make your acquaintance." He shook her hand vigorously before resuming his seat. "Sorry to have barked at you like that, but those other females were a sore trial to me. Not a one of them could speak a word of the blasted language. Now, on to business. When will you be able to leave London? I should like to have my mater home before the week is out."

Sara blinked at the duke. Was she hired then?

The door opened again, and the young secretary entered, smiling at Sara with approval. "Well, Miss Belding, I see you have survived the German Inquisition. May I be the first to welcome you to our happy family?"

"Don't rush your fences, boy." The duke scowled at the man. "Make your introductions first, 'less you want her to think the lot of us are queer in the attic." He turned back to a mystified Sara. "Miss Belding, I should like to introduce my youngest boy, Cedric."

"It's Sanford, actually." The young man took her hand with a laugh. "I've just been sent down from Cambridge, and Father is still angry with me."

"Insolent puppy." The duke beamed at his youngest with obvious pride. "He put a snake down his tutor's . . . er . . . robe. What pluck, eh, Miss Belding?"

Sara agreed it sounded pluckish to her, and glanced hopefully at the duke. When he realized she was staring at him he cleared his throat.

"Now, Miss Belding, I don't know what you were paid at your other post, but I'm fully prepared to be generous." He named a figure that made Sara's eyes widen in disbelief. Surely she had misunderstood.

"I beg your pardon, Your Grace," she said in a weak voice, "but what did you say?"

"One hundred pounds per annum," he repeated, his thick brows meeting over his pug nose. "If that's not enough, say so. Nothing's too good for my mater."

"I . . . no, Your Grace, the figure is quite sufficient, I assure you." Sara was shocked. The sum he had named was almost twice what she'd been offered for her teaching post, and more than she had hoped to earn. There was no way she could refuse such a position, she realized with a sinking heart, wondering how she was going to break the news to her aunt.

"Excellent," the duke repeated, rubbing his hands together with relish. "Mater will be pleased. She can't abide English servants, and my Effie, that's my wife, don't you know, has been at her wits' end. I shall take you to meet them." He leapt to his feet in a move agile for one of his girth. "They are with company now, but I daresay they won't mind. Come along, then."

"I believe I shall tag along." Sanford fell into step behind them. "I'm hoping to persuade Mother I have been punished long enough. Making me act as Papa's secretary during these interviews was most cruel, don't you agree, Miss Belding?"

"Most cruel," Sara agreed, hiding a smile at Sanford's ingenuous tones.

"Not that it was all bad," he continued as they climbed the stairs to the second floor. "Papa may not have cared for our other applicants, but I found at least one of them worth a second look."

The saucy blonde flashed in her mind, and she gave him a knowing look. He was a very likeable young man, open and full of life. She silently wished him luck with the blonde, thinking she would undoubtedly lead him a merry chase.

"Here we are," the duke said, pausing before a closed door and straightening his cravat with a nervous hand. "Mater is a bit deaf, but sharp as a tack for all her four-and-eighty years. Just make sure you speak in her good ear, and you'll be fine."

There was a small group of ladies clustered in front of the fireplace, and the sight of one of them made Sara stop in midstep. No, it couldn't be. She willed herself not to panic. Surely there was more than one woman in London addicted to that dreadful shade of orange.

But even as this comforting thought was winging its way to Sara's heart, the woman in question turned around, blue eyes widening in surprise.

"Why, Sara," Lady Mallingham exclaimed in delight. "Whatever are you doing here?"

For a brief moment Sara feared she would swoon. Never in her wildest dreams had she imagined such a contretemps, and she could think of no graceful way to extricate herself. She was well and truly caught. The only thing left for her to do was to brazen her way through and pray for a miracle.

"Aunt Agatha." She managed a weak smile. "How . . . nice to see you."

"Eh? You are related to the countess?" The duke waddled forward to stare at Sara in confusion. "Why didn't you say so? Lady Mallingham and my Effie are bosom friends."

"I . . . er . . . had no idea the families were acquainted," Sara stammered, her cheeks pinking in embarrassment as she searched for some diversion. She glanced around the drawing room, which was decorated in the Grecian mode, and her glance fell on an elderly woman swathed in a mound of shawls. Hostile black eyes peeked out of a lined face that was almost prodigiously ugly, and Sara was quick to recognize the woman as the duke's beloved "mater." Sensing a possible distraction, she gave the ancient creature an encouraging smile.

"Good afternoon, Your Grace," she greeted the woman in precise German. "I hadn't meant to intrude upon you. My name is Miss Sara Belding."

At hearing her native tongue, the woman broke into a toothless grin and let fly with a virtual torrent of words. Before Sara could begin to reply to even half of what was said, a tall woman with fading red hair stepped forward to greet her.

"You're here about the position, aren't you?" she said, her eyes softening with pleasure. "How wonderful! We were beginning to fear it would never be filled." She turned to the countess, who was glaring at Sara with dawning comprehension. "You never said your little niece was a linguist."

"I had no idea she was," came the tart reply. "The dear child is a never-ending source of surprises. Is that not so, my love?" The row of yellowed teeth she flashed at Sara did little to reassure her.

"Good heavens," the duchess exclaimed as she took Sara's hand in hers, "your poor hand is like ice! Come closer to the fire and warm yourself before you take a chill." She bustled Sara forward, urging her onto one of the lyre-backed chairs.

"Do you think we ought to send for a doctor?" the duchess asked Lady Mallingham worriedly. "I believe you said she has recently been quite ill?"

"Oh, no, Your Grace, I am quite well, I assure you," Sara spoke quickly. "But I thank you for your concern." Lord, what was she going to do now? she wondered with growing desperation. Judging from the fury snapping in her aunt's eyes, it wouldn't be very long before she was exposed as the traitor she felt.

"Are you quite sure you are feeling all right?" the countess asked in sharp tones. "You are not behaving at all like yourself."

Sara closed her eyes in resignation. There was no hope for it. She would have to confess all. "Yes, Aunt," she said quietly, opening her eyes to meet Lady Mallingham's hostile gaze. "I am sorry to have deceived you."

"Eh?" The duke scowled in confusion. "Deceived? What's going on here, Effie?" He frowned at his wife as if she were responsible for the mystery.

"It would appear our 'companion' neglected to gain her aunt's approval before applying for the post," the duchess replied with gentle understanding. "Is that it, Sara?"

"Yes, Your Grace," Sara mumbled, giving the notion of swooning careful thought. Or better still, she could die. She reasoned if she were dead then she'd be safely out of it, and it would be left to the duke and her aunt to haggle over her lifeless form.

"The devil you say!" The duke was properly shocked, and gave Sara an accusing glare. "I've never heard the like!"

"Calm yourself, Edgar." The duchess was accustomed to her husband's delicate sensibilities. "I'm sure Sara meant no harm."

"Indeed I didn't, ma'am," Sara agreed, shooting her aunt a guilty look. "And I most certainly didn't mean to upset you, Aunt Agatha. But the position sounded so perfect I felt I had to apply. I . . . I knew you wouldn't be pleased, but . . ."

"Of course I wouldn't be pleased!" Lady Mallingham exclaimed, her eyes taking on a watery sheen. "Why should I be pleased when I have been so cruelly betrayed? I would not have thought you capable of such a thing, Sara." Her voice quavered slightly. "I thought you had come to love me."

Sara leapt from her chair and hurried to her aunt's side. "I *do* love you," she said, kneeling beside the countess's chair. "But I thought I was doing what was best for us all. I can't expect you to support me forever, and times are hard—"

"Excuse me, my dear," the duchess interposed, laying her hand on Sara's shoulder, "but I think it would be best if you and Agatha continued your discussion at home. I'm sure you'll understand that we couldn't engage you against the wishes of your family."

"Of course." Sara swallowed her disappointment. All things considered, she would have liked the position. "And again, I apologize for any inconvenience I may have caused you."

"Think nothing of it," the duchess soothed with admirable nobility. "I'm sure we'll have no trouble finding someone else, will we, my dear?" She turned a meaningful smile on the duke, who was trying to explain the goings-on to his mystified parent.

"Eh?" He glanced up. "Oh. No, my love, no trouble at all. Although this means we won't be going home to Langden just now."

Sanford, who had been listening to the drama in bright-eyed silence, straightened with interest at this pronouncement. "I say, Miss Belding, you're a dashed angel of mercy! I have been praying we might remain in London, and now we shall!"

"Sanford!" His mother shook her head at him in exasperation.

"I'm sorry, Mama," he replied blithely. "But it's the truth, you know. *Vincit omnia veritas,* to quote my Latin professor. 'Truth conquers all things.'"

"I know what it means," she said with an indulgent laugh. "Your mama isn't hopelessly dim. Now, be a good boy, and go finish your papa's journals. If you promise to stay out of trouble for the rest of the day, I may even forget that I am put out with you and let you accompany us to the theater."

"It will be as you desire, Your Grace." He sketched a courtly bow. "Or as my French instructor would say, *'C'est—'*"

"Sanford," the duke interrupted with an impatient roar, "go!"

"Oh, very well. But I don't understand how you expect me to become an educated man of the world if you never let me apply what I have learned. La-

dies," he said, turning to Sara and Lady Mallingham
with another bow, "it has been a pleasure. I'm sorry
you won't be joining us, Miss Belding. I daresay
you might have taught me some dashed fine
phrases."

The silence in the black-and-yellow carriage was
fraught with tension as Sara and the countess made
their way to her home through St. James's Park. Every now and again Lady Mallingham would sniff
audibly and dab at her eyes with a crumpled handkerchief, making Sara writhe with remorse. By the
time they reached her aunt's home she was so consumed with guilt she would have done anything to
restore the lively glint to the countess's blue eyes.

She decided to wait until they were safely indoors
before prostrating herself at her aunt's feet, but the
moment they stepped into the vestibule pandemo-
nium erupted around them.

"Miss Belding, you are found!" Mr. Jenks, her
aunt's formidable butler, descended upon them, his
usually impassive face shining with such enthusiasm that for a moment Sara thought he meant to
embrace her. He stopped a few feet short of where
she stood frozen with shock and bent a paternal
frown on her. "We have been looking for you,
miss," he admonished in stern tones.

Before Sara's tongue could uncleave itself from
the roof of her mouth, the door to her aunt's drawing room burst open and the earl rushed out, his
jacket discarded and his cravat loosened by agitated
fingers. "Where have you been?" he thundered, his
strong hands descending upon her shoulders in a
bruising hold. "You've been missing all afternoon!"

"I . . . I wasn't missing," Sara stammered, staring up into Brant's dark face in amazement. "I was . . ."

"Aunt Agatha." Brant had only just noticed the countess, and was frowning at her. "Do you mean to say Sara has been with you all this time?" His hands were still resting upon Sara's shoulders, but neither of them seemed aware of the fact.

"My lord, if you would but listen to me for one moment, I could—" Sara tried again.

"She most certainly has not!" Lady Mallingham snapped, shooting her red-faced niece an indignant look. "She was walking the streets seeking employment!"

"What?" Brant's hands tightened around Sara's delicate flesh, drawing her against him.

"Yes!" Lady Mallingham continued, one hand clasped to her breast in a dramatic gesture which might have alerted the earl had he noticed it. "You may only imagine my shame when the Duke of Langden burst into the room where I was visiting with his wife and mother to introduce us all to his mother's new companion." She glared at Sara in silent accusation.

"Lord Mallingham, Aunt Agatha, if you would let me speak, I can explain everything." Sara was determined to have her say. "You are making too much of this. I wasn't 'walking the streets' for employment. There was an advertisement in the *Times,* and—"

"I am going to my rooms," Lady Mallingham interrupted in a quavering voice. "I am simply too heartsick to hear another word. Sara, I leave you to make your explanations to your cousin." And she turned to ascend the stairs, her head held with regal pride.

Aware of the gawking servants crowding around them, Brant grasped Sara's arm and pulled her into the drawing room. Once the door had closed behind them, he turned to face her. "Well?" he drawled, folding his arms across his broad chest. "I am waiting, Cousin."

Sara felt her temper flaring at the arrogant words. She was willing to acknowledge that she had wronged her aunt, but she owed her cousin nothing. Had it not been for his nefarious plotting behind her back, she would never have found herself in her current predicament. She lifted her chin another notch and crossed her arms in deliberate mimicry of his stance.

"Well," she shot back, "and what is it you are waiting for, *Cousin?*"

Brant's lips tightened in fury. He had arrived at his aunt's home fully prepared to do battle with Sara, only to find the household in an uproar over her disappearance. She hadn't been seen since before luncheon, and none of the servants could recall seeing her leave. A quick search of her rooms revealed her clothes were still hanging in her wardrobe, relieving him of his initial suspicion that she had bolted. But as time passed and no trace of her was found, his relief turned into worry. He was debating whether or not to send for the authorities when she arrived.

But as was often the case whenever he was around Sara, his emotions underwent a radical change. The gratitude he felt that she was safe and not lying dead in some filthy gutter quickly turned to exasperation at the havoc she had raised. Fixing her with a cold, unwavering stare, he said, "I am waiting, Cousin, for your apology. Your 'explanation' doesn't interest me in the slightest."

Sara's hands clenched into small fists. "Then I am afraid, sir, that you are in for a very long wait indeed. I have no intention of apologizing to you. This is none of your concern, and I will thank you to keep out of it."

The years of command were all that kept Brant in control of his temper. Except for the muscle ticking in his lean jaw he managed to hide the fury he felt at her words.

"You are forgetting I am your guardian," he said, his voice deceptively calm. "Your behavior is most assuredly my concern, especially when you insist upon conducting yourself like a hoyden. But as it happens, I am referring to another matter."

"And what might that matter be?" Sara asked sweetly, her eyes flashing at his insult. Hoyden indeed, she seethed, her resentment mounting.

"Your promise to me." Brant met her defiant gaze with unwavering censure. "In case it has escaped your memory, you gave me your word you would remain with Aunt until the Season had ended. Is this how you honor your obligations?"

Sara's cheeks burned at his hit. Remembering what Jane had said, she tossed her head back in silent challenge. "My word was to a man I thought to be a gentleman," she said coldly. "A promise I considered void when I learned you were conspiring with Lord Cherrington behind my back. Yes," she added at his stunned expression, "I know all about your little campaign to marry me off! It's too bad for

you, sir, that I am not one of your soldiers. If I
marry, it will be because *I* choose to do so, and not
because I am following orders!"

"Why, you little—" Brant was speechless with
incredulity. Either the minx was part witch, or one
of his co-conspirators had a devilishly loose tongue.
Not that it mattered, he supposed. Now that she
was aware of his machinations she would doubtless
enter a nunnery, if only to wreck his careful planning. Knowledge that all his work was for naught
set fire to his control, and his temper flared out of
hand.

"Damn you, Sara!" He forgot himself so far as to
curse, his hands snaking out to grab her and pull her
against him. "I was only doing what I thought best
for you," he continued, shaking her angrily. "You
are my responsibility, and—"

"I am *not* your responsibility!" Sara answered,
struggling to free herself. "I am a grown woman,
not some simpering child you can order about. I will
do as I please, and when the Season is over it will
please me to leave, and there is nothing you can do
to stop me!"

To the woman listening at the keyhole this
seemed an ideal moment to stage her entrance.
Straightening her gown with a determined tug, she
pushed open the door and staggered into the room.

"My heart," Lady Mallingham gasped, her hand
going to her chest as she collapsed in a soft rustle of
orange silk before the horrified eyes of the two
combatants.

Chapter Nine

Shock held Brant and Sara immobile. Then they moved as one to where the stricken countess lay on the Aubusson carpet. Brant reached her first, his fingers going to the base of her throat, searching for some signs of life. When he felt the weak but steady pulse beneath his touch, his shoulders sagged in relief.

"She's alive," he murmured, raising dark blue eyes to Sara's anguished face. "But I think she would be more comfortable in her rooms."

"Yes, of course," Sara answered, forcing herself to rise despite her shaky legs. "Shall I call for a footman to help you?"

"No, I can manage on my own." He lifted Lady Mallingham's limp form in his arms as if she were no more than a child. "If you would be so good as to get the door?"

He carried his aunt up the stairs with Sara trailing at his heels. She raced past him and flung open the door to Lady Mallingham's room, then rushed to the canopied bed to throw back the orange silk counterpane as Brant laid his precious burden down. Her aunt's maid, alerted by the cries of the other servants, followed them into the room, barking out orders like a sergeant-major.

"Miss and I will see to Milady," Miss Pimms snapped, elbowing Brant aside with ruthless efficiency. "Mind you go fetch a proper doctor for her ladyship. *Now,* if you please," she added when he hadn't moved quickly enough to suit her.

"Yes, Miss Pimms." He was too well trained a soldier not to recognize the voice of command when he heard it. "But first I would like a word with my cousin." He placed his arm about Sara's waist and guided her from the room.

"I must be off," he said, tucking back a strand of hair that had fallen from Sara's neat bun during her wild race up the stairs. "I promise to return as quickly as I can. Will you be all right until then?"

"Yes, my lord," she replied, touched by his thoughtfulness when his mind must surely be distracted with worry. "I shall be fine."

"Good. Take good care of our aunt until I return. And Sara?" His fingers curled about her elbow, staying her as she turned to go.

"Yes?" She gazed up at him expectantly.

"Don't worry," he whispered, tracing the trembling curve of her lip with a gentle finger. "I won't let anything happen to Aunt Agatha. I love her too, you know."

"I know," she said, smiling tremulously.

"I'm glad." His eyes glowed with a warm light as he ducked his head, replacing his finger with the most fleeting of kisses. "Chin up," he murmured, a teasing smile lifting the corners of his mouth as he raised his head. "We'll soon have her back and terrorizing us. You'll see."

After he departed Sara went back into the room to help Miss Pimms. The maid had already begun undressing the countess, and Sara hurried forward to assist her. Between the two of them they soon had her changed into a warm nightgown and tucked between the scented linen sheets. Their ministrations had roused Lady Mallingham slightly, and she murmured incoherently before drifting off into a fretful slumber.

While they awaited the doctor's arrival Sara conducted a cursory examination of her aunt, calling upon the skills she had learned at her papa's side. Miss Pimms watched her with a sharp eye but made no move to interfere, seeming to trust the young woman's abilities. When Sara had finished examining her aunt, the taciturn maid spoke for the first time.

"Will my lady be all right, miss? Her color's not so bad."

"I'm no doctor," Sara answered, her brow puckering with worry. "But I can find no obvious symptoms which would indicate a heart ailment. Her pulse is strong, and her extremities are warm to the touch, but without listening to the heart there is no way I can be certain. At least her breathing is easier," she added, watching the steady rise and fall of her aunt's chest.

"The Deverleighs are a hearty stock," Miss Pimms said, nodding her graying head knowingly. "Take more than a few twinges to lay them low."

There seemed to be no reply to this, and fortunately for Sara the redoubtable maid didn't seem to expect one. As they sat waiting, Sara occupied herself by studying her aunt's bedroom. Like the countess herself, the room was a charming mixture of elegance and eccentricity. Delicately carved pieces of Sheraton and Hepplewhite stood beside ornate Chinese cabinets, and a jumble of mementos and curios littered every surface. She was admiring a portrait of Lady Mallingham as a young bride when Brant returned, a solemn-faced physician in tow.

The physician, whose name proved to be Dr. Davies, took one look at Lady Mallingham and ordered all but Miss Pimms from the room, insisting he must have privacy in which to examine his patient. Sara would have remained, but Brant led her out into the hallway, smoothing her protests with a gentle murmur.

"Why don't you go to your rooms and rest?" he suggested, eyeing her pallid face with concern. "You can do no more here, and it won't do Aunt any good if you collapse as well."

She paused uncertainly, acknowledging the sensibleness of his suggestion, yet reluctant to leave her aunt's side. She'd only be a few doors away, but she feared putting even that much distance between them. Her papa had died while she was absent from the room, and she'd never forgiven herself for that. If something happened to her aunt as well . . .

As if sensing her melancholy thoughts, Brant gave her shoulders a reassuring squeeze. "Go on," he said softly. "I promise to call you the moment there's any change. At least go change your gown," he urged when she hadn't moved. "It's damp, and you'll take a chill."

Sara glanced down at her black dress in surprise. So much had happened in the past few hours she hadn't given her appearance a thought. "Very well, sir," she said, agreeing to his request. Now that he mentioned it, the gown was uncomfortable. "If you will excuse me, I shall be but a moment. What of you?" she asked hesitantly. "Will you be remaining here?"

"I'll be in the drawing room," he answered, pleased she was being sensible about the gown. He had been expecting to have a fight on his hands. "Shall I order some tea for us?"

That sounded agreeable to Sara, and after murmuring a quiet good-bye she hurried to her rooms to change. Matty was waiting when she arrived in her rooms, expressing horror at her mistress's bedraggled condition.

"Why, miss, why ever be you wearing that old thing?" she scolded, turning Sara around to unfasten the lacings. "And your pretty hair all scraped back that-a-way. See what happens when you don't have Matty do for you? I vow I have never seen the like. . . ."

Sara didn't waste any energy answering Matty's stern lecture. The moment her hair had been brushed out and she'd been laced into a clean gown of soft yellow cotton, gently ruffled at the neck and cuffs, she gathered up her woolen shawl and raced down the stairs to join Brant.

He had already ordered tea, and was lifting his cup to his lips when she dashed into the drawing room. "That was quick," he drawled, pleased to see she had brushed her hair out of the ugly bun. The sight of her glorious hair pulled back in the confining bun had angered him almost as much as her damned defiance, and he had longed to tear out the restrictive pins. However, none of these emotions was evident in his face as he extended a hand to her, indicating she should join him on the small settee.

He had donned his black jacket before rushing out to fetch the doctor, but his cravat had been hastily tied. This small imperfection in his usually

immaculate appearance was oddly reassuring, and
Sara was smiling as she sat down beside him.

"I hope you're hungry." Brant noted her smile
with relief. "Cook has outdone himself this time."

Sara gazed at the delicately tinted petit fours, as-
sorted sandwiches, and fresh biscuits in dismay.
Despite her hunger, and the tempting array of food,
she wasn't sure if her churning stomach could tolerate even a mouthful. Brant was watching her
closely, and correctly interpreted the small frown
knitting her brow. He poured a cup of tea for her,
then filled a plate with a variety of cakes and sandwiches.

"We mustn't insult Armand," he said, pressing
the plate upon her with a stern look. "You know
how temperamental the French can be."

Sara accepted the plate with good grace, knowing
it was useless to argue with her cousin once he had
made up his mind. She drank the tea thirstily and
was nibbling a petit four when Dr. Davies entered
the room. The sight of his somber face destroyed
the little appetite she had, and she placed the plate
on the table. Her hand instinctively sought Brant's,
and she felt comforted at his touch.

His fingers closed protectively around hers as he
faced the doctor. "How is our aunt?" he asked in a
firm voice, hiding his own fears for Sara's sake.

"The countess is resting comfortably, and is in no
immediate danger," Dr. Davies replied in the soothing manner of one accustomed to anxious relatives.
"I have every confidence that she will make a complete recovery. In the meanwhile, I've given her a
mild sedative, and she should sleep until morning."

"Thank God," Sara whispered, her eyes closing in relief. "Oh, thank God."

Brant sent a similar prayer winging heavenward. Despite his optimistic words to Sara, he had been secretly fearing the worst. He had seen death too many times to hold out much hope for his aunt. "Can you tell us what is wrong with her?" he asked, when he trusted himself to speak. "She seemed to think it was her heart."

"Oh, no." On this point the doctor was more than happy to reassure them. "Her ladyship's heart is as strong as ever, considering her advanced years. But like as not I would say the countess is suffering from nervous exhaustion, doubtlessly complicated by a severe emotional shock. What she needs most is complete quiet and relaxation, which is why I am suggesting you remove her to the country as soon as it can be arranged."

"The country?" Brant frowned in confusion. "Do you mean Mallingham? But she hasn't been there in years. Wouldn't such a long journey be too dangerous in her condition?"

"Not if it were undertaken in small stages," Dr. Davies replied expansively. "Your estate is located in Devonshire, I believe?" At Brant's nod, he continued, "Well then, if you were to make a leisurely trip of several days—and in a comfortable coach, mind, and not one of those dashed curricles all you young blades fancy—then I foresee no impediment. Your aunt's maid strikes me as being the reliable sort, and I am sure we may depend upon her to follow my instructions to the letter."

Brant mulled this over, his active mind already making plans and arrangements. He disliked the notion of leaving London when Parliament was in session, but his aunt's health must be foremost in his thoughts. There was also the small matter of Sara's Season. Although she had made a respectable showing, she had yet to receive an offer or at least an offer he would consider. His lips twisted in memory of the two obvious fortune hunters who had dared press their suits with him. He had made swift work of the scoundrels, tossing them out of his study with a deadly word of warning as to what would befall them if they were to approach Sara again.

The thought of Sara made him frown as he realized she had been uncharacteristically silent since the doctor's announcement. He slid her a worried glance, noting her pale complexion and trembling lips with concern. Her golden eyes were shimmering with unshed tears, and he found himself wanting to brush them away. He shook off the troubling sensation and turned his mental powers to the problem at hand.

"Very well, Dr. Davies," he said, picking up the familiar reins of responsibility. "I shall arrange everything at once. When do you think it will be safe to move her ladyship?"

"I should wait until the end of the week at least," Dr. Davies answered thoughtfully. "Give Lady Mallingham time to adjust to the idea. In the meanwhile take care that she eats proper meals, and that she doesn't become too active."

"Of course." Brant nodded. "Will there be anything else?"

"No, but should her ladyship suffer another spell, mind you send for me at once. Now if you will excuse me, my lord, I must be off."

Brant rose to his feet, extending a hand to the doctor. "Thank you for coming so quickly, Dr. Davies," he said, shaking the older man's hand. "I am most grateful, I assure you."

"You are most welcome, your lordship," the physician replied, hiding a secret grin at the memory of the wild-eyed young man who had burst into his surgery, barely giving him time to gather up his bag before carting him off. He turned to Sara, acknowledging her with a bow. "And you must be her ladyship's niece. You mustn't look so distraught, my dear. We shall soon have your beloved aunt returned to good health."

Sara managed a shaky smile on his behalf. "Thank you, Doctor," she replied in a soft voice. "It was good of you to come."

Brant excused himself to escort the physician from the room, leaving her alone with her painful thoughts. She sat in rigid silence, reliving every moment of the past afternoon. Not since her papa's death had she suffered such an emotional upheaval in her world, and then, as now, she was almost overwhelmed by a deep sense of guilt. A shudder of agony shook her slender body as she covered her face with her hands.

"Sara, what is it?" Brant had returned and was kneeling in front of her. "Are you all right?"

"It's my fault," she whispered in a broken voice, dropping her hands to stare at him in helpless pain. "If you could have seen her face when she realized what I had done . . ."

Brant's arms closed about her, pulling her gently against his warm chest. "Hush now, you mustn't say such things," he said, stroking her hair with a shaking hand. "Aunt is going to be fine, you'll see. You mustn't blame yourself for what happened."

Her arms slipped tightly about his neck as she pressed closer to his strength, like a small child seeking the safety of its parent's arms. "It is my fault," she sobbed bitterly. "It *is*. You heard Dr. Davies: 'a severe emotional shock.' She was so upset by what I had done. So hurt. If I hadn't applied for the post this would never have happened. If she d-dies then it means I have k-killed her . . ."

Brant drew back at once. "Don't even think such things!" he thundered, administering a small shake. "Aunt Agatha isn't going to die, Sara. Do you hear me?" He shook her again. "She's not going to die!"

He sounded so strong, so sure of himself, that Sara collapsed against him, accepting the sweet comfort of his words. She sobbed in relief as he continued holding her, his touch all that was gentle and good. Finally she regained control of herself, and drew back with a watery sniff.

"Better now?" he asked in a gentle whisper, wiping the tears from her cheeks with the pads of his thumbs.

"Much better, thank you, sir," she murmured, ducking her head in embarrassment. "I'm sorry for weeping all over you like this," she continued with a nervous laugh. "I'm not usually so missish, I assure you. It is just I . . ."

"Hush." He laid a silencing finger against her lips. "Pray don't insult me with an apology. I'm your cousin, and—despite all that has happened between us—I hope I am also your friend. To whom else would you turn for comfort? And I am to be called Brant, remember?"

"I remember," she answered when his finger shifted to stroke the curve of her jaw. "But what shall we do now? Do you really intend removing Aunt to your country estate?"

"As soon as possible," he said with a nod, moving away from her to pull from his pocket a white lawn handkerchief, which he then offered to her. "May I count on your assistance?"

"Of course, my . . . Brant," she amended, startled by his words. Surely he didn't think her so churlish as to refuse, she thought, wiping her cheeks with the soft fabric. "I shall be only too happy to help in any way that I can."

"I know you will." He smiled in understanding. "I trust you implicitly, Sara, I want you to know that. If I have led you to believe otherwise, then it is I who must apologize. Will you forgive me?"

"If you will forgive my behaving like a spoiled, petulant child." Sara was moved by his honest declaration, and knew she had to respond with equal openness. "I was wrong to have applied for the post without first discussing the matter with you. Or at least, *trying* to discuss it with you," she added, her golden eyes dancing with laughter.

He saw the animation returning to her face and smiled in response. "We do seem to talk at cross-purposes, don't we?" he agreed with a soft chuckle. "I fear it is because we are too much alike; both of us too stubborn and proud for our own good."

"It would seem to be so." Sara laughed, feeling as if a great burden had been lifted from her shoulders. Despite her concern for Lady Mallingham, she felt years younger, as carefree and happy as a child. She flashed Brant a bright smile, suddenly eager to begin the journey. Much as she had enjoyed London and the pleasures of the Season, she was a country girl at heart, and she longed for green meadows and the sweet, open air.

"Tell me about Mallingham," she demanded with enthusiasm. "I know it is in Devonshire, but how big is it? How many rooms does it have? What are your stables like? Will I be able to go riding?"

Brant laughed at her excited questions. "You may most certainly go riding with me. In fact, I'm looking forward to showing you my estate. As for the rest of it, you must wait and see for yourself. Mallingham is not so easily described. You must see it for yourself to truly appreciate it."

"Oh, but—"

"Not another word," he insisted, shaking a warning finger at her as he helped her to her feet. "There is too much that needs doing for us to be sitting around and prattling. If we mean to be in the country by next week, then 'tis time we got started."

The rest of the week passed in a blur for Sara and Brant. While he was kept busy by his Parliamentary duties and by seeing to the financial aspects of the move, she oversaw the closing of the two houses and arranged to have the necessary staff transferred to Mallingham. Priscilla and Jane came in response to her urgent summons, joining her in the drawing room where they took over the dreary job of canceling her remaining social obligations. When she tried to express her gratitude, Jane waved her thanks away.

"Think nothing of it, Sara dearest. That's what

friends are for, after all. Isn't that so, Priscilla?" She turned to the younger girl sitting beside her on the gold-and-white-striped settee.

"Of course," Priscilla agreed, her expression wistful as she gazed at Sara. "I'm more than happy to be of assistance, although I shall miss you most dreadfully. Now I shall have but one friend in London," she added as her hand closed shyly over Jane's.

"Nonsense." Sara was touched by Priscilla's declaration. "Why, you have many friends in Society! Only look how popular you've been this Season."

"Oh, society friends." Priscilla shrugged her slender shoulders. She was wearing a new gown of leaf-green muslin trimmed with bands of deeper green velvet, and looked enchantingly delicate. "The men are only nice to me because they think me pretty or because my fortune interests them. And the women are friendly because they hope to meet Hugh through me. None of them truly cares for me for myself, as you do."

"What ladies are interested in Hu—in your brother?" Jane looked up, her fine brow wrinkling in annoyance. "I hadn't thought him to be interested in the petticoat line."

"He's not." Despite her unhappy thoughts Priscilla managed a rueful smile. "It is *they* who are interested in *him,* for all the good it does them."

Jane busied herself examining the hem of her dark blue gown. "I don't see why they should bother," she muttered in a petulant voice. "He has the manners of a barbarian, and very little to recommend him in the way of intelligent conversation. And his attitude toward females is positively medieval! I'm only surprised he hasn't auctioned you off to the highest bidder the way some men do even in these so-called enlightened times of ours."

"Oh, Hugh would never do that!" Priscilla's green eyes widened at Jane's suggestion. "He loves me, and he has assured me I need never marry unless my affections are truly engaged. He's the dearest brother alive, and he's really not so terrible once you get past his bluster. It's just that he is shy, as I am."

"Hmph. About as shy as a troop of Turkish brigands," Jane grumbled before turning to Sara. "Have you any idea how long you will be in the country?" she asked curiously. "Or will that depend upon the countess's health?"

"It will depend upon my aunt," Sara replied, wondering at Jane's sudden interest in Lord Tressmoore. Until now she had thought her friend devoted to the memory of her late husband, and therefore uninterested in men. Oh, well, it was none of her concern.

"Will you be returning for next Season?" Jane demanded with a pointed look. She knew of Sara's plans to seek employment once the Season ended, and wondered if Lady Mallingham's illness had changed that. Privately she hoped it had, although she would support her friend whatever her decision.

Sara glanced down at her blue gown, searching for an answer. Since her aunt's collapse she had avoided all thoughts of the future. Her only concern now was for the countess, and she had deliberately closed her mind to all else. But now that the matter of her future had been directly raised, she knew she could no longer ignore it. What *was* she going to do?

"Well, of course she shall be returning," Priscilla

said with a laugh before Sara could reply. "The Deverleighs are her family now, and we are her friends. Where else would she go? Unless she has a beau in the country?" She flashed teasing green eyes in Sara's direction. "Have you, Sara? You can trust us not to tell a soul!"

Sara smiled at Priscilla's gentle raillery. "None that I am aware of," she replied good-naturedly. "I've never been in Devonshire, and in any case I'm sure I shall be much too busy nursing my aunt for such things. But I will miss you both. Perhaps you can come for a visit once the Season is ended?" It was the first time she had extended such an invitation, but Brant and Aunt Agatha did say she should consider their home to be hers as well. Besides, she would be lonely in the country.

Both ladies accepted at once, and after a somewhat emotional farewell they took their leave, promising to exchange letters once Sara was comfortably settled. After they had gone Sara returned to the study to finish the last of her remaining correspondence. When that was done, she smoothed out the skirts of her gray dress and went up to visit her aunt.

Under Dr. Davies's express orders she saw her aunt but once a day, and then for never more than one hour. Brant was under the same restriction, and although they complained about it when they were alone, they nevertheless complied with the doctor's orders. After all, they assured each other, the important thing was that the countess rest so that she might recover from her attack.

The invalid was propped up against the lace-edged pillows, and her face lit up at the sight of her niece.

"Ah, Sara, there you are." She beamed, holding out her hand. "I thought you had forgotten your poor aunt. Come give me a kiss."

Sara did as she was bid, depositing a warm kiss on Lady Mallingham's lined cheek. She noted her aunt was dressed in a new bed-jacket of her favorite orange trimmed with swansdown, and smiled in pleasure. The fact that her aunt was again taking interest in her appearance was a good sign. "Of course I haven't forgotten you," she scolded gently, settling onto the orange brocade chair beside her aunt's bed. The cream-colored drapes were partially opened, admitting a small stream of sunlight which fell across the canopied bed, illuminating the countess's features.

Sara thought she looked a little pale, and reached for the carafe on the bedside table. "Jane and Priscilla were here," she explained, pouring some of the scented barley-water into a glass and handing it to her aunt. "Didn't you get my message?" She pressed the glass to Lady Mallingham's lips, silently bidding her to drink.

"Wretched stuff," the countess grumbled, but she did take a few tiny sips before lying back against her pillows. "Now what is it you were saying?"

"My message," Sara repeated worriedly. "I sent you a message that my friends had come to visit. Do you mean you didn't receive it?"

"Message?" The older woman's blue eyes grew cloudy. "Oh, I daresay I did. But one day is so much like the other, that I suppose I forgot. I seem to forget so many things these days." She sighed heavily.

Sara's heart pounded in concern. Her aunt's absentmindedness was almost as distressing as her continued weakness, and she made a note to mention both to Dr. Davies the next time she saw him. He would be calling upon them tomorrow to examine the countess preparatory to their long journey. Brant planned to be present, and Sara knew he was just as anxious as she was.

"Why are you so quiet today, my dear?" Lady Mallingham queried in a tired voice. "I hope you're not overdoing things. We have servants aplenty, and I don't want you tiring yourself like this. Promise me you will be more careful."

"I will, Aunt," Sara assured her soothingly. Since her illness the countess had become obsessed with both her and Brant's health. It was as if being confronted with her own mortality made her fear that death was imminent for them all.

She turned away from her aunt to pick up a book from the bedside table. It was a gothic horror story filled with grisly specters and swooning virgins; Sara considered it most dreadfully written, but Aunt seemed to enjoy listening to her read it.

"Now let me see, where did we leave off yesterday?" she asked, flipping open the leather-bound volume.

"I believe that villain Decasirillo was about to entomb poor Evalina," Lady Mallingham decided, settling back against her pillows with an eager sigh. "Really, I can't help but think the dratted gal is somewhat lacking in intelligence. Who would be so

foolish as to follow a ghost down a secret passage, I
ask you? Ah, well, no matter. Read on."

"Yes, Aunt Agatha." Sara hid a smile at her aunt's
tart observation. "Yes, here we are. 'Evalina's terrified heart beat within her bosom like a trapped
sparrow struggling to be free. Just as she was certain
she must surely expire from the horror of the scene
before her, her straining ears picked up a faint, me-
tallic scratching . . .' "

The journey to Mallingham took place as
planned, and once the countess had been safely
bundled into her carriage they were on their way.
Lady Mallingham and Miss Pimms traveled in their
own carriage, as Dr. Davies felt it would be more
restful for her. This left Brant and Sara, chaperoned
by Matty, to ride on ahead. After an initial wariness
they soon fell into a comfortable companionship,
conversing easily as they made their way west.

In deference to Lady Mallingham's condition they
paused often, stopping for the night at local inns.
Sara couldn't help but compare this journey with
her first trip to London. Then she had traveled by
common mail coach, sitting atop the swaying con-
veyance, as she had lacked suffcient coin to ride inside. It had been a rough, difficult journey, and
there were many times when she fought against
tears as the icy winds tore at her thin cloak.

Now she rode in undreamed-of luxury, her every
whim catered to when they stopped to take their
meals. Instead of a threadbare cloak, she was draped
in a warm mantle of soft pink wool, a heated brick
at her feet to keep out the chill. She would be a liar

if she pretended not to enjoy the attention and the comfort, but at the same time she feared it. What would become of her if she grew too accustomed to such treatment? How could she hope to return to her former life after this? Sometimes it seemed as if that other life had been a mere dream, a nightmare, and this was the only reality.

She knew such thinking to be dangerous, as were the thoughts which teased her days and tantalized her nights. She tried banishing them, but they returned of their own accord, torturing her with their forbidden sweetness. Sitting across from Brant and listening to Matty exclaim over the passing scenery, Sara vowed to control her errant thoughts. She knew that only misery would follow if she allowed such thoughts to become unfulfilled dreams.

"Oh, Brant, it's beautiful!" Sara gazed at the yellow brick house glowing golden in the fading rays of the setting sun. Like many houses of its period, it had been built in the shape of an *E* to honor Good Queen Bess. The front part with its Doric columns and expansive porch had been remodeled during the first years of the present king's reign, and it seemed to Sara as if the house were holding out its arms in welcome. She shook off the fanciful notion and turned a dazed smile upon Brant.

"You are quite right, Cousin," she said, her voice soft with wonder. "Mere words couldn't possibly describe all this. It must be experienced."

"I'm glad you agree." Brant studied her enraptured expression with contentment. He could remember vividly the first time he had seen Mallingham. He had been a mere lad of six, but he had fallen in love with the old house. It had seemed to him to be a magic castle, glowing with warmth and welcome. Even before he learned he was to be his uncle's heir he had regarded Mallingham as his. Knowing that Sara shared his love for his ancestral home filled him with an odd sense of rightness, and he realized he'd been longing to bring her here, to bring her home.

"Leave off, Pimms, I refused to be carried into my own home as if I were a demmed invalid!" Lady Mallingham's sharp tones rang out, shattering the unnatural stillness that had fallen between Sara and Brant. They both turned in time to see the countess alighting from her carriage, her thin frame draped from head to foot in an orange cape.

"Aunt." Brant hurried forward to assist her. "Are you certain you wouldn't rather wait for the litter?"

"Stuff!" Lady Mallingham snapped indignantly. "I don't know what is the matter with the lot of you! Can't a body have a simple attack of the ague without everyone carrying on as if it were the plague! I walked into this house as a young bride almost fifty years ago, and I shall walk in now. You may carry me out when I am dead, but as for now, step aside. It's cold out here, and I want my tea. Come along, the pair of you, and stop dawdling." She swept past Brant and through the front door.

Brant turned to Sara, his blue eyes twinkling with amusement. "Well, my lady, it seems we have been given our orders." He bowed to her with a courtly manner. "Welcome to Mallingham."

Chapter Ten

Life in the country soon settled into a comfortable pattern. Sara rose early each morning for a ride with Brant; then they shared a cozy breakfast before going their separate ways. At his request she took over the running of the house, seeing to the duties Lady Mallingham usually performed as lady of the manor. She also visited daily with her aunt, keeping to the schedule they had set in London.

When they had been there less than a fortnight she went into her aunt's room to find the countess sitting up in bed, her blue eyes sparkling with lively interest.

"Good morning, Aunt Agatha." Sara greeted her aunt with a warm kiss. "You're looking very well this morning. Did you have a restful night?"

"Pah, I am tired of sleeping," Lady Mallingham grumbled, although she was smiling. "I'll have an eternity to sleep once I am dead. But Sara, there is something I have been wanting to discuss with you."

"And what might that be?" Sara smiled at her aunt's eagerness.

"I think it is time we had a dinner party."

Sara blinked in astonishment. "I beg your pardon, ma'am?" Surely she couldn't have heard aright.

"I want to have a dinner party," Lady Mallingham repeated with marked impatience. "And I want you to arrange it."

"But Aunt, it is much too soon," Sara protested

weakly. "We have been here but a short while, and in any case your health is much too . . ."

"And what if we have only been here a few weeks?" the countess interjected briskly. "When my Henry was the earl, we gave a huge supper ball on the very night of our arrival. And my health, missy, was never better. Hartshorn and water, that's all a Christian soul ever needs. Besides, the neighbors will be wanting to meet you. They are probably thinking it dashed queer you haven't been formally introduced to them as yet."

This at least was true, Sara mused. She and Brant had already encountered several of their neighbors on their morning rides, and while at church she had caught more than one speculative glance being cast her way. They had put about the news of her aunt's poor health, and the neighborhood ladies were holding off on their calls. The next move was up to them, and a dinner party was without doubt the most efficient means of meeting everyone all at once.

"Very well, Aunt." Sara bowed to Lady Mallingham's desires, knowing she was right. "It shall be as you wish. Have you any suggestions as to whom I should invite or what I should serve? This is all very new to me, I fear."

"For a first dinner party, it's best to invite everyone," Lady Mallingham answered, laying a finger on her lips. "Otherwise someone is bound to be offended. The Hallsingforths are still in London, so we won't have them to contend with, which is no small blessing, I assure you. And the Martindales are in mourning for their son. But other than that, might as well invite the neighborhood."

"The entire neighborhood?" Sara squeaked, visions of trying to stuff the population of Devonshire into her cousin's formal dining room filling her head.

"Well, not every milkmaid and field hand, of course." Her aunt cast her an exasperated look. "I am referring to the gentry. The Wilsons, the Pettingtons . . . everyone." She waved her hand vaguely. "Oh, and mind you don't forget the vicar. He's a pompous old goat, but still he must be included. One mustn't insult God, as my Henry used to say. All in all we shouldn't have more than twenty or thirty guests."

That sounded a slightly more manageable figure to Sara, and the rest of the visit was spent discussing the menu. They had just decided upon local trout followed by capons and a baron of beef when Miss Pimms entered the room, her stern face set in disapproving lines at the high color in her mistress's cheeks.

"Time's up, miss," she informed Sara in a voice which brooked no opposition. "We mustn't tire her ladyship."

"Nonsense, Pimms." Lady Mallingham tossed her maid a defiant scowl. "When will you leave off treating me like a doddering old fool?"

"When you stop acting like one," came the tart reply. Miss Pimms tolerated insubordination from no one, not even her employer.

Sara left the two older women happily engaged in an exchange of insults, and went down to the small study which had been set aside for her use. The study was in the rear of the house and faced the formal gardens. It was decidedly a lady's room:

small, and furnished with delicately carved furniture and soft, pastel colors that reminded Sara of the flowers blooming outside the French doors. Settling at her dainty oak desk with its curved legs and polished top, she dipped her quill in the crystal inkwell and began drawing up invitations.

When she had done all that she could, she went to the kitchens to discuss the proposed menu with the cook. Her mind was so preoccupied with her plans that she paid no mind to where she was going and crashed into Brant as he was stepping out of the library.

"I beg your pardon," he said, his arms automatically going about Sara's waist to steady her. "I didn't see you standing there. Are you hurt?"

"Not at all, sir," she answered breathlessly, her heart pounding from the shock of their collision. Or at least that was what she told herself. Certainly it could have nothing to do with the feel of his body pressed to hers, or the warm, spicy scent of his skin as he bent over her. Blushing at the wayward direction of her thoughts, she burst into hasty speech.

"Actually, my lord, I fear 'tis my fault. My mind was elsewhere, and I wasn't paying proper attention to what I was doing. I only hope I haven't caused you an injury."

Brant glanced down at the delicate woman he held in his arms, and his lips tilted in a rueful grin. "Oh, I daresay I'll survive," he drawled, thinking he had never seen Sara in greater beauty. Her hair was worn down in silky waves caught back by a simple violet-colored ribbon matching the gown she was wearing, and her cheeks were rosy with healthy color. Country life seemed to agree with her, he mused, aware of a strange sense of relief coursing through him. He had been worried she would grow bored with the slower pace here, after the gaiety of London.

"But tell me," he teased, reluctant to let her slip away just yet, "what were you thinking of that made you grow so careless? Are you still fretting over Aunt? She is much improved, I assure you."

"Oh, I know that," she stammered, wondering if she should demand he release her. "In fact, she is insisting we have a dinner party as soon as I can arrange it." She studied his strong face curiously. "What do you think?"

"I think it is an excellent suggestion," he replied in a decisive voice. "I haven't entertained nearly enough since inheriting the title, and it is time I began." He smiled down at her. "Will you do me the honor of serving as my hostess?"

Sara was taken aback by his request. "But that would hardly be seemly. Your aunt is lady here, and she—"

"Is in no shape for anything so demanding," Brant finished for her. "She will doubtless put in an appearance, but we mustn't allow her to exert herself so soon in her recovery." He saw the troubled, guilty look which flashed across her expressive features at his words. Although it was the reaction he had been wrangling for he felt a surge of remorse at her obvious distress, and sought to assuage her unhappiness.

"Come, Sara," he pleaded, his tone deliberately cajoling. "Say you will be my hostess. If you refuse, I'll be forced to approach Miss Pimms, and you know I am terrified of her. Please?"

The thought of the tight-lipped Miss Pimms decked out in satin and jewels was nearly Sara's undoing. She could almost see her—sternly informing the squire that there would be no pudding for him until he ate his peas. She bit her lip to hold back the laughter bubbling up inside her. She had almost regained her composure when she caught sight of the pleading expression on her cousin's face. He looked so much like a hopeful little boy begging for a treat that she was unable to contain herself a moment longer.

"Oh, very well, you shameless beggar," she conceded with a laugh, her soft voice laced with amusement. "I should be honored to act as your hostess. But mind you behave yourself," she added, waggling a threatening finger beneath his nose. "I'll have none of your mischief-making at *my* party, sir, and so I warn you!"

His arms dropped to his sides as he stepped back from her. "Yes, General!" he answered, snapping her a sharp salute. "As you say, General!"

"Very good." She nodded her approval. "Just keep behaving like a proper little soldier and we should get along famously. Like a certain gentleman of my acquaintance, I do not tolerate insubordination."

"Yes, sir, General." He clicked his heels together with military precision. "Will that be all?"

"That is all." She inclined her head with regal hauteur. "You may consider yourself dismissed."

"Thank you." He lowered his arm with relief. "Now unless you have further orders for me, might I suggest we adjourn for lunch? I had forgotten how hungry all this soldiering can make a fellow."

Following luncheon Sara went off to consult with the housekeeper while Brant returned to his books. Or at least that is what he intended to do. But rather than going over the accounts with his estate agent, he spent most of the time staring out the window. As had been the case during these last few weeks, his mind was totally occupied with thoughts of Sara.

She had looked lovely this morning, he mused, his mouth softening in a reminiscent smile. They had spent most of luncheon laughing over an incident which had occurred on their ride. He remembered how natural he felt whenever he was with Sara; how good it felt just to see her smile.

He was an aloof man, and the years of command had only added to the sense of isolation he so often felt. Even with Felicia he seldom had dropped his guard. He had decided it was simply his nature, and never gave the matter another thought. Then Sara had entered his life, and suddenly he found himself experiencing emotions which were as puzzling as they were pleasing.

"I beg your pardon, my lord." Brant's agent cleared his throat nervously, hoping to reclaim his employer's wandering attention. "But will there be anything else?"

"Eh?" Brant glanced up to find the other man regarding him with a quizzical expression. Realizing he had been staring off into space like the veriest moon-calf, he ducked his dark head over the ledger and pretended to study the tidy column of figures. "No, Cranston, everything seems to be in order here. You have been doing an excellent job."

"Thank you, my lord." Cranston's amusement at

the earl's distracted manner was hidden behind a
carefully bland expression. Usually Lord Mallingham went over the estate books with a mag-
nifying glass, questioning entries and offering
compliments and criticisms as he saw fit. Today,
however, he had scarcely glanced at the books;
his attention was clearly elsewhere. The agent
permitted himself the tiniest of smiles as he spec-
ulated on the exact cause of his lordship's distraction. He had been hearing the most delicious
gossip from below-stairs. . . .

"If you won't be needing me then, my lord, I shall
be returning to my duties." Mr. Cranston rose to his
feet and began gathering up the books they had already examined. "Miss Belding has expressed a desire to see our mill, and I thought to take her there
this afternoon."

Brant glanced up at his words. "I wasn't aware
my cousin was interested in such things," he said
with a frown, wondering why Sara hadn't asked
him to escort her to the site.

"Oh, but she is," Cranston replied assuredly. "In
the few weeks she has been with us she has been to
the shearing sheds and the home farm, and of
course she has ridden out with my good wife to
visit with some of our older tenants. I . . . er . . .
assumed you knew, my lord." He faltered at Brant's
dark scowl.

"No, Cranston, I didn't," Brant answered, envisioning Sara's laughing excitement as she explored
his vast, sprawling estate. He shook off the intriguing vision and turned his attention back to his manager.

"If Miss Belding wishes to see the mill, then you must by all means take her," he said decisively, picking up one of the books and studying it with unseeing eyes. "Just mind that she doesn't become overly tired. She was quite ill this winter, and I don't want her to suffer a relapse."

"Very good, Lord Mallingham, I shall see to it at once." The agent was almost to the door when Brant spoke again.

"Cranston . . . wait."

"Yes, my lord?" He glanced at his employer inquiringly.

"What do you think of Miss Belding?"

Cranston almost dropped his ledgers. "I beg your pardon, Lord Mallingham?" he asked faintly. "What did you say?"

"What do you think of Miss Belding?" Brant repeated, feeling as surprised by his question as his agent had been. The question had popped out of his mouth of its own volition, and he could see no way of recalling his words. "That is," he said, determined to save what he could of his pride, "do you think she is contented here in the country?"

Cranston's brow cleared at once. "Oh, yes, my lord. As a matter of fact, I was remarking to Mrs. Cranston only this morning how easily Miss Belding has fit into our life here at Mallingham. I daresay there are many young ladies who would not find country living to their liking. But then, Miss Belding is country-bred, is she not?"

"Yes," Brant replied, considering his agent's words carefully. "She is. Thank you, Cranston. You may go."

* * *

In the end, planning the dinner party wasn't nearly so arduous a task as Sara anticipated. After receiving her invitation, Mrs. Pettington, the local squire's lady, donned her best bonnet and hurried over to Mallingham to offer her assistance. It was an offer Sara accepted with alacrity, and the two ladies soon had the situation well in hand. Although the party hardly measured up to London standards, it still promised to be the talk of the neighborhood for many weeks to come.

On the night of the dinner party, Sara agonized over what to wear, donning and discarding dress after dress, until her maid took matters into her own hands.

"Your purple gown, miss," Matty announced, pushing Sara gently onto the bench in front of the mirror. "And your pretty hair down with a strand of pearls woven through it."

"Pearls?" Sara was uncertain. "But won't that be a trifle grand? This is a country party after all, and—"

The knock at the door cut short her weak protest, and Miss Pimms rustled in, the familiar jewel case clasped in her hands. "Her ladyship says as I was to assist you," she informed Matty in her brisk tones. "Is that the gown she'll be wearing?" She indicated the dress draped across the bed.

"Yes, Miss Pimms." As usual, Matty was properly cowed by the older maid's presence.

Miss Pimms inspected the gown with its layers of filmy skirts and heart-shaped neckline before nodding her approval. "The Mallingham amethysts," she said decisively, flicking open the case and holding it out for Sara. "They was a present from old King Henry to the third Lady Mallingham back when he was between wives. Like as not the old goat would have offered for her but for the fact her husband was still alive, and more than capable of looking after his own."

Sara stared down at the stunning arrangement of perfectly shaped, creamy pearls strung together with square-cut jewels the exact shade of her gown. "They're beautiful," she whispered, stroking the smooth perfection of the stones with a reverent finger. "I have never seen anything so lovely."

"They are a picture," Matty agreed, picking up the heavy necklace and fastening it around Sara's delicate throat. "And they do look so grand on you, miss. You ought to have your portrait painted wearing them, like all the Deverleigh ladies. Have you seen their pictures hanging in the Long Gallery? All them lovely ladies in their fine court dresses and this very necklace about their throats. History, miss, that is what you're wearing."

"Don't forget the bracelet," Miss Pimms instructed, keeping a sharp eye on Matty. "My lady says she's to be all rigged out like a proper Deverleigh. All the county will be here to see her, and she should be dressed as befits a lady."

Matty did as ordered, securing the bracelet's jeweled clasp around Sara's wrist before slipping the earrings into her lobes, and the ring with its large square-cut amethyst onto her finger.

Sara stared down at the exquisite jewel on her hand, turning it so the purple caught the light and flashed it back with brilliant fire. History, she thought sadly. A stone to be handed down from

father to son, before being placed on the hand of a
chosen bride. Would Brant one day give this ring to
the lady he made his wife? The thought was not a
pleasant one.

After thanking the two maids for their assistance,
Sara went to her aunt's room to present herself, a
ritual they had established in London. Her aunt was
dressed and waiting when she arrived, and her
wrinkled face broke into a smile at Sara's appearance.

"My dear, you look positively *stunning,*" she
gasped as Sara stood before her. "Turn around, I
want to see all of it."

Sara did as her aunt instructed, the fragile layers
of violet-colored silk swirling around her in a blur
of color. When she next faced her aunt, the older
woman was beaming with pride.

"You look like a duchess, my love," she said, her
eyes suspiciously bright. "A queen. And I'm glad to
see you wearing the amethysts; for I must own that
I have never cared for them. Purple is such an odd
color, don't you think? But on you they look quite
lovely, and that gown shows them to their best advantage."

"Thank you, Aunt." Sara leaned forward to place
a grateful kiss on the countess's cheek. "And may I
say, ma'am, that you're looking quite dashing as
well? That's a new gown, I take it?" She gestured at
the velvet gown her aunt was wearing. Although
cut in the current mode, it was fashioned in the
brilliant flame-orange Lady Mallingham favored.

Her aunt preened like a young girl three-quarters
her age. "As a matter of fact, it is," she said in

pleased tones. "Brant ordered it up from London as a surprise. Do you like it?"

"Very much," Sara replied honestly. "The gown . . . er . . . suits you."

"It does, doesn't it?" The countess stroked the soft velvet with her finger. "It was something of a shock, I must admit. Not the gown, of course, for Brant is always offering to pay my modiste's bills, but rather 'tis the color that surprises me. Really, Sara, you would not credit it, but your cousin has the most appalling taste in clothing. The last gown he fobbed off on me was in the most dreadful shade of blue. Can you imagine? Me, in blue." She shook her head in amazement.

"No, Aunt." Sara smiled softly at her cousin's actions toward the elderly lady they both loved. "I can't imagine you in such a color."

Brant was standing at the bottom of the stairs discussing planting techniques with Mr. Cranston when the rich sound of feminine laughter made him glance up at the two ladies descending the staircase. The smile of welcome vanished from his face as he caught sight of Sara guiding their aunt down the stairs. He felt the breath leaving his lungs as he stared at Sara, unable to tear his eyes away from her glowing beauty.

Her slender body was outlined in a delicate shade of violet silk, and her warm brown hair fell in shimmering waves to the creamy shoulders exposed by the low-cut bodice of her stylish gown. His eyes widened as he recognized the jewels glowing against her skin. The Mallingham amethysts. He raised his eyes to Sara's and, for the measure of a heartbeat, blue eyes meshed with gold in a moment of total intimacy.

"Well, don't just stand there gaping at us like a moonling," Lady Mallingham snapped as the ladies neared the bottom of the stairs. "Come help your poor aunt negotiate the last of these demmed stairs. I've no desire to come tumbling down them like a drunkard. A fine entrance *that* would make."

"My apologies, Aunt." The countess's strident tones released Brant from his temporary paralysis, and he moved forward to offer his aunt his arm. "If I appeared moon-struck is it because I have been rendered speechless by the sight of two goddesses descending my staircase."

"Pah, you have the devil's own tongue," Lady Mallingham retorted, albeit with a delighted smile. "As if you even noticed me. Your attention was all for your cousin, and don't think I didn't notice. Not that I blame you. Regular vision, ain't she?"

"That she is, Aunt." Brant turned to a brightly blushing Sara. "Allow me to be the first gentleman to say how lovely you look," he said, his deep voice husky as he carried her hand to his lips for a brief kiss. "Once the other men see what a vision you are, I fear I may be trampled in the rush to your side."

"Your lordship is too kind." Sara managed to speak over the furious pounding of her heart. "It would seem that not only have you deprived the devil of his tongue, but you have done him out of his charm as well. But then, Aunt, you did warn me he could be as charming as Old Nick when he put his mind to it, did you not?" She turned to Lady Mallingham eagerly, anxious to put an end to the dangerous sensations that were threatening to swamp her reason.

"Of course." The countess stared at her nephew with almost maternal pride. "We Deverleighs are noted for our charm. And just so you won't think we ladies behindhand in the art of paying compliments, allow me to note that you are looking *devilishly* handsome as well. In that jacket of plum satin you make the perfect foil for our Sara."

Sara glanced at Brant through half-lowered lashes. She'd thought almost the very same thing when she'd first spied him waiting for them. His dark head had been bent attentively toward Mr. Cranston, his expression solemn as he listened to whatever the agent had been saying. The sight of his broad, muscular shoulders encased in the deep purple satin had made her pulse race, and she'd suddenly wished she could have seen him in uniform. How handsome he must have looked, she mused, so strong, and proud, and fine. Then he had glanced up, and from the moment their eyes had met she'd been unable to look away.

She had felt forever changed by that single look. Changed in ways which terrified her, because to admit to those changes would be to admit the one truth she had been denying for what seemed forever. She was in love with Brant.

"Thank God that is over," Lady Mallingham grumbled, leaning down to rub her aching feet. "I was beginning to think we would have to set the dogs upon them before our guests would leave. But it went quite well, I think." She shot her niece a loving smile. "Congratulations, my dear. Your first party was an unqualified success."

"Thank you, my lady," Sara answered dutifully, turning the night's events over in her mind. But everything seemed misty and unformed, like a dream she tried to recall upon wakening. Only one memory stood out clearly, and that was when Brant had raised his glass, calling for a toast to his beautiful hostess. That moment was frozen forever in her heart, and she knew that even when she was a very old lady, she would remember the look in Brant's eyes as he gazed at her across the crowded table.

"Sara?" A bony elbow prodding her ribs brought her upright, and she turned to her aunt.

"I'm sorry, ma'am," she said, feeling more than a little foolish at being caught daydreaming. "What did you say?"

"Nothing of interest, or so it would seem," Lady Mallingham replied with a knowing smirk. "Well, if you two young people will excuse me, 'tis time I had these old bones in bed. No, remain where you are," she ordered when they both made to rise. "I ain't so feeble I can't make it to the doorway without assistance. I see Beechton standing there by the door. He can call Pimms to help me. Until morning then." She brushed a quick kiss on each of their cheeks before departing, calling for the footman.

After the countess had gone an uneasy silence descended upon the tiny room. Sara stared down into her glass of wine, trying to think of something light to say. But the discovery of her love had left her tongue-tied, and she wanted nothing more than to be alone so that she could absorb all that was happening to her. When she had endured all that she could of the oppressive tension, she set her glass aside and rose to her feet.

"I believe I shall retire as well," she said, making her tone as polite as possible. "I fear I have become too accustomed to country hours for such dissipation. Good night, Cousin." She turned toward the door, praying for enough strength to make it to her room without disgracing herself, but it was not to be. She had barely taken two steps when Brant called out to her.

"Sara, wait, I should like to have a word with you." He stood and walked over to where she was waiting, studying her averted face with an enigmatic gaze.

Sara's eyes closed in a silent plea for control. "Certainly, sir, what is it?" She raised inquiring eyes to his. "Did you want something?"

"I was hoping for a walk in the garden," Brant answered, his frown deepening at the obvious signs of strain in Sara's eyes. "But if you're too tired, I daresay it can wait until tomorrow."

The thought of walking through the sweetly scented garden with Brant was too tantalizing to resist. Even as her brain was urging her to accept the excuse he had offered her, Sara found herself saying, "Oh, no, a walk in the garden sounds the very thing. I'll just go and fetch my shawl—"

"Nonsense," Brant said, tucking her hand beneath his arm. "The evening is quite warm yet. And in any case, we shall only be out a short while. As if I should risk exposing you to a chill." He shot her a reproachful pout.

Sara ducked her head, hiding her smile at his words. "You are quite right, sir," she murmured, her tone properly penitent. "I can't imagine what I was thinking. It must be the wine which has so affected my reason."

"Do you mean to say you are bosky?" Brant demanded, eyeing her with exaggerated interest. "How intriguing." They were out on the terrace now, and his arm settled comfortably about her waist as he guided her down the marble steps. Although it was well past midnight the light shining from the full moon illuminated their path, making everything about them glow with a faint, incandescent light. A lover's moon, Sara thought dreamily, before turning her attention back to the man walking beside her.

"Well, I shouldn't bother taking advantage of the situation were I you," she answered his teasing remark with a provocative toss of her head. "I'll have you know my guardian is an ogre of respectability who would soon call you to account were you to trifle with my affections. And," she added with obvious relish, "he is said to be a crack shot . . . for a man of his age."

"I am quaking in my boots," Brant drawled, enjoying Sara's teasing even as he was admiring the play of moonlight and shadow across her upturned face. "Although I must protest your description of me. I will ignore your brattish reference to my age, but an 'ogre of respectability'? Surely, ma'am, that is overdoing it a bit?"

Unable to resist the allure of her creamy skin, Brant stroked a tanned finger across the curve of her cheek. It was, he marveled silently, almost the same color as the pearls resting against her throat. But the texture was much smoother, softer, and his finger dipped lower to play with the necklace.

"An ogre," Sara insisted, hiding her response to his touch behind a nervous laugh. She prayed he wouldn't detect the throbbing of her rebellious heart, or sense the fine tremor which shook her at the feathery brush of his finger on her skin. Stepping back, she pretended a lightness that she didn't feel.

"Now that you have lured me out into the moonlight, what is it you wanted to say? It is grown quite late, and in another moment I will be nodding off altogether."

"Aunt's birthday is at the end of August," he replied, his voice matching hers for lightness. "Since tonight's affair was such a success, what do you think of holding a costume ball in her honor?"

The question caught Sara unawares, and she stared at him in blank surprise. "A costume ball?"

"Mmm." He nodded, smiling at her reaction. "I thought it might be amusing. They were all the rage when Aunt was a young girl, and I believe she said that is where she met my uncle. I also thought we might invite some of our friends down from London. The Season will be ending soon."

Sara brightened at the thought. She had been writing to Priscilla and Jane since her arrival, but missed their company. Besides, her inner voice assured her, the more people who were around them, the greater her chance of hiding her love for Brant.

"I think it is an excellent notion!" she enthused with forced gaiety. "Will we have dancing, do you think? If so, we'll need an orchestra of sorts."

"It would hardly be a ball without dancing," he

pointed out with a maddening grin. "And I quite agree with you about our need for an orchestra. Only look at the mischief we got into without benefit of proper musical accompaniment."

Sara paled at the reminder of that afternoon. She had relived that moment a hundred times in her dreams, eventually coming to the conclusion that she had blown the incident all out of proportion. Brant's teasing words seemed to confirm this, for he was too much of a gentleman to make light of the matter had it truly been as she remembered.

"Quite true, Cousin." She managed a credible laugh, hiding her unexpected pain. "We certainly can't allow our guests to gallop about the ballroom hopelessly out of step with one another. Now that that is settled, I will be seeking my bed. The very thought of organizing a costume ball has me reeling with exhaustion. Good night." She turned and fled back into the house before Brant could stop her.

Brant stared after her, his hands balling into tight fists. Blast it all to hell, he damned his own loose tongue with scathing fury. Whatever had possessed him to say such a thing to her? He deserved to be horsewhipped for reminding her of that moment in the music room.

Sara had joked about being bosky, but perhaps it was *he* who had overimbibed. Certainly something had to account for his behavior and the fact that since walking out into the gardens with Sara he had been aching to take her into his arms and kiss her. And not just a brotherly kiss . . . as he had kissed her on the day Aunt Agatha had collapsed.

He had wanted to kiss her passionately. Completely. The way a man would kiss the woman he loved and wanted above all others. His fists clenched tighter as his body responded to the sweet image of Sara in his arms, and it was some time before he was able to turn and follow her into the darkened house.

Chapter Eleven

The house was all at sixes and sevens the next day, and it was well past noon before Sara was able to get away for her ride. Brant had been called out earlier on an emergency—a young farmer who had cut himself on a scythe—and he still hadn't returned. In a way she was relieved, for her nerves were decidedly raw after last evening's encounter. But, on the other hand, it would have been nice to have caught at least a glimpse of him . . . if only from a distance.

She smiled ruefully at her conflicting emotions. Perhaps the writers of those Minervian novels her aunt was addicted to weren't so very far off the mark after all, she mused. Certainly she had been behaving as addlepated as any lovesick heroine these past few days. Shrugging off her fanciful thoughts, she donned her topaz velvet habit, and tugged her high-crowned hat lower on her forehead before urging her horse into a canter, leaving the groom who was to accompany her standing in the dust.

She hadn't ridden very far when she heard a familiar sharp whistle. She reined in her mount and waited expectantly as Brant galloped up beside her.

"Good morning, Brant," she greeted him with a happy wave of her small riding crop. "How are you feeling this mor—"

"Damn it, Sara, what do you mean riding off without your groom?" His harsh voice cut into her cheerful greeting, and his dark brows met in a thunderous scowl as he glared at her. "I thought I had made it plain you were never to ride out alone. What if you had fallen?"

Sara's smile vanished at his cutting tones. "I beg your pardon, my lord," she said, her chin coming up with stubborn pride. "I had no idea the use of your stables was forbidden to me. I'll return at once." Her small gloved hands tightened on the reins as she jerked her horse around.

"Sara." He leaned over and caught hold of her mare's bridle. "Don't go."

Sara glared up at him, not giving an inch despite the softening she could see in his forbidding expression. "Yes, Lord Mallingham?" she asked in chilling tones. "Is there some objection to my riding back to the stables? I can walk if that is what you prefer."

To her surprise Brant tossed back his head and laughed, making his bay stallion dance with nervousness. The small rebellion was easily controlled with a lithe move of his strong hands, and then he was grinning at her with unabashed enjoyment. "That is what I adore about you, Sara," he told her, his blue eyes bright with laughter. "There is noth-

ing the least bit missish about you. You aren't one
of those milk-and-water females who swoon whenever a fellow shouts at them. You shout back."

"If you're intimating that I'm a shrew . . ." Sara
began hotly, only to be interrupted by another low
rumble of laughter from Brant.

"I meant nothing of the sort, hellcat," he told her,
still chuckling at her mutinous expression. " 'Twas
meant to be a compliment, so kindly pull in your
claws before I decide to trim them for you. Now
come, I'm in a hurry and I've no time to dawdle. I'll
escort you back toward the stables."

Sara sniffed loudly, electing to ignore his provocative teasing. He released her bridle, and they
turned back in the direction of the manor house. It
was a warm day with just a hint of a breeze to stir
the tall grasses, carrying with it the delicate scent of
wildflowers and the gentle buzzing of bees. Except
for the sound of their horses and a distant barking
dog, the silence was unbroken. They'd only ridden a
short distance when Brant spoke.

"I'm sorry for snapping at you. But I've only just
come from the Creightons', and I fear I was distracted."

"How is Mr. Creighton?" Sara asked, touched by
his quiet apology. She knew Brant to be prouder
than most men, and she knew he did not apologize
easily. "Is his arm badly cut?"

Brant nodded, his expression grim. "It looks as if
he may lose it," he said. "The doctor is with him
now, but there is precious little he can do. If the
bleeding can't be stopped . . ." His voice trailed off
meaningfully.

Sara bit back an exclamation of horror. As the

daughter of a country physician she was well acquainted with such injuries. She also knew what the loss of an arm could mean to a farmer. Even if he survived the amputation and subsequent infection, how could he hope to work his land? She was about to ask Brant this very question when he said, "I've assured Joel that if . . . if the worst should happen, he needn't worry about his family. And if he lives, I've promised to make him my steward. He's a dashed fine farmer, and he knows this land better than any man. I was on my way to fetch Mrs. Cranston when I saw you tearing hell-for-leather across the field. Remind me to scold you later on the matter of your recklessness," he added, giving her a weary half-smile.

"I will," she promised, then asked curiously, "Why were you looking for Mrs. Cranston? Is there something I can do to be of help?"

Brant hesitated a moment, then said, "Anna— that is Joel's wife—is heavy with child. The doctor is worried that the shock of Joel's injuries may send her into early labor, and he already has his hands full tending Joel. Mrs. Cranston has helped the midwife before, and I thought it might be a good idea to have her on hand . . . just in case."

"Oh, well, if that is all you need her for, then why are we waiting here?" Sara tugged her horse to a halt and turned toward Brant with a willing smile. "I can help deliver a babe."

Again Brant hesitated. "Sara, this is no place for a lady. Joel is badly cut, and there is blood everywhere. And if Anna should go into labor—"

"Then I will be there to help," Sara interrupted in a firm voice. "Brant, you have said before that I am no milk-and-water miss, and so I am not. I am the daughter of a country sawbones, and I have helped him deliver dozens of babies. I know what to do, and as far as the blood is concerned"—a wise, womanly smile softened her features—"well, it is obvious you have never seen a babe being born. I won't swoon, I assure you."

Brant studied her face, feeling his heart tightening with the most curious sensation. "If you're certain you won't be upset," he said hesitantly, his eyes meeting her earnest gaze, "then perhaps it would be all right."

"I am certain," she said, reaching out to cover his hand with hers. "Brant, if it were your wife lying helpless, wouldn't you want someone to help her?"

The vision which her words conjured up made his head swim, and it was several seconds before he could trust himself to answer. "Yes," he said, his voice husky with emotion. "I would want someone to help my wife. Let us be off, then."

It was almost dark before they were able to leave the small cottage. Dr. Preston had been able to save Joel's arm, while Sara had tended to the young wife. Despite her obvious anxiety over her husband, she hadn't gone into labor, and it was Sara's belief that she would carry the babe to full term. But just to be safe, Brant arranged for the midwife from the next village to be in attendance. She would stay with the Creightons until the babe came, and help to care for Joel.

Once all had been arranged to Brant's satisfaction, they made to take their leave. They had just bidden the midwife farewell when Anna reached out a shy hand to touch Brant's sleeve.

"I thank ye for your kindness, my lord," she whispered in a timid voice. "God bless both ye and your young lady."

"You're most welcome, Anna." Brant patted her thin, work-worn hand comfortingly. "Just mind you stay in bed until the child is born. Don't fret about the chores. I'll be sending someone over to do them until Joel is on his feet again. All right?"

"Aye, my lord." Anna's eyes closed on a contented sigh. Brant waited until he was certain she was asleep, and then turned to escort a drooping Sara home.

The countess was waiting for them when they returned to Mallingham. She had been frantic with worry all afternoon, and the door had scarcely closed behind them before she was ringing a peal over their heads.

"And where have the pair of you been?" she demanded, fixing them with an angry glare. "It is nigh on eight o'clock, and you have been gone for hours! That dratted butler would only say that one of the tenants had been hurt and that you . . . Great God in heaven, Brant! What has befallen you?" Brant had moved forward into the light, and the countess's eyes widened in horror at the sight of him. "You are covered with blood!"

Brant stared down at his stained shirt. "Yes," he said with weary disinterest, "there was a great deal of blood." His arm tightened around Sara's waist as he guided her toward the stairs.

"But what happened? Are you injured? What is wrong with Sara?" Lady Mallingham trailed after them, barking out questions like an agitated terrier. "Blast it, Brant, at least tell me if I should send for the doctor!" she cried, planting her hands on her hips and glaring up at him in frustration.

Brant took pity on his aunt and called out over his shoulder, "We are both uninjured, Aunt, and the doctor is with Joel Creighton. Now if you will excuse us, I wish to get Sara into bed before she drops. She is asleep on her feet."

Once he reached the top of the stairs he sent a footman scurrying for Sara's maid, then half led, half carried her to her rooms. They halted outside her door, and he set her down, cupping her face in his large palms, studying her wan features with obvious concern.

"I want you to promise me you will rest all day tomorrow," he said, brushing his thumb over the soft curve of her cheek. "I shouldn't have let you work so hard today. You are exhausted."

"So are you." Sara's hand crept up to push back the lock of dark hair which had fallen across his broad forehead. His skin was pleasantly warm, and she could feel the rough beginnings of his beard as she stroked her fingers over his jaw. On one level she was shocked by her audacity in touching him in so intimate a manner, but she didn't care.

When he dragged a gentle thumb over her trembling lips, she repeated the caress with a light touch of her fingers. She felt his lips parting beneath her fingers, and then he was bending over her, his mouth seeking hers in a warm kiss.

The touch of his lips filled Sara with the sweetest of longings. Even as she was telling herself that this must not be, she was responding with all the love in her heart. It felt so wonderful that she held nothing back, surrendering all that she was into Brant's keeping.

"Sara," he whispered huskily, feeling her uninhibited response with wild exultation. His arms lifted her closer as he deepened the kiss with sensual mastery. Only the knowledge that they were standing in the hallway where anyone might see them kept him from kissing her the way his heart was demanding he should. He raised his head reluctantly, his breathing uneven as he gazed down at her. "Are you all right?" he asked, his strong body trembling with the effort of control.

"I . . . I'm fine," Sara stammered, aware of the furious pounding of her heart. It echoed the pulse she saw beating in Brant's tanned throat, and she knew he had been as moved by their embrace as she. The knowledge filled her with a curious sense of feminine satisfaction, but before she had time to dwell on the matter Matty came hurrying toward them.

"Miss, will you look at you now," the maid scolded, brushing past Brant. "Still in that filthy habit, and looking that tired." She shot Brant a reproachful glare, clearly blaming him for her mistress's condition.

"Your valet is waiting for you, my lord," she informed him with a cool sniff. "I'm sure you'll be wanting to get out of them dirty things. Good evening to you."

Brant accepted his dismissal with good nature. After mouthing a good night to Sara he went to his rooms. As Matty had said, his valet was waiting for him, his thin face registering displeasure at the bloodstained clothing.

When he'd finished bathing and shaving, Brant devoured a hasty meal of fresh fruit and rare roast beef layered on thick pieces of warm bread. After giving orders that Sara was to be fed as well, he crawled into bed too exhausted to go down and face his aunt. His last thought just as sleep claimed him was the warm feel of Sara in his arms, and when he slept, his dreams were filled with the sweetest of memories.

Sara and Brant spent the next few weeks working together in close harmony. As if by mutual consent, they never spoke of the kiss. Brant continued treating her with the same tolerant affection he had always shown her, but now there was an added softness in the way that he spoke with her, looked at her. Sometimes she glanced up unexpectedly to find him watching her, his blue eyes dark with emotion, and she knew he was remembering the burning intensity of that moment.

Joel's arm had all but healed and his wife had been delivered of a fine son when the Deverleighs' houseguests began arriving. The Season had ended some weeks before, but this was the first opportunity they had had to make the long-awaited visit. Sara was delighted at seeing Jane and Priscilla, and once they had paid their proper respects to Lady Mallingham, she carried them off to her room for a private coze.

The cream-and-rose-colored room adjoined Sara's bedroom, and was furnished with the same daintily carved cherrywood furniture. The walls were covered with a deep rose moiré satin, while an Aubusson carpet glowed softly in the light spilling through the pale pink sheers hanging on the tall windows. While Priscilla and Jane admired their surroundings Sara ordered tea to be brought in to them, and soon the three friends were giggling and laughing together as if they had never been parted.

They had just finished laughing over the latest *on-dits* from London, when Jane cocked her dark head to one side and demanded to know what the deuce was going on.

"I beg your pardon?" Sara wiped some crumbs from the skirts of her flowered gown. "But whatever are you talking about? Nothing is 'going on.'"

"Really, Sara." Jane laughed, tucking her feet beneath her black-and-white dress as she settled on the rose settee. "You know full well what I mean, so pray don't dissemble. What is going on between you and your esteemed cousin? When you left London you were all but at daggers drawn with him; now the pair of you are as cozy as a pair of weevils!"

Sara's blush rivaled the roses on her gown. Was her love for Brant so obvious? she worried, nervously pouring another cup of tea. Lord, she hoped not. It would be beyond mortifying if anyone were to guess her closely held secret.

"Oh, Jane," Priscilla admonished her friend in her gentle voice. "One cannot exist in a perpetual state of acrimony. Sara and Lord Mallingham are cousins, after all; of course they have mended their differences. And they did so before they left London, if you'll remember."

"You're right, of course." Jane accepted Priscilla's censure with a good-natured shrug. "I had forgotten about that. But in my defense, Priscilla, allow me to point out that Sara was as mad as the very devil at her cousin, and I don't blame her a whit. Finding out that one has been made the object of a military campaign is enough to put any female's back up. Which reminds me," she added with a glance back a Sara, "how are things going on the battlefield? Is he still attempting to marry you off to the first eligible man who offers for you?"

Sara seized upon the topic eagerly, thankful to draw attention away from her and Brant's relationship. "Actually, he seems to have abandoned his plans. At least, I have seen no evidence of any further plotting. We have been very busy these last few weeks, and with my aunt so ill there is no question but that I will remain with her."

Jane nodded in understanding. "But what of when she is well again? What of *your* plans? Will you be seeking another position?"

This was the first Priscilla had heard of the matter, and she demanded to know what they were discussing. Sara obliged by telling her everything, including the details of her ill-fated excursion to the Duke of Langden's, something she had never told Jane. When she had concluded her story Priscilla sat back, shaking her blond head in amazement.

"Do you mean you applied for a post without first seeking your guardian's permission?" she asked in faintly shocked accents. "Sara, how did you dare?"

Sara knew a slight hurt at Priscilla's words. She had been hoping, if not for her friend's approval of

her actions, then at least for her understanding. She
was trying to decide how best to respond when Jane
gave another peal of laughter.

"Oh, for pity's sake, Priscilla, don't be such a
pea-goose! Sara wasn't applying for a post in a
bawdy house, after all. There is nothing wrong with
seeking employment as a companion. And Lord
Mallingham is *not* Sara's guardian. He has no right
whatsoever to tell her what to do."

"Oh, I didn't mean to criticize you." Priscilla's
green eyes matched the elegant gown she wore. "I
only meant, how could you be so brave? *I* could
never do anything half so daring."

"Yes, but you don't have an overbearing male
plotting to marry you off to the first man who will
have you," Sara grumbled, her temper stirring with
reminiscent pique. "You told us yourself your
brother would never force you to be married against
your will."

"Yes, that is so," the younger girl answered, an
odd look darkening her expression for a moment.
She shook her head as if trying to dislodge an unhappy thought, then smiled back at Sara and Jane.
"Well, I still say what you did was uncommonly
brave, and I for one salute you." She lifted her cup
in a mock toast.

"Here, here." Jane raised her cup in response. "To
Sara. May she always be so successful in thwarting
her cousin's evil schemes!"

In his study Brant was also enjoying a reunion
with his friends. After Hugh filled him in on the
news from Parliament, the three men settled into

the comfortable moroccan leather chairs set before the fireplace, a decanter of Madeira on the table between them. Both Marcus and Hugh had discarded their jackets upon entering the sunlit study, and their cravats were loosened about their throats. They were sharing reminiscences about some men who had served with them on the Peninsula when Marcus snapped his fingers.

"Good gad, I almost forgot to tell you," he said, stretching out his booted feet with a sigh. "Peter Kelton spoke with me on my last night in London. You remember him, don't you? Johnny Frammington's cousin?"

Brant had a vague recollection of an earnest young man with thinning brown hair and a rather retiring disposition. "Yes." He nodded slowly, twirling his glass in his hand. "He's some sort of scholar, isn't he?"

"Of Greek antiquities," Marcus clarified. "He's not as well heeled as Frammington, but he does quite well. There's an inheritance, I believe, and I've heard he has a rather comfortable living in Kent."

"Indeed." Brant smiled at Marcus's description of the other man. "May I ask why you have brought up this paragon of masculine virtue? You sound rather like a matchmaking mama sizing up a prospective suitor," he added teasingly, his dark blue eyes reflecting the color of his broadcloth jacket.

Marcus flushed in embarrassment. "Well, actually," he grumbled, thrusting a hand through his dark blond hair, "I mention him because he was asking after your cousin Sara. Unless I miss my guess, I think he means to offer for her."

Brant's smile vanished. "Are you certain?"

"Fairly certain," Marcus said. "He spoke at great length to me about her beauty, her intelligence, all that other drivel men spout when they're about to make an offer. Then he asked me for your direction and hinted he would be writing you a letter within the next several weeks. 'An urgent missive,' I believe he called it," he added with a low chuckle.

"Family's good," Hugh volunteered, rubbing a large hand over his jaw. "And the fellow seemed a right'un, even if he ain't in the army," he qualified hastily.

Brant frowned, the hand which was resting on the table tightening into a fist. "Did he ask if Sara had a dowry?" he demanded, his jaw hardening at the memory of the two fortune hunters who had already approached him. If this Kelton fellow thought to make use of Sara in such a manner, he would break his scrawny neck!

"Not at all." Marcus was regarding Brant with undisguised curiosity. "I mean, he ain't *that* big of a gudgeon, even if he is a bit prosy. Besides, I recall hearing he has over five hundred pounds a year, so it's not as if his pockets are to let. No, he's genuinely fond of Sara, I am sure of it."

"He's too old for her," Brant decided, quickly reversing his objection. "Sara needs someone lively, who is interested in more than a bunch of dusty books."

"Fellow's younger than I am, and I ain't seen forty yet," Hugh protested, obviously put out. "Besides, everyone knows 'tis best to marry off a young chit to an older man. Keeps 'em in their place. Rosefield's offered for m'sister, and I am contemplating the matter. A duke after all, even if he is a Whig. She could do much worse."

"Rosefield!" Marcus leapt to his feet and glared down at Hugh with narrowed eyes. "My God, he's almost fifty! How can you even think of marrying Priscilla to that gouty old lecher?"

"He ain't a lecher," Hugh denied indignantly, his chest swelling beneath the dun-colored coat. "Leastways he ain't one for a duke. And he's only gouty every now and again. Besides, what does that matter? Priscilla would be a duchess, and she'd never want for anything."

"I can't believe you are serious about this," Marcus continued, pacing the confines of the book-lined room in obvious agitation. He stopped in front of Hugh's chair, staring down at the older man with flaming eyes. "I thought you to be a man of honor," he said in a cutting voice. "But to sell your beautiful sister to that gross mountain of flesh . . ."

"I say, that's doing it a bit too brown, old boy!" Hugh's massive brows met over his nose in a pugnacious scowl. "Rosefield's a dashed fine fellow, and he claims to be fond of my Priscilla. Do you think I'd let her marry just anyone? And what is all this to do with you, I should like to know? You ain't her brother!"

"I don't have to be her brother to object to seeing her sold into virtual slavery!" Marcus shot back furiously. "Everyone knows of Rosefield's dissipations. My God, they are said to have offended even Prinny! To even think of Priscilla in his care . . ."

"I think the journey up here must have left you tired," Brant said as he interposed himself between his two friends, fixing Marcus with a warning glare.

"Might I suggest you retire to your rooms and rest until tea? Afterwards I'll take you to my stables. I have some new hunters my man sent up from Tattersall's, and they're prime bits of blood. Would you care to see them?"

The new topic was accepted grudgingly, and they made plans to meet at Brant's stables following tea. Hugh downed the last of his Madeira and, after bidding Marcus and Brant a somewhat stiff adieu, left to go to his rooms. Marcus lingered a few minutes longer, staring down into his wine with a worried frown.

"You really don't think he'll force her to marry him, do you?" he asked in a gruff voice.

Brant glanced up from his own perusal of his glass. "Who? Do you mean Rosefield?" Marcus nodded curtly. "Of course not. You know Hugh positively dotes on his lovely sister. He would never make her do anything she found distasteful."

"Rosefield!" Marcus repeated, shaking his head in disgust. "How can he even consider it? The man is an anathema to all that is decent. Why doesn't Hugh just sell her to the old king and be done with it? He may be blind and half-mad, but at least he is relatively harmless."

"I agree with you about Rosefield," Brant admitted slowly. "But in the eyes of the world it would be considered an excellent match. He is one of the wealthiest men in England."

Marcus sank deeper in his chair. "Wealth isn't everything," he grumbled. "And I doubt you would consider the match quite as excellent if it were Sara the old lecher was after. Would you?" His sherry-brown eyes flicked at Brant in challenge.

"Don't talk nonsense," Brant snapped, setting his glass on the table with a loud thud. "Rosefield hasn't shown the smallest interest in Sara."

"But what if he did?" Marcus pressed, leaning forward to watch Brant's reaction. "What if he came to you tomorrow and offered for Sara? What would your answer be?"

The thought of Rosefield's slack lips tasting Sara's sweetness, his age-splotched hands caressing her tender flesh, filled Brant with murderous fury. Without pausing to think what his words might reveal to his friend, he snarled, "I'd tell the old bastard to go to hell, and then I would drive him from Mallingham."

A satisfied smile crossed Marcus's face as he lifted his glass of wine to his lips. "That is what I thought," he said, cocking an eyebrow at Brant. "Something tells me this is going to be a most interesting summer."

The house party rose early the next morning, and while Brant took the men out to inspect the stables, Sara took the ladies on a tour of the house. It was Jane's and Priscilla's first visit to Mallingham, and they expressed awe at the lovely old home and the sense of history which permeated each room. They were pausing in front of the portraits in the Long Gallery when Jane gave a sudden exclamation.

"I have it," she cried, her gray eyes shining with delight. "It's the perfect solution!"

"What are you talking about?" Sara asked in a wary tone, remembering Jane's last "perfect solution."

"The costume ball, silly." Jane laughed at her friend's obvious suspicion. "It's in less than a week, and I have been fretting over what I would wear. I did bring something with me—a Chinese robe my brother brought me from Macao—but this is much better. We shall all go as ladies from the court of King Henry the Eighth."

"Oh, Jane, how clever!" Priscilla clapped her hands like a pleased child. "I have always longed to wear a farthingale." She paused uncertainly, a small frown marring her pleasure. "But will we have time to sew something up, do you think?"

"There are several trunks of clothing in the attic," Sara suggested, caught up in her friends' enthusiasm. "As long as we are careful, I don't see why we shouldn't be able to borrow something."

This met with much approval, and the three of them trooped up to the attic where they spent the rest of the morning rooting through the old trunks in search of the perfect costumes. When they had found what they were looking for, they carried the gowns down to Sara's room so that they could model their finds.

Jane had found a dress of deep scarlet velvet with wide sleeves slashed to show the ivory satin beneath. There was a small snood of dark gold mesh set with garnets that went with the gown, and when Jane slipped it over her dark hair she looked every inch the proper Tudor lady.

Priscilla's gown was of sky-blue satin, the bodice of which was heavily encrusted with seed pearls and gold embroidery. It also had a farthingale, and Priscilla's soft green eyes gleamed with pleasure as she modeled it for her friends. But it was Sara's gown which elicited the most praise. It was, the three ladies agreed with mutual sighs, quite the loveliest gown any of them had ever seen.

Cut in a rich purple velvet, with a wide, square-cut neckline, the sleeves were puffed like little balloons at the armholes, than narrowed and became close-fitting with a ruffle of lace at the wrists. Like Priscilla's gown, the bodice had been heavily embroidered, and the faint gleam of precious stones could still be detected lying against the brilliant fabric.

"Oh, Sara, how very beautiful you look," Priscilla exclaimed with a romantic sigh. "Just like one of the paintings come to life! And your dress fits so well it might have been made for you. Mine is a trifle tight."

"So is mine," Jane agreed, tugging at her bodice. "Also it is terribly musty. Do you think we should risk placing them in the sun to air out, or would that ruin them?"

Sara was uncertain on this point and rang for Matty, who immediately consulted with Miss Pimms. It was decided that the gowns would be cleaned, then placed in a cedar press for airing. That problem resolved, the ladies went back downstairs to join the men for luncheon.

After the meal Sara slipped upstairs to look in on her aunt. She found the countess lying on her blue-and-white brocade chaise longue, an open book on her lap and a faraway look in her eyes. When she heard Sara enter, she turned her head toward the doorway.

"Good afternoon, child," she greeted Sara, flashing an absentminded smile. "I was hoping you'd come see me today. Come closer, dear, I have something important to discuss with you."

"Of course I meant to see you today," Sara said with a laugh as she crossed the sunlit room to her aunt's side. "Don't I always come visit you after luncheon? Now"—she dragged one of the lyre-backed chairs over and sat facing Lady Mallingham — "what is it?"

"What do you think of Priscilla Tressmoore?"

The question puzzled Sara. "Well, ma'am, that is difficult to say," she answered, choosing her words carefully. "She's one of my dearest friends, of course, and I'm quite fond of her, but—"

"No, no, no." Lady Mallingham waved her hand impatiently. "I mean, what do you *think* of her? Do you think she would make a good wife for your cousin?"

The blood rushed from Sara's face, and for a moment she feared she would swoon. "I . . . what did you say?" she managed in a reedy voice.

"Really, Sara, I wish you would pay attention when I am speaking to you," Lady Mallingham grumbled, pulling her orange robe closer about her and folding her arms across her chest. "I asked you, and quite clearly too, I might add, if you think your friend Priscilla will do as a bride for my nephew. She is quite beautiful, and he does have a penchant for blondes . . . or so I have been told. Also she is well dowered, and a sweet widgeon from all accounts. And the families have known each other forever . . . which is always important. All in all I think it would be a suitable match. Don't you agree?"

Sara's heart, which seemed to have stopped beating, now resumed that function with such an agonizing intensity it felt as if it would burst from her chest. She closed her eyes in painful defeat.

"Has he offered for her yet?" she asked quietly, steeling herself for the answer.

"Not yet," Lady Mallingham admitted with obvious disgust. "But he *has* been most particular in his attentions, don't you think? He always made sure to dance with her at least once at every ball we attended, and he speaks of her constantly. And now he has invited her and her brother up for a visit—unless it was your idea to invite them?" She looked at Sara questioningly.

"No, Aunt," Sara replied, remembering the night in the garden when Brant had first mentioned inviting Jane and the Tressmoores for a visit. At the time she fancied he had done it to please her. But now . . .

"Well, there, you see?" Lady Mallingham crowed in triumph. "It is obvious he dotes on her. And about time, too, I should think. He is almost thirty-three now, and it is past time he was setting up his nursery and seeing to the succession. I have been fair distracted with worry, I can tell you. But now I can rest peacefully, knowing he is settled."

"You . . . you speak as if all is arranged," Sara said, wondering how she could appear so outwardly calm when inside she was slowly dying.

"Well, surely it is only a matter of time." Her aunt sounded so smug Sara could have screamed. "She is young, she is pretty, *and* she is here. If she has half a brain in her blond head, I daresay she can finagle an offer out of him. You must have a private word with her, Sara, and tell her what she must do.

Men are such backward creatures. A lady would expire of old age before one of them ever got around to proposing. It is up to us ladies to take such matters into our own hands, and so you must tell her."

"Yes, Aunt," Sara mumbled unhappily, envisioning Priscilla and Brant together. They would make an attractive couple, she acknowledged, swallowing her bitterness. He with his dark hair and flashing blue eyes, she with her blond curls and dimpled smile. Her sweetness would offset his haughty arrogance, and if he loved her . . . Sara's mind stopped abruptly, refusing to follow the thought to its logical conclusion.

Chapter Twelve

The stack of letters waiting on his desk was the first thing Brant saw when he walked into his study. He picked them up and was flicking through them disinterestedly when he came across two letters addressed to Sara. The first was from the Duke of Langden, and the second was from Peter Kelton.

Brant frowned down at the second letter, and toyed with the idea of opening it as he took his chair behind the massive cherrywood desk. He told himself that as Sara's guardian he had that right, but in the end he decided against it. Sara would not thank him for it, and he could well imagine her fury, should he presume to open her mail. She would doubtless have his guts for garters for such a breach of her privacy, he thought, a reluctant smile touching his lips as he set the letter aside with the other.

The next letter he glanced at was also from Kelton, but this one was addressed to him. He tore it open, his expression becoming increasingly foreboding as he read the meticulously penned lines. As Marcus had expected, the letter was a formal declaration of his intentions regarding Sara.

He listed his sources of income, his fortune and prospects, his family's connections, even his academic credentials . . . as if Brant would care a whit that he took honors in Greek and Latin. He also wrote at length of his "tender regard" for Sara, concluding the letter with an earnest plea that Brant would find his humble suit acceptable, and grant him permission to address Sara.

Brant leaned back in his chair, his heart at war with his head. Kelton's offer was all he had once hoped for. He was well born, and if not exactly wealthy, he was at least comfortably situated. His reputation was impeccable, and he seemed a decent enough fellow. He could be trusted to take every care of Sara. That was just the problem, he realized, his tanned face paling at the enormity of his discovery. He didn't want Kelton to take care of Sara. He didn't want any man taking care of Sara, save him. He was in love with her.

The shock of his realization kept him frozen to his chair. He loved her. He loved her temper, her pride, her gentle affection for his aunt, and the way she carried herself with such dignity. Lord help him, he even loved her independent spirit, and her fierce determination to make her way without any help from anyone. He shook his head in disbelief, staring at the portrait of his uncle with unseeing eyes.

Since inheriting the title, he had given the subject of matrimony as little thought as possible. But whenever the subject did come up—usually as a result of his aunt's hectoring—he would vaguely imagine that he would find some sweet, dutiful chit from the country, marry her, and be done with it. He would still have his other interests, and all in all his life would remain just as he wished it. He had never thought to marry for love. In fact he hadn't even believed in the emotion . . . until now.

There was a sharp rap on the door and Marcus entered, his blond hair tousled by his recent ride. "I say, those new horses of yours are prime goers," he said, flinging himself onto the chair facing Brant. "That Terrington is a wonder. If you ever decide to put him to stud be sure to . . ." He broke off at the expression on Brant's face. "What is it? What has happened?"

Brant ducked his head, hiding his face from his too-sharp friend. "Nothing is wrong," he said, his voice rough with strain. "I was just thinking, that is all."

"Cut line, old fellow," Marcus advised, swinging his booted feet lazily. "The rest of the world might believe that taradiddle, but I do not. Now, what is it? Is there anything I can do to be of assistance?"

Brant was touched by his friend's obvious concern and the understanding in Marcus's eyes. Sighing heavily, he extended the letter to him. "From

Kelton," he said, watching Marcus's face as he read the letter. "You're right, he wants to marry Sara."

"I can see that." Marcus's eyes twinkled as he scanned the letter. "Lord, he is a prosy devil, isn't he? 'I humbly beseech and implore that your lordship will accept my petition and grant me the honor of asking for Miss Belding's hand in matrimony.' Good gad, why doesn't he just ask for your permission, and be still?" He continued reading, pausing every now and again to chuckle over a particularly convoluted phrase. When he was done he handed the letter back to Brant.

"Well, it looks as if we have done it," he said, looking pleased. "My congratulations, Mallingham, on another mission successfully completed. When may we expect the joyous event to take place?"

Brant glanced down at the letter in his hand, his fingers tightening around the paper until it rattled. "I'm not sure that it will," he said, forcing himself to speak coolly. "There are . . . other considerations."

"What other considerations?" Marcus demanded with a puzzled frown. "He's wealthy enough, and Lord knows he has the breeding and position. It ain't like he's a country schoolteacher without a penny in his pocket! What else is there to consider?"

"Sara's feelings in the matter, for one thing," Brant snapped, casting the viscount a dark scowl. "I don't even know if she likes this Kelton fellow. And I have no intention of forcing her into a marriage she would find distasteful."

"Of course you haven't," Marcus replied calmly. "But if she accepts Kelton's offer, would *you* have any objections? You don't seem all that pleased, if you don't mind my saying so."

Brant shrugged, powerful shoulders rippling beneath his dark jacket. "My objections, as you call them, are my own affair," he said stiffly, not wishing to confess his newfound love to anyone, even his closest friend. "Let us say that I am not . . . favorably disposed toward the match."

"I see." Marcus rested his chin on his cupped hand, studying Brant's stiff expression with avid interest. "Does this mean you will refuse Kelton's suit?"

Brant's lips tightened as he faced the unpalatable truth. "The decision is not mine to make," he said through clenched teeth. "Kelton has written her a personal letter, undoubtedly telling her of his feelings for her. I will give it to her."

"And if she returns his affections and accepts his offer?" Marcus asked, hiding his smile in his hand.

"If she accepts his offer, then I will reconsider the matter," Brant answered, his fingers crumpling the letter into an untidy ball.

"Please, miss, mind you stand still," Matty implored through a mouthful of pins. "However am I to get this hem straight with you hopping about like that?" They were standing in Sara's sitting room, gazing into the cheval glass the footman had dragged in from the bedroom.

"I'm sorry, Matty." Sara subsided at once, contenting herself with merely turning her head to better see her own reflection. The gown had only come out of the press that morning, and with the ball in less than two days' time there were still some alterations to be done. Matty had just finished pinning the hem when Brant walked into the room, his blue eyes widening at the sight of Sara in the velvet gown.

"Your lordship." Matty scrambled to her feet, bobbing a respectful curtsey. "I was just finishing Miss's gown. Lovely, ain't she though?"

"Quite lovely," Brant agreed, finding his voice at last. He recognized the gown. It was the one Katherine Deverleigh, Lady Mallingham, had worn to have her portrait painted, and it looked every bit as breathtaking on Sara as it did on his beautiful ancestor. Looking at Sara, her soft shoulders gleaming against the rich velvet, he could understand why the king had become infatuated with the countess.

"Is there something you wanted, my lord?" Sara asked, feeling a quiver of uncertainty rush through her at the intensity of his gaze. She felt absurdly vulnerable standing in the center of the room . . . exposed. As if he could see through to her most intimate thoughts. Blushing at what those thoughts were, she managed to free her gaze from his and glanced nervously away.

"Yes." Brant gathered his wits together and dismissed Matty with a wave of his hand. "You may go," he said. "I'd like a word with Miss Belding in private. But mind you stay close. I'll only be a moment."

"Yes, your lordship," Matty answered, her eyes flicking between her young mistress and the earl. "I'll just be in the other room, then." She scurried out of the sitting room, leaving the door discreetly ajar.

When they were alone Sara stepped down from the small stool she had been standing on. Her knees were shaking so badly that she stumbled and would have fallen, had Brant not stepped forward to catch her in his strong arms.

"Thank you." She laughed breathlessly. He was so close she could see the fine lines fanning out from his blue eyes, and the subtle, spicy cologne he always used teased her senses. Her hands flexed against his shoulders as she levered herself away from him.

"What was it you wished to say, sir?" she asked, her voice shaking despite her attempts to appear cool.

"These came for you a few days ago," he said, pulling the packet of letters from the pocket of his brown coat and handing them to her. "I apologize for not giving them to you sooner, but I fear they slipped my mind." His eyes rested on her face, alert for any betraying sign of emotion. "I trust they aren't urgent."

"I'm sure they're not," Sara replied absently, turning the letters over in her hand. At the sight of the first letter, the blood rushed into her face. Good heavens! Why on earth would the Duke of Langden be writing to her?

Brant saw the telltale color spreading across Sara's cheeks, and his hands tightened into fists. That tore it, then. It was evident Sara must feel something for the damned scholar.

The second letter brought a puzzled frown to Sara's face. Who was Peter Kelton? Then she remembered a rather earnest young man she'd met at Lady Pettyforth's soiree. His name was Kelton, was it not? She had spoken to him several times since then, now that she thought of it, listening politely as he prattled on about the ancient Greeks. He was very sweet, and she had felt sorry for him. But she couldn't understand why he had written to her; she scarcely knew the man! She placed both letters on the table and turned back to Brant.

"Thank you for bringing these to me," she said, wondering why he was looking so fierce. "Was there anything else you wished to say to me?"

"Is that the dress you will be wearing to the ball?" he asked, realizing he had been staring at her like one bewitched.

"Yes." She stroked the shimmering velvet with a fingertip. "Jane thought it might be amusing if we all dressed as ladies from King Henry's court. We found them in the attic and fell in love with them." She paused, then cast him an uncertain look. "It is all right if we wear them, isn't it? We didn't think to ask permission, but . . ."

"Of course you may wear them," Brant assured her. "You must know that anything I have is yours. I was just thinking how very beautiful you look in Katherine Deverleigh's court gown."

"She wore this at court?" Sara was delighted by this piece of news. "How intriguing!"

"Mmm." He nodded. "In fact, she was wearing this very gown the first time Henry ever saw her. That is why he had the amethysts designed for her. The stones were to match her gown, which was said to be the very shade of her eyes, while the pearls were to set off her white skin. Which reminds me, it would please me if you would wear the amethysts to the ball, including the small tiara designed to accompany the set."

"The king sent her a tiara as well?" Sara asked with a raised eyebrow. "That was daring of him."

Brant shook his head. "The tiara was from her husband, Christopher. It is said to have cost more than the whole of the original set."

"Why did he buy it then?"

"Because," he answered in a knowing voice, "she was his wife, and a Deverleigh always keeps what is his. The tiara was Christopher's way of telling Henry that Katherine had no need of any title the king might bestow." He reached out a finger to brush a stray curl back from her forehead. "Will you wear them for me, Sara?"

"All right," she said, her skin flushing at his touch and the midnight-blue gleam in his eyes. "Thank you, Brant."

"You're welcome." His voice was husky as he continued touching her. "Sara, would you promise me something?"

"Certainly." She glanced at him curiously. "What is it?"

Brant paused, searching for the right words. "Before you accept an offer . . . any sort of offer at all, I want you to come and see me first. Will you do that for me?"

"Of course, but . . ."

"Promise me," he repeated, his hands dropping to her shoulders as he pulled her against his chest. "Promise that you will speak with me before accepting any offer. However . . . however tempting that offer might be. Do you agree?"

Sara's eyes closed as she absorbed the warm pleasure of his hands resting on her bared shoulders. "Yes, Brant," she sighed, her voice soft and low. "I promise."

Brant swallowed in relief. At least she wasn't going to accept Kelton's offer out of hand, he thought, slowly relaxing his grip on Sara. He smiled down at her as he stepped back.

"I will see you later then," he said, watching her as she turned away from him. "And Sara?"

"Yes?" She glanced at him uncertainly.

"Save a waltz for me."

After he had departed Matty came back into the room, her manner oddly subdued as she finished pinning up the hem. When they were done, Sara changed into a pale blue dressing gown, telling Matty she was going to rest until dinner. The moment she was alone, she tore open the letter from the duke.

My Dear Miss Belding, she read,

I hope your aunt has recovered from her unfortunate illness. You might advise her to try drinking a pint of ale each afternoon. I make a practice of this, and it has done wonders for my gout. Now as to the reason for this letter.

We were able to fill the post after all and returned to Cornwall that week. Unfortunately the female we hired, a Fraülein Horstmann, proved to be a dashed loose screw who ran off with the under-footman. I am writing to see if you are still looking for a position and if so, if you would like to come and join us here at Langden. With your family's permission, of course.

The pay will be the same as we discussed in London, and we could arrange that you might have some holiday so that you could see your beloved aunt when you pleased.

If you should like the post, please write back at once as we are most anxious to fill the position.

Your humble servant,
Edgar Grosbey, Duke of Langden

Sara lay back on her couch, the letter fluttering to her lap. The offer stunned her, for she had thought the position to be lost to her. In the two months since that fateful afternoon so much had happened, she had scarcely given the matter a thought. Until her aunt was well there was no possibility of her leaving . . . or so she had told herself. But Lady Mallingham was recovering now, her strength returning with each day. Perhaps it *was* time Sara looked to her future . . . especially if Brant was contemplating marriage.

The very thought made her eyes close in pain. There was no way she could remain with the countess if Brant were to marry Priscilla. It would destroy her to see his happiness, to watch Priscilla and Brant together. She folded the letter and put it aside, unable to contemplate her bleak future any longer.

Sighing, she picked up the letter from Mr. Kelton, her eyes growing wide with disbelief as she read his startling proposal of marriage.

He wrote that his mother had declared it was time he took a bride, and after careful consideration he had decided that she possessed all of the qualities he deemed suitable in a wife. He went on to describe what he termed his "tender regard for her delicate sensibilities," and ended the letter with a request that she make him the happiest of men by accepting his hand in marriage. Nowhere in the four-page letter did he once mention the word *love*.

Now here was a pretty kettle of fish, she thought, tucking the letter into the pocket of her dressing gown. How on earth was she supposed to reply to such an insulting proposal? What a very strange day it had been. Brant had just made her promise she would consult him before accepting any offers, and now she had to consider not one offer, but two. One for honest employment, and the other for what could only be termed a marriage of convenience.

Her frown deepened as she wondered how Brant knew of the offers. The letters had been sealed, so she knew he hadn't opened them. There was no way he could have known about the offers . . . unless he had been corresponding with the duke and Mr. Kelton.

But that was nonsense, she told herself. Brant had been as mad as the very devil when she had applied for the post. He had even spoken of writing the duke a strong letter on the matter, so she could hardly believe he would have changed his mind in so short a time. The duke's letter was obviously a coincidence, she decided, which only left Mr. Kelton's letter as suspect. Judging from the pompous, condescending tone of his proposal, he was hardly enamored of her. So why had he lit upon *her* as his intended?

A sudden suspicion dawned, bringing her upright on the couch. Jane had teased her about Brant's "campaign," and she had answered that she'd seen no evidence of it. Well, here was evidence aplenty! It was obvious the deceitful creature had been up to his old tricks all along, and rather than abandoning

his efforts, as she mistakenly presumed he had, he
had been plotting to marry her off to Mr. Kelton.
He couldn't wait to get her off his hands now that
he was finally settling down . . .

No. She stopped abruptly. The thought was un-
worthy of her. She knew Brant was fond of her in
his own way, and that he'd never force her into
anything so distasteful as an arranged marriage. He
might not return her love, but he did hold her in
some regard. Kelton had most probably written him
asking permission to pay his respects to her, and
Brant was letting her know he approved of the suit.
Why else would he have made that odd request that
she consult him before deciding on her course of
action? Perhaps he feared she would refuse, and he
wanted the chance to convince her.

Well, no matter, she decided glumly. There was
no way she would tie herself to a marriage of convenience. The duke's offer, however, was another
matter. Whether Brant married Priscilla or not, she
knew she would have to leave Mallingham. She
couldn't remain and risk having Brant learn of her
love. She would sooner die than have him look at
her with pity. No, she would have to go. It was the
only way. She picked up the letter from the duke,
mentally composing her letter of acceptance.

By the night of the ball Mallingham had been
transformed into a magical wonderland. Exotic
flowers brought from London had been placed in
tubs about the brightly lit ballroom, along with pots
of roses from the garden. The gardeners and maids
had been busy all morning arranging flowers and

small, flickering fairy lights, until the whole of the ballroom and garden looked like an enchanted forest glen. Flowers were everywhere, even woven along the curved banisters, and their heady perfume mingled with the softer musk of the scented candles. The dance floor had been polished to mirror brightness, and the French doors were open along the far wall, admitting the softest of summer breezes. Sara knew, even before hearing the delighted gasps of the guests, that her ball would be the talk of the county for years to come.

Sara, Priscilla, and Jane had made quite an entrance into the ballroom, and their costumes were received with much enthusiasm. The gentlemen of Mallingham were equally well received, and she heard several whispered compliments on their costumes. Brant wore a velvet doublet and a wide starched ruff, his athletic legs encased in a pair of white hose, while Marcus went as a Roman soldier, his blond head covered by a leather helmet. Even Hugh went in costume as Admiral Lord Nelson, and Jane teased him unmercifully about his chestful of medals.

After seeing to her guests' comfort, Sara went to check on her aunt, who was holding court at the dowagers' bench. She found Lady Mallingham reclining on a couch Brant had ordered carried down from her sitting room, and when she saw Sara, she gestured for her to join her.

"Quite a little turn-out, eh?" she said, nodding at the crowded dance floor. "You are to be congratulated on all your hard work, my dear. I think I can promise that this night will be talked about for years to come."

"Thank you, Aunt Agatha." Sara kissed the crown of snow-white hair atop the countess's head. "But why aren't you in costume? I know you're still far from well, but—"

"And what would you call this?" Lady Mallingham bristled in feigned indignation as she indicated her demure gown of ivory-and-rose silk. "It most certainly is a costume, and a highly effective disguise, I might add. Three of our oldest neighbors walked right past me with scarce a nod. Had it not been for this"—she unfolded her orange ostrich-plumed fan—"they would never have recognized me."

Sara laughed as she settled beside her aunt. "How very stupid of me not to have realized that you are incognito," she said, smiling as she surveyed the glittering crowd. "And I believe you are right about the ball, ma'am. It does seem to be a success, don't you think?"

"More than you shall ever know," came the cryptic reply as the countess took a dainty sip of champagne. "Which reminds me, my dear, do you recall the other afternoon when I said I thought Brant was contemplating offering for Miss Tressmoore?"

Sara's pleasure with the ball vanished at the countess's words. "Yes, Aunt Agatha," she answered in a strained voice. "I remember."

"Well, I heard it from Pimms, who heard it from Mr. Cranston, that Brant has sent to London for his mother's betrothal ring!" Lady Mallingham's blue eyes sparkled with delight. "What is more, he and Lord Tressmoore were holed up in Brant's study for the better part of two hours this afternoon, and they called for a bottle of champagne when they were done!"

"Then . . . then he has offered for her?" Sara's stomach lurched, and the room swam about her.

"Well, not yet, of course." The countess was staring at her with concern. "But I daresay he will be making an offer before the night is out. Sara, child, what is it? You are as white as chalk!"

"I . . . the heat . . ." Sara stumbled to her feet, feeling panic overwhelming her. She had to get out of there before disgracing herself. "I am unwell—" she muttered, backing away from the couch. "Pray excuse me—" She turned and bolted for the French doors with single-minded determination.

Brant was discussing wheat prices with one of his neighbors when he saw Sara's headlong flight into the garden. He paused long enough to mumble a polite excuse, and then he was hurrying to his aunt's side.

"What is wrong with Sara?" he demanded, frowning toward the French doors Sara had just dashed through. "Is she ill?"

"I am sure I don't know." Lady Mallingham blinked up at him guilelessly. "I was just congratulating her on her offer from Peter Kelton, and the next thing I knew she leapt up and ran out of here like a madwoman."

"Do you mean she has *accepted* him?" Brant roared, unmindful of the nearby guests who were listening to the exchange with avid interest.

Lady Mallingham was not so lost to the proprieties, and cast her nephew a warning glare. "Will you kindly lower your voice?" she hissed. "People are staring. And of course she hasn't accepted . . .

not yet. But she will be accepting an offer once it is
made in proper form. I have no doubt that she will
make a lovely bride, and so I told her. The next
thing I knew she was dashing out of here like—"

"Damn, she will *not* marry that pompous bag of
wind!" Brant swore feelingly, then whirled on his
heels and stalked in the direction Sara had just run,
his shoulders squared in determination.

Lady Mallingham made sure he was out of sight
before signaling the footman. "Is that special champagne I ordered brought up from the cellars chilled
yet?" she asked when he came to her side.

"It is, Lady Mallingham."

"Excellent." Lady Mallingham's smile of satisfaction deepened. "You may wait half an hour and
then open it."

"Yes, my lady."

Sara made it as far as the rose garden before pausing to catch her breath. She had barely recovered
from her wild flight when she heard the sound of
running footsteps behind her. Suddenly a pair of
strong arms were closing about her, hauling her into
a possessive embrace.

"Just what the devil do you think you are doing?"
Brant shouted, shaking Sara none too gently. "I told
you to speak to me before accepting an offer, and I
meant it! You are not going to that addlepated fool,
do you hear me? I forbid it!"

Sara threw her head back and glared at him
through pain-filled eyes. She remembered the duke
had said she would need her family's permission
before he would hire her, but she was damned if she

would let Brant stop her. "I am sure Aunt will give me her blessing," she said, her chin coming up in defiance. "Your permission is not needed, your lordship, I assure you."

"The devil it isn't," Brant shot back, goaded beyond endurance. Even in the most deadly of battles he had never been this enraged. This was the most important battle of his life, he realized with hardening resolve, and he was determined to be victorious. He made a superhuman effort to regain control of his temper.

"Come, Sara, be reasonable," he said, realizing he was goading her into defiance. "You can't mean to go through with this. You must know he doesn't love you."

Sara stared up at him as if he had run mad. "Of course he doesn't love me," she said, anger temporarily giving way to confusion. "What has love to do with anything, for heaven's sake? It's only a position, after all."

"A position!" Her words set fire to his temper once more. "Is that how you regard marriage?" He administered another shake.

"Marriage?" she squeaked, certain Brant was the worse for drink. It was the only possible explanation for his behavior.

"Don't play the innocent with me," he said, drawing her into a tight embrace. "Aunt has told me you are thinking of accepting a proposal tonight, and so you shall. *My* proposal." He ducked his head, taking her lips in a kiss of unleashed passion.

At first Sara fought him, confused and alarmed by his words, but as the kiss deepened, she found herself surrendering to his urgency. Her lips parted beneath his, welcoming the intimate touch of his tongue against hers. When he finally lifted his head, Brant's breathing was ragged with desire.

"I love you, Sara," he whispered hoarsely, his eyes bright as he gazed down into her flushed face. "How can you even think of leaving me?"

"You . . . you love me?" Sara whispered, trembling with hope and fear.

"I love you," he repeated, bending to kiss her soft mouth with aching tenderness. "Don't leave me, my darling," he pleaded in a husky voice. "I should go mad without you."

"But what about Priscilla?" Sara asked, her hands cupping Brant's face as she stared up at him. "Aunt said you were going to offer for her."

"Priscilla?" His brows pleated in confusion. "Why should I offer for her? She is a sweet child to be sure, but she is much too young for me. Actually," he said, his frown becoming thoughtful, "I think Marcus is going to propose to her. He and Hugh were in my study for the better part of the morning coming to terms."

"Aunt Agatha," Sara said, speaking quite distinctly, "told me you were offering for Priscilla. She also said you had sent for your mother's betrothal ring."

Brant pressed a kiss against the palm that was resting on his cheek. "Why would I offer for Priscilla when I am mad with love for you?" he asked in a low, provocative voice that made Sara shiver with delight. "And now I think 'tis time you took pity on me and told me what your feelings are toward me. Do you love me, Sara?" He spoke teasingly, but she could feel the tension in the hard body pressed to her softness, and see the uncertainty darkening his eyes.

She tugged his head down to hers, reassuring him with the sweetest of kisses. "You must know that I adore you," she murmured, drawing back to smile up at him. "Why do you think I was so determined to leave? I thought you meant to marry Priscilla, and I loved you too much to stay."

Another kiss was exchanged before Brant gave a soft chuckle. "I still can't believe you thought I meant to have her," he said, shaking his head in amazement. "As I said, she—" He stopped abruptly. "Did you say my aunt told you I was going to propose to Priscilla?"

"Yes. She said you'd been thinking about it for days."

"She told *me* you had accepted Peter Kelton's offer," Brant said slowly, his lips tightening with suspicion.

"But how would she know that?" Sara demanded, her brow wrinkling in confusion. "I never told a soul! In fact the letter never left my . . ." Her voice trailed off as she remembered discovering Miss Pimms hanging her robe back in the wardrobe. She hadn't thought much of the incident at the time, but now . . .

"Miss Pimms!" she exclaimed indignantly. "She must have found the letter in my pocket and showed it to Aunt Agatha!" Her eyes met Brant's in a moment of shared comprehension and her indignation fell away. In the next moment they were both overcome with laughter.

"That witch!" Brant laughed, swinging Sara in a

joyous half-circle. "That meddlesome, cunning, wonderful old witch! She has outsmarted us all!"

"Do you mean she has plotted all this? Just to bring us together?" Sara was torn between outrage and delight. "I was right about her from the start! She is an absolute dragon!"

"But such a wise old dragon, my love," he said, the kiss he bestowed upon her lips rife with emotion. "Sara, I love you. Please say you will marry me."

"Gladly, my darling," Sara responded, blinking back tears of happiness. "Nothing would give me greater pleasure than to become your wife."

They spent several more delightful moments in the garden before Brant drew back. "Remind me not to wear a ruff next time I make love to you," he murmured with a wicked chuckle. "The damned things are devilishly uncomfortable."

"Yes, my lord." Her eyes sparkled up at him mischievously. "I shall be sure to remind you upon some appropriate occasion."

They began kissing again, when the sound of someone clearing her throat penetrated their private world. They turned as one to find Lady Mallingham standing there, her arms akimbo as she glared at them.

"Am I to take it that the pair of you have finally come to your senses?" she demanded in a querulous tone.

"Yes, Aunt," Brant replied, folding Sara against his chest. "You may be the first to congratulate us. Sara has just done me the honor of agreeing to be my wife."

"Well," the countess snorted with obvious impatience, "it certainly took you long enough! I was beginning to think I should have to lock the pair of you in the dungeon before you came to the point. Now leave off your lovemaking for a few minutes and come back into the ballroom. The guests are waiting to drink a toast in your honor. And straighten your ruff, Brant. It is crooked."

"Yes, Aunt." Brant did as he was ordered before offering his arm to Sara. Just as they were about to enter the house he called out to Lady Mallingham.

"Aunt?"

"Yes?" She glanced over her shoulder at him.

"Thank you," he said softly.

"You are most welcome." Her teeth flashed in a delighted smile. "Now that the two of you are to be safely leg-shackled, I believe I shall turn my attentions elsewhere. That Mrs. Broughton is a lively minx. Just what Lord Tressmoore needs to keep him in line." And she strode into the ballroom, all traces of her infirmity gone.

Brant and Sara exchanged amazed looks, then burst out laughing again. They shared a final kiss, and followed their aunt into the crowd waiting to toast the beginning of their life together.

The End?

The end of a book is never really *the end* for a person who reads. He or she can always open another. And another.

Every page holds possibilities.

But millions of kids don't see them. Don't know they're there. Millions of kids can't read, or won't.

That's why there's RIF. Reading is Fundamental (RIF) is a national nonprofit program that works with thousands of community organizations to help young people discover the fun—and the importance—of reading.

RIF motivates kids so that they *want* to read. And RIF works directly with parents to help them encourage their children's reading. RIF gets books to children and children into books, so they grow up reading and become adults who can read. Adults like you.

For more information on how to start a RIF program in your neighborhood, or help your own child grow up reading, write to:

RIF
Dept. BK-1
Box 23444
Washington, D.C.
20026

Founded in 1966, RIF is a national nonprofit organization with local projects run by volunteers in every state of the union.

About the Author

Joan Overfield's first novel is generously colored with a rich tapestry of social as well as moral history about the Regency period of England. As a former social studies teacher, Joan has incorporated her knowledge of English upper-class life with a sprinkling of humor to create this 1987 winner of the Golden Heart Award from the Romance Writers of America. She lives in Washington State, where she enjoys an active membership in several writers' groups.